king's salacious secrets

Pretty Little Robots
Book Two

jerri chisholm

WISE WOLF
BOOKS

WISE WOLF BOOKS
An Imprint of Wolfpack Publishing
wisewolfbooks.com
9850 S. Maryland Parkway, Suite A-5 #323, Las Vegas, Nevada 89183

This is a work of fiction. All of the characters, organizations, publications, and events portrayed in this novel are either products of the author's imagination or are used fictitiously.

Cover design by Wise Wolf Books

Paperback ISBN 978-1-957548-91-3
eBook ISBN 978-1-957548-67-8
LCCN 2023941064

king's salacious secrets

one

· · ·

AN ENGINE HUMS OFF in the distance, leaves rustle, a woman coughs. I wake.

The brightness is dazzling, that's the first thing I notice —stripes of white and orange, and it strikes me that perhaps I'm outside. Aunt Jo will be cross that I've been so careless— sleeping outdoors! But no...That's not right.

I don't live with Aunt Jo anymore.

No, I live...I live at Strath Glen—yes, that's right. I'm betrothed to a tall fellow—the perennially icy viscount, that's who. And I sleep in the guest quarters that have three large windows overlooking Airo-Aurora's mighty birch forest. Yet, something tugs at me. It reminds me that right now, I'm far from my bed. Far from the palace, even.

Memories—blurred ones—come cascading back, circling through my brain like pinwheels, and I draw in a sharp breath.

No. No, that won't do. Those recollections must be false —perhaps I'm still sleeping. I must be. I close my eyes again. I drift into a light, dreamless slumber. The cycle repeats itself, of that I'm dimly aware, until finally, the urge to sleep is less overwhelming. But my head thumps like it's jammed with cotton balls and I wish wakefulness hadn't come so soon.

Really, I should be deciphering where I am, what's going on, but it's only when a breeze catches me across the face that I squint both eyes open, meaningfully now.

Questions enter my mind concerning my whereabouts: *where*? But also, *how*? *Why*? *When*?

I blink down at a blue jumpsuit, rumpled and covered with dirt. Cracked concrete fans out beneath me, and overhead is a patch of metal—a bus stop, maybe. Lifting my gaze even further, I make out uneven lines and glinting surfaces off in the distance. The Sky Center, I realize, and something in my stomach drops.

"Sweets, is that you comin' to?"

A redheaded woman I've never seen before appears in front of me, her face hovering just inches from my own. A second later, it's gone. With a groan reverberating from the bottom of my stomach, I prop myself up on my elbows, determined to speak with her. Determined to get some much-needed answers. Instead, my gaze snags on a lawn-green helicopter that sparkles under the scintillating sun. It looks strangely familiar, that machine, and the sinking sensation in my stomach grows worse.

Like coins from a slot machine, details come back to me.

I commandeered that machine—the blue jumpsuit that I wear is because I'm dressed for flight.

I took Wolfe Rocksavage—the viscount of Airo-Aurora and, thanks to the Mainframe slotting us together against all odds, my fiancé—to the neighboring country of Myopia for a work meeting.

I made a detour on the ride home and discovered what was hiding at those coordinates in Ashville Range: an army of Mavericks controlled entirely by the Mainframe.

And...and I learned of Wolfe's most tragic past: his wife, and child, killed by a beast in the woods.

Difficult details to process in the sky, and certainly still now.

But then what? What went wrong? How did I get from that sparkling green beast to here, heaped inside a bus stop, barely able to fight the merciless pull of sleep?

Something flickers way off in the distance, distracting me from my thoughts. An object—a pole? Whatever it is, it extends itself taller and taller—

"You awake?"

The flickering pole solidifies into that of a very tall man. Wolfe, I realize with a jolt. That's his frown way up there. That's his voice that barks down at me.

And then I inhale sharply, as though I've just been slapped in the face. My stomach doesn't simply sink, it flips, and I fight off the sudden urge to vomit. Because a memory has just formed in the back of my brain. An awful one. One of the world going dark as Wolfe and his uncle, the King, stare down at me.

Sedate her.

Those were the words Wolfe muttered as he pushed me into the arms of the bluecoats and Doctor Lebwitski, the man I've come to fear above all else. I had thought Wolfe was on my side, that he was trustworthy, an ally, and then: *Sedate her.*

"You awake?" he asks again.

I'm too full of emotion to put thought into words, but immediately I regret it, as he doubles over to better inspect me. Those metallic eyes are flashing slivers as they scrutinize my every detail.

"Get away from me," I fire at him, or I try to, but the sedative hasn't completely worn away, and my words come out slurred and sandwiched together.

"What's that, now?" he snaps. Impatient, as ever.

"Get away from me," I repeat, clearly this time.

"Oh, that. I take it you have some recollection of the

events leading you here? Good. I don't have time to explain it all at any rate—my uncle's waiting in the limousine as we speak. I came only to update you on something that requires your immediate attention."

I blink, and when I open my eyes again, Wolfe has disappeared. Then a voice that bears his hallmark disinterest whispers in my ear: "That army spotted in Ashville Range. I've convinced my uncle that you think it just that: an army, to protect our nation-state, nothing more. I assured him you suspect nothing of the override chips. Clear?"

Saliva gurgles in the back of my throat.

He must take it for agreement, as he continues briskly, "It goes without saying, your behavior going forward must be no different. Suspicion, especially now," he adds, in a dreary tone, "must not be aroused."

More confused than before—something I didn't think was possible several minutes ago—I open my mouth. A thousand questions sit on the tip of my tongue, but already he's turning on his heel. I call for him, but it's too late. Almost immediately, he becomes nothing more than a shadowy pole that evaporates into the distance. My sense of hopelessness grows, alongside an ember of anger.

That's it, then? That's all the explanation necessary after he shoved me heartlessly into the hands of the enemy? And what about my current predicament, lying like a puddle on the grounds of the Sky Center, barely able to move?

Seconds pass, then minutes. For a while, I consider returning to sleep—a better way to wait out the sedative— but my mind is turning in too many directions for rest to come. Too many emotions, too much injustice, too much building wrath. All I can do is bide my time and wait.

———

AN HOUR LATER, I'm finally able to pull myself to my feet using the plexiglass walls to support me. I scan the horizon. No distant hum of an engine, no black behemoth, no sign of life anywhere. The red-headed woman, clearly Wolfe's messenger, has gone, alongside the man himself.

Well, then. Abandoned in a bus stop by the man I'm destined to wed in just two short months—isn't that the stuff girls dream of.

I roll my eyes, debate crying, then begin inching forward, out of the bus stop, around the blue glass of the Sky Center, and finally, after an eternity, along the winding drive lined with pear trees. By the time I reach the street, my insides swirl with nausea and my head aches more with every step. Still, with no other choice, I drag myself forward along the avenue, teetering along the narrow sidewalk as cars race by next to me.

When the time comes, I turn without hesitation to the Mainframe.

two

. . .

SEVERAL MINUTES LATER, I drop with relief onto a swivel chair. Tufts of cotton escape from small tears, and it squeaks with every minute movement, yet a sense of warmth and contentment washes over me as I settle into the familiar seat. To make matters even better, I'm all alone, aside from an employee stationed in the corner of the room who sleeps soundly.

The computer screen in front of me flickers to life, dates appear along the left-hand column, and I select one at random. Joanne? Bruce? Joanne. Time? Dinner hour—more likely for our three to be home. I slip earphones on and wait while the Mainframe pulls up that precise moment from my mother's life. My heart races with anticipation.

And then I'm staring down at a plate with mashed potato and peas, a fork and knife cut through a piece of chicken, and the rest of the world...the rest of it ceases to exist. Next, a young girl with long, bushy hair fills the screen, her nose buried in a book—and I think to myself that I haven't changed all that much. The visual feed shakes and the sound of my mother's laughter echoes through the earphones, and even though it's distant and tinny, it makes everything hurt all at once. I see my father, too, motioning toward me, and I know without listening that he's imploring me to put the book down, instructing me to eat. It's a friendly argument we had at least once a week, right up until the day he and Mom died, and I hurt even worse.

The younger version of myself rolls her eyes, puts the book aside, and picks up a knife and fork. The video feed shakes once again...more laughter from my mother.

I flip the screen off and stare at my lap.

Deep breath, Alex.

Strange. I don't remember it being so difficult before. So heart-wrenching. But, it's been weeks since I've been here, visiting my parents' memories, and so maybe that's why it catches me off-guard.

I sit for a long time, and once the hurt subsides, at least somewhat, I think about the day. This morning, and all the developments since. The sedative has completely worn off now, and for the first time in hours, I'm completely lucid and thinking clearly. I can recall all the horrific details of the trip to Myopia, yet still, the sight of Wolfe staring down at me as a needle is plunged into my neck is the hardest to ignore. That's saying something, too, considering the discovery we made at Ashville Range—the army of Mavericks amassed by King, and controlled entirely by override chips.

Then there's the fact that I came so close to having an override chip implanted in my own brain. And, finally, the truth of Wolfe's past, now in plain sight before me. He had a wife, and a child. And both, woman and infant, were killed deep in the woods. There had been rage there, on his part, and resentment. He hated his wife, both before and after the tragedy. But his love for the child had been true.

Seismic developments with far-reaching ramifications. Heart-wrenching details. And yet that face, those eyes, peering down at me...it haunts me. Eyes so emotionless that nothing whatsoever had flickered inside. Cold, calculating and void of feeling. And now he wants everything to be the same, like it's that easy to block out that sight, that memory. Like it's that easy to restore my trust in him.

No. I can't trust him...I can't do any of it.

What I should be focusing on, instead of Wolfe, is that I've blown the curious case of the scrolls wide open. I've discovered the secret trying to be conveyed—the override chip program plus the army of robotized Mavericks—and that's worth a pat on the back. And yet I still haven't discovered who my messenger is, or why Timothee and Jill's names would be wrapped up in all this.

Or, frankly, why I would be wrapped up in it, either.

What I need to do to answer those questions, I realize slowly, is track down my caller. And I know the caller comes from this very building, don't I?

Carefully I stand, more excited than before, and approach the Mainframe employee in the corner of the room. He continues to sleep soundly, so I clear my throat. His snores stop, but he doesn't lift his head. I clear my throat a second time and announce: "Ashville Range."

He peers dozily up at me. "Ashton who? Don't know him." He lays his head down again.

I don't think this man is my mystery caller. Clearing my throat for a third time, I ask, "Where can I find the others employed by the Mainframe, please?"

"The employees?"

"Yes, them. The technicians, to be specific."

He appraises me with slightly more interest; still not very much. "What do you want with them?"

"I'd like to have a word, that's all."

"What kind of word?"

"I'd like to ask them some questions," I say tactfully.

"Why?"

"I'm curious about some things."

"What things?"

"Things...related to their job."

"Can't do. This here's the only public place, but don't fret," he adds, yawning. "Once your Selection comes up, you'll be able to see a bit more."

"My Selection has come and gone—"

"It has? Shouldn't you be at work?"

I rub my head, trying to soothe the thumping pain that has grown worse over the past minute, either from this insipid conversation, or from standing. I thank the man who looks set to return to sleep, then step into the cold corridor of the Mainframe. The lobby's to the left, and to the right are double doors, sealed shut. Last time I was here, they hung wide open, the guards and custodians alike distracted by a party with the technicians in the heart of the Mainframe. No such luck today, but that doesn't deter me from giving them a try.

Nothing. No give whatsoever. But, there is a keypad, and I roll up my sleeves, entering first the year, then the address—

"Oi!"

When I turn, I see a familiar guard clad in olive green bearing down on me. Surprise cuts across his face, he comes to a standstill. "What are you doing here?"

"You left my company without so much as a goodbye," I say to Sedaris, the guard that Wolfe tasked to watch over me during that brief yet intractable period of punishment.

He smirks. "Your boyfriend gave me the boot after he saw me getting too familiar. His words, not mine. Looks like I shouldn't have taken words with you, after all."

"And yet now we're able to converse freely. Isn't that nice?" I ask, with a trace of sarcasm.

"A real treat. How are you out and about anyhow? Didn't Slevenia take over my post?"

"Was that her name? She never did mention it. Anyway,

the viscount rescinded his orders shortly after you were replaced. No more guards on my tail."

His brow lifts. "That a fact?"

"That surprises you?"

"You have a way about you, that's all. Didn't take you all that long to free yourself, now did it."

"It took longer than I would've liked," I assure him.

"Nah, you've got a way," he concludes, then he gestures to the keypad I was hunched over a second ago. "And now here you are, poking around the Mainframe. Gets a person thinking."

"Consider me curious, that's all." Before he can interrupt with another snide comment about my curiosity or having some way about me, I say as politely as possible: "On that note, I'm interested in meeting the technicians that work here. Can you please point me in their direction?"

"You want to speak with the technicians," he echoes, as though the request requires some clarification.

I nod. "I'd consider it a personal favor for an old friend."

He chuckles. "Now I'm beginning to see why you've got everyone running scared."

"Oh?"

"Bold little thing behind those big eyes, don't you think?"

"I wouldn't say that, no."

"Aye, well, think again. Anyhow, out you go."

"Just—"

"Don't make me say it again."

"But—"

"You already made me lose one post," Sedaris reminds me. "You're not about to make me lose another."

I can't argue the point, and I trail silently behind him to the exit. A minute later, I stand outside, the Mainframe's doors sealed shut behind me. I won't get my hands on those technicians easily, that much is clear. And yet someone inside beckons to me with those damn scrolls. To what end?

And why, I wonder for the hundredth time, are Jill and Timothee wrapped up in all this? Then I snort. I could use Jill's connections—or even her strength—to get inside the Mainframe, that's for sure. That or Timothee's computer skills to hack my way in.

Right now, though, I realize with a sinking feeling, I have nowhere left to go but home. And my home is that draconian palace soaring overhead, with its glistening windows and spindles catching the late afternoon sun. An enigmatic recluse for a sinister ruler, and home to the man I'm destined to wed, the one that has only ice running through his veins. Yet despite all that, I can't help but admire the strange beauty that is Strath Glen. Without realizing it, I've fallen in love with those cornices, the pillars, even the weathervanes. I've come to admire the neat rows of windows, the drafty stables, the well-pruned shrubs. Even the plenitude of the interior alongside the eerie décor is less off-putting than it once was.

If it weren't for the occupants who fill me with dread, I might actually enjoy the climb up the steps toward the towering front doors. But occupants there are, plenty of them, and my pulse races as I draw nearer, my fingers shake at the prospect of seeing King or Wolfe. The thought makes me break into a sweat. It makes me want to run far, far away.

"You get left behind at the airport or something?" Jill shouts from her spot next to the front door. Half her mouth twitches into a smile and she makes a show of checking her watch. "Your fiancé arrived back here hours ago."

"As a matter of fact, I was left behind," I reply, and even though my voice is curt, I feel a rush of relief at seeing her familiar face. A friendly one, too.

"Get out of here."

"I wish I was joking, believe me."

"But wasn't it your fiancé you were piloting?"

"Correct again."

She considers me, then spits over the banister. "You okay, princess? You look like you've seen a ghost."

Far worse, I think to myself, but of course, I can't say that. I can't say a thing, not when the Mainframe will have a permanent record of it. I can't act differently, either, if Wolfe's to be believed. So, I force myself to smile. "Nothing that a warm shower can't remedy."

"That and a slug to your fiancé's nose," she adds, winking. "Want me to take care of it?" She cracks her knuckles.

"If anyone gets to punch him, it's me," I assure her as I pat her shoulder. Then I walk across the threshold, more nervous than before. All those sounds—palace sounds—hit me at once. The drilling from way up high, the laughter emanating from below, the argument in the library. The parrot screams in Devonshire, a gust of wind rattles the door behind me, and it's dizzying—all of it. But, I catch the sound of a voice singing an aria from Bishop's Aisle, way up on the top floor—King—and all those other sounds vanish, like they're sucked into a vortex. Goosebumps slip over my skin at the prospect of seeing King for the first time since the fiasco at the Sky Center, but in a stroke of luck, the aria fades into the distance.

It's immediately replaced with the sound of high heels echoing across the black polished floor. The Queen.

She cocks her head to the side when she sees me, smiling sweetly. "You dirty birdie, you!" she exclaims.

"Uh, yes," I acknowledge, looking down at my filthy blue jumpsuit. "I'm on my way to change right now," I assure her.

"Enjoy your evolution!" she trills as she sweeps by me and into the library.

I stare after her. Yes...the artificial intelligence that powers the override chips could definitely be strengthened. But I remember all those floating heads upstairs along Bishop's Aisle—the victims of early experiments with chip implantation, and I wonder if the Queen's override chip is a bit experimental, too.

"Always a killer!" screeches the parrot from Devonshire.

"Move, move!" shout a group of well-dressed women. Princess Aubrey's personal milliners, I think...and I'm smacked across the face with a powder-pink hat box.

Cradling my cheek, I edge sideways, where I'm almost flattened by a dozen men in fedoras. "Run, chicken-little!" one of them shouts at me with a glowering look over his shoulder.

"Always a killer!"

I slip behind a Ming vase and wait for the bustle to fade, and when the corridors are empty, I take the stairs up to the second floor two at a time. Almost there. Almost to the confines of my room, and I don't think I've ever been so happy to see the dizzying, bizarre House of Mirrors. Through a world of black and white I go, my reflection bouncing from one mirror to the next, my pallid appearance impossible to ignore—

"Dearest, a late return from the Sky Center, isn't it?"

I trip over my feet, just barely stopping myself from landing flat on my face, then spin around to see Wolfe's mother, the duchess, considering me. Her gaze lingers on my red cheek and the patches of dirt along my jumpsuit. "Y-Yes, well," I stutter. "I, um, missed my ride."

"Do you mean to say that my son forgot you?"

I know the woman enough to sense that it's a loaded question. "Uh—"

"There you are, sister! I've been looking for you all day long!" Evie, Wolfe's younger sister, studies me. "Did you know that my dearest brother returned to the palace hours ago? And in what a mood—my! Whatever happened?"

Two sets of Rocksavage eyes lay into me, waiting patiently for an answer, and here I am, too exhausted, too overwhelmed to string a simple sentence together, let alone something half-intelligent that won't ignite further interest or investigation into the dreaded adventure.

Theater, Alex, I remind myself. Life's a theater—especially here at Strath Glen.

So, I plaster a smile on my face and wave my hand dismissively. "Nothing but a misunderstanding," I trill. "A misunderstanding that caused me to miss my ride."

"Oh, poor sister!" Evie shouts, laying a hand upon my shoulder. "You must be absolutely ready for a long old sleep." Then her gaze meanders down my jumpsuit, her eyes rounding with horror at the dirty patches. "After a bath, of course," she adds tactfully.

I smile graciously at Evie, but my smile fades when I catch sight of the duchess. She's astute, just like her son, and it's painfully obvious right now that she doesn't believe a word.

three

· · ·

THE NEXT MORNING, there comes a knocking at the door, and it pulls me from my sleep. A shame, too, as it had been a pleasant dream, one of life back in Quire, the aroma of Aunt Jo's meat pies in the air, the fire crackling, laughter abounding, even as a tall, unknowable shadow lingered in the corner.

The knocking comes again, louder this time, and I push away the covers, grumbling. When I finally open the door, it's Gerard, the head butler, standing there, his suit perfectly pressed, his white button-up starched, his hands tucked professionally behind his back.

"Yes?" I ask, between yawns.

"A message, miss, from the viscount."

My brow furrows and I peer at him. "Oh?"

"He asked me to pass along his apologies for not seeing you home from the Sky Center," he begins.

I resist the urge to roll my eyes. Some apology, coming through the butler rather than said to me in person. Cowardly, too.

"And to remind you," Gerard continues, "of this evening's dinner, taken at its normal time, as usual."

Ah. So, the apology, lame as it was, had been a ruse. Attend dinner, keep up appearances—*that* had been the real message. I thank the old butler, then head to the closet to pull on riding clothes, the most sensible and comfortable of the palace's offerings. Finally, after I'm dressed and ready for a day I'd rather avoid, I take a moment and stare at my reflection.

Funny. My face betrays none of the emotion currently boxed in my chest—the tidal wave of anger rolling in whenever I think of Wolfe, the lightning bolt of fear I experience when I think of King, the bluecoats, or Doctor Lebwitski. It reveals none of the secrets I've uncovered, either—shocking ones, *damning* ones. So...perhaps keeping up appearances will be easier than imagined.

Later that day, however, after hours of avoiding the royal family at every turn, I stand outside the doors to Carnegie Reserve, frozen. Nerves erupt in my belly. There's legitimate fear there, of course. After all, if King discovers that I know of the override chips, I'll have one planted in my own brain—rendering me as good as dead.

I'm lucky to have avoided it yesterday, frankly. One little misstep and I'll almost certainly meet that terrible fate. Yes, even though I hate to admit it, Wolfe's right. Every conversation I have must now be disguised. And the scrolls...I must now take efforts to conceal even them. Tailing King to learn more of his deranged ways is no longer a possibility, either—not really. Nothing can make him suspicious, or I'm done for.

But there's another reason I falter outside Carnegie, and it's not King, and it's not fear. It's the viscount, simply put. Yesterday morning I'd counted him an ally. I had trusted him, and now that trust has been laid to waste. How much of what he said on the helicopter had even been true? How much involvement in the override chip program has he really had? And, most pressing, where do his loyalties truly lie?

I don't see how I can act normally around him when so much has changed.

I take a deep breath and remind myself that I have to try. I resign myself to being polite, civil. I'll eat some dinner, make chit-chat, then retreat to my quarters. A straightforward plan, one that gives me some semblance of security.

But as soon as I swing open Carnegie's door, I realize that the evening will be anything but ordinary, and all thoughts of my plan, if I can even call it that, go out the window.

There's a full, thunderous party underway. The only light comes from the thousands of colorful fluorescent tubes that zigzag across the walls and hang in twirling streamers from the chandeliers. Neon confetti rains continuously from the ceiling and sparklers erupt every few seconds in each of the corners. The choir sings gospel with fervor, the vultures sing along as they dance.

"Sister!" Evie shouts, grabbing me by the wrists. She spins me merrily in a circle, then adds in a scolding tone, "What a boring old outfit for Matthew's homecoming, my!"

"Sorry?"

"Have you not heard the news? Heavens! It's a rock you live under, positively!"

"I was away from the palace yesterday," I remind her as my stomach squeezes ever so slightly. Being out of the loop makes me nervous, or maybe it's the prospect of change doing it. After all, it's difficult enough to keep up with the pace of the household as it is. "What happened?"

"Dear Matthew, sister! Aubrey's husband, of course. He's only just arrived. Do you see him there?" She points through a sea of people to a man with a close-shaved head and a navy-blue suit embellished with gold tassels. "He came as soon as he got wind of the pregnancy," she adds, with a whisp of admiration. "He's *very* serious about his role as a father, I think. Oh, how terrible of me! How was your day? Did you get some much-needed rest last night? And soap? Did you sort out the misunderstanding from yesterday's excursion? Was my brother impressed with your piloting skills?"

"One could say that," I say tactfully as Evie pulls me forward, deeper into the crowd. She places a glowstick around my neck while I help myself to a glass of champagne.

Aubrey, dressed in swaths of bubble-gum lace and with her hair spun into a towering updo, steps in front of us. She kisses Evie on the cheeks and exclaims, "Can you believe my luck!"

"Cousin?"

"A rave in my honor," she exclaims, sounding giddy, then she links arms with Dear Matthew, who appears at her side, and together they make the rounds through the crowd, nodding at guests, shaking hands with the more senior members of their social circle—the very definition of courtly. A façade of marital bliss, too. One as artificial as the one me and the viscount will hide behind in just two paltry months. The thought makes me feel like a deflated balloon, and I find myself hoping for a far better future for Evie.

I'm distracted a second later, for it's at that very moment that I spot him across the room, dressed in grey, towering over the crowd, deep in conversation with...who else...King! And the deflated balloon sensation grows worse.

As Evie shrieks happily with some girls from a west-side estate, I watch Wolfe and King through the near darkness. The ruler of our nation-state must say something amusing because half of Wolfe's mouth flickers into a smile. It's just a fleeting moment, a hint of laughter at his lip, but it's enough to turn my stomach. His allegiance to King and to his own position of power have always been manifest. My own conceit is to blame for thinking otherwise, really.

But the realization doesn't make me hurt any less.

A moment later, I turn away, deciding I'd rather observe the falsities of Aubrey and Dear Matthew, both clearly masters of the craft. Maybe if I observe them closely enough, I'll pick up a few tips.

Tethered at the elbow to each other but otherwise turned to the crowd, they move in lockstep. A dash of the hand here, a flash of teeth there—a winning combination, judging by the gleeful faces left in their wake.

Eventually, I yawn and face up to it: hiding in my room is far more appealing than play-acting for this crowd. And really, I've already made an appearance, haven't I?

I start for the door, looking forward to an evening curled up with a book before me, when a gloomy voice sounds in my ear: "I assume introductions have been made."

I turn to see Wolfe peering down at me with that disinterested expression of his plastered across his face. "Introductions?" I echo.

"To the man of the hour, naturally." He tips his head in the direction of Dear Matthew. Right now, King's arm is draped over Dear Matthew's shoulder, and yet, as I watch, King's watery eyes flick with intention over the crowd, stalling on me.

I stand straighter and try to ignore the shiver going down my spine. But between King's gaze and the fact that Evie and her mother stand within earshot, I realize that falsities really are imperative. So, with effort, I tuck both hands behind my back and lift my chin politely to Wolfe. "Not formally, sir, but we have exchanged words at the Rose Ceremony. Sir."

His gaze narrows at this last *sir*, and his mouth puckers ever so slightly. He knows I'm being false, but he says nothing about it. Instead, he clears his throat and continues, "Tell me what was said at the Rose Ceremony."

"God help you."

He frowns openly, his brow scrunching in the middle. "Pardon me?"

"God help you. That's what your cousin-in-law said to me."

"Evie, you are too young to be drinking," he chides, and he snatches the glass from her hand without removing his gaze from mine. "What prompted such an utterance?"

"Perhaps you should ask him. Sir."

Eyes flash like a warning. "I am asking you, now."

"It was nothing more than a conversation with Aubrey herself that prompted it, if you must know."

"Tell me of that conversation, then."

"Is this an inquisition?" I ask in my sweetest voice.

He folds at the waist and says quietly between clenched teeth: "It's called making conversation. Something those engaged to be married tend to do."

"Those engaged to be married tend not to desert the other in a bus stop, and yet here we are," I counter.

His eyes sweep purposefully over the people standing nearby. "Do recall what I said to you at that bus stop," he reminds me.

"If I'd forgotten, I wouldn't be standing here in the first place," I point out.

He leans back on his heels, looking mildly disconcerted. "Meaning..."

"Meaning that we should discuss the weather," I finish coolly.

His lips press into a thin line. Then he clears his throat, gathering himself, and says brusquely, "I am now curious. What conversation with my cousin prompted Matthew to utter something so unusual?"

"If memory serves me, she was busy enlightening me on how little I will please you. *Sir*."

"Viscount, cousin-in-law," comes a voice from over my shoulder, and then Matthew's pushing toward Wolfe, he's clenching Wolfe's hand in his as Aubrey teeters on her stilettos charging after him. "I'll be needing your advice on all matters of things now that I'm taking up residence at yours, and with a babe en route!"

Wolfe merely nods, curt as ever, gaze fixed my way. He's annoyed with me, that much is clear. I suppose I am being rude. And I *did* decide to take the helicopter to Ashville Range, breaking the rules in the first place. And yet that transgression is nothing compared to his—

"This little thing is all yours, I presume?" Dear Matthew continues, and without waiting for a response, he wraps an arm around my waist and taps my behind. It makes Aubrey's mouth pinch, though I don't think it's Matthew she's jealous of. Almost immediately, she's distracted by a mob of gushing young women who place their hands over her stomach and bombard her with well-received questions.

Wolfe grumbles something indecipherable.

"I've seen you before, doll," he adds to me. "Don't think I forget so quickly."

"And yet your disposition has markedly changed since," I remind him.

"A change in circumstance sometimes requires as much. And here's me calling the kettle black. I've been led to believe you herald from a modest neighborhood, thrust into palace life against all odds, hmm? If that doesn't change a person—"

"On the contrary."

He squeezes me tighter. Then he pushes his face close to mine so his mouth is tight against my ear. His breath is hot; he smells like salt: "You don't wish to be here anymore than I do. I can see it all over that sweet little face of yours. Blink if I'm right—gotcha! So, doll. Looks like you and me have a special connection, and so soon—"

"What's this?" demands Wolfe, gesturing to Dear Matthew. "A man of your rank, whispering secrets to my fiancé right in front of me. Do it again and see." Just as quickly he turns to his father and launches into a boring-sounding conversation regarding a trade agreement, completely forgetting about my existence.

I sigh. Nothing but optics here, from every angle, and here I am, forced to join the masquerade.

"Amelia Earhart, with bunny ears. That's what I'll call you," roars King a moment later as he steps in front of me and pinches my nose.

I swallow, hoping that the reference to Earhart, a female aviation hero who disappeared many generations ago, isn't a vaguely concealed threat. I drop into a curtsy, ignoring the way my heart hammers, and say, "Good evening, King. A lively event tonight."

"For a lively fellow! A tremendous turnout, too! My heart's a flutter! I see the two of you are getting acquainted?"

"Uh...indeed. It seems we have quite a bit in common, both being lucky enough to be betrothed to royalty."

"My mighty Mainframe made you a superstar, didn't it, my dearest twinkle?"

"Um, yes, King," I say politely, determined to be pleasant, and agreeable, and the opposite of threatening.

"Speaking of your betrothed," he continues, "quite an adventure in the skies with yours yesterday, hmm, Amelia Bunny-Ears?"

In my peripheral vision, I spot Wolfe turning his watchful eyes upon us. "One I'm still recovering from," I say carefully, fingering my neck where the syringe had entered.

"Nasty business, that," agrees King, his eyes catching in the neon light so they glow orange. "I'm afraid there was a mix-up at the Mainframe, and my prized bluecoats thought you were in a tizzy. An attempt to calm you, is all. I trust the sedation left you no worse for wear?"

I cough to disguise a snort of laughter. Just how stupid does he think me? Very, evidently. And yet, he had said himself that he doesn't find me stupid in the slightest... It had been Wolfe who had insisted that I was, and now I understand why. After all, if King thinks I'm stupid, I'm much less a threat, meaning my survival is far more likely.

"My dearest?" prods King, fluttering his eyelashes for effect.

"No...no worse for wear, King. An understandable mistake," I add generously, as go-go dancers begin to flood Carnegie.

"Tremendous!" shouts King, though I'm not sure if he's referring to me or to the dancers.

"Papa!" shouts a new voice that belongs to James. "Heavens, go to Mother at once. Her gown is wedged between the tables, near to the tattoo artist. I'm afraid she'll be inked any second if she keeps lingering."

"Daises," mutters King, and he disappears into the darkness.

Before I can breathe a sigh of relief, James takes up his spot. He lifts my hand and begins fastening glow sticks to my wrist. "You're positively glowing, my flower," he coos, then he kisses my fingers. "Dear Matthew," he calls, "have you met this little one? Don't mistake her for a bore, not in the slightest."

Matthew steps toward us and repositions his arm around my waist. "I was just chatting with her, matter of. Her fiancé told me to take the heave-ho, but, in all honesty, I think she'd like to say the same to him."

James shakes with laughter. "It's only natural! But is it true?" he asks me. "Would you rather a prince by your side?"

I'm spared from answering by Evie returning to the

conversation and tutting her tongue. "I told you, cousin, about this. Stop sniffing about, and you," she adds to Dear Matthew in a scolding tone, "keep your hands to yourself."

"Don't bother yourself, Evie," interjects Wolfe lazily.

All four of us look at him. Quite a turn from the man casting threats a minute ago. Then he steps closer, and Matthew's arm drops at once. Whoever this man is, Dear Matthew, he is cautious around Wolfe. His bravado extends only so far. And yet, I don't want to depend on my fiancé for anything since where did it get me last time? Drugged and forgotten about in a bus stop miles from the palace, that's where.

I wait for the others to return to their conversations, then approach Dear Matthew, determined to both make an alliance and gain some vital information that's long been leaving me wondering. "I'd like a word," I say. "In private."

His eyebrows shoot up and he whispers something to James, who suddenly looks gleeful. I ignore it and lead Matthew away, but not before Wolfe notices. In my peripheral, I see him frown so deeply it makes the angle of his mouth sharp and unpleasant.

Perhaps at one point I would've felt badly, but not any longer.

I lead Dear Matthew to the far side of Carnegie, where it's quietest, and we stand in front of a fluorescent light in the shape of a heart. "You and I really do have a lot in common, you know."

"Look, babe. You're not really my type—"

"What? No. I mean we have a lot in common since we've both been betrothed to royalty."

"Oh, yeah. So?"

I shake my head, beginning to regret my decision to steal Matthew's ear. "Listen, my feelings toward the viscount have no bearing on what I'm about to ask you. Do you understand?"

He spreads his arms. "Whatever you say, doll."

"My name is Alex."

"Alright, Alex. I'm listening."

"Since your marriage to Aubrey, until today, you have resided elsewhere—"

"And you want to know how I swindled my way into it, isn't that right?" He laughs. "And you think it has no bearing on your feelings for that arse, yeah?"

"I feel for him the same way he feels for me, I can assure you. There's no reason to laugh at his expense."

"You defend him, even though you clearly don't like him. But what of his feelings for you? He sure was quick to stop me from whispering sweet-nothings in your ear, wouldn't you say? Oh, sure, he's never liked me. Does as the boss-man does, and the boss-man's never thought me up to his precious princess' snuff. But still, he must care about you in some capacity."

At these last words, I glance through the crowd in Wolfe's direction, I find him staring at me from the very spot I left him. He looks completely disinterested, his face like a mask, except for the fact that his gaze doesn't shift away from us for even a moment, no matter the number of inter- ruptions that pull at his jacket-sleeve. "Not him," I clarify, even though there's a whisp of satisfaction I feel, torturing Wolfe as I clearly am. "I wish to discuss you. How is it that you were able to reside elsewhere?"

"You'll never be able to pull it off, doll. I wanted to be here as little as Aubrey wanted me here. So, aces. You... You've got a different situation. If the viscount wants you here, then here you'll stay. Besides, the viscount is King's apprentice. He won't stand for his fiancé living elsewhere, not for a second. The whole palace is theater, haven't you noticed? What of me, huh? Do you think I want to cozy up to yours? Listen, kid. You seem all fine and good, but don't buy anything I'm selling. And if you want to survive life here with this lot, you might want to start working on your own act." With a sidelong look, he disappears, clasping arms with Aubrey, who appears at his side as if from thin air. The meet and greets, complete with the wrist swishes and toothy smiles, continue as if they never stopped in the first place.

"Sister," Evie gushes a minute later, grabbing my arm and pulling me through the crowd. "Tell me *everything*. Why is it you wanted Dear Matthew's ear? You're driving my brother mad, I'm *sure* of it. And speaking of him, did you see who just turned up?" We finally emerge through the throng, and she points toward the punch bowls.

Claudia stands there in a tight dress, chatting breezily to the duchess. They look like old friends, and for a reason I can't ascertain—especially given how much anger I feel toward Wolfe right now—it leaves me with a sour taste in my mouth. The whole day does—yesterday, too—and no matter which direction I turn, it's only made worse by each and every development.

How much I'd give to leave it all behind, to return to my rightful home in Quire—

"Well, sister? The curiosity is killing me, absolutely!"

"With Dear Matthew," I explain, coming back to reality, "I was curious as to his living arrangements until now, that's all. As for Claudia, do you know what she's doing here?"

"I don't have the foggiest. Nobody tells me a thing, remember? I suppose she's ready to return to the party circuit, the shock of not being betrothed to brother having finally worn off. That must be her fiancé, there." She points to a boxy man who carries her purse, and I notice Wolfe contemplating him, too.

I sigh because something tells me that Dear Matthew's homecoming won't be the only change to life at Strath Glen. Not at all.

four

. . .

THE EXCITEMENT SURROUNDING the arrival of Dear Matthew and the return of Claudia to Strath Glen's party scene wanes little in the days following. Festivity is tactile in the air, and each evening laughter rings louder through Carnegie. Drink is indulged in with particular earnest, and each event lasts longer and later into the night.

The advice I received from Dear Matthew and the viscount is not forgotten. I must keep up appearances. I'd even be wise to take it further, to adopt a false act to see me through life here at the palace surrounded by false acts.

But always I've been true to myself. Never have I been one to put on a show. So, instead of joining the ongoing party, I've taken refuge in my quarters, hoping that my absence won't be noticed amidst all the madness.

The dullness of the slow passing days is something I've come to loathe, but at the very least, it's allowed me to stay out of sight of Wolfe and King. And, if Claudia's return to the palace has rekindled a romance between her and Wolfe, so be it. Whatever moments of fleeting tenderness we've shared in the past have been shattered apart by his callous treatment at the Sky Center.

I nip what I can from the kitchen throughout the day, careful to stick to the servants' stairs and underused corridors to avoid my soon-to-be family, and the evenings are so riotous that I really don't think I'm missed anyhow.

The rest of my time is spent contemplating, thinking, planning.

There's no longer any question that the Mainframe's Selection system must be dismantled, the override chip program must be overturned, King must be sacked. But, of course, none of that is readily doable, particularly for a lone girl from Quire. And yet something has to be done. Too many people are getting slotted into lives that don't interest them, and when their dissatisfaction becomes known, they are tampered with—an override chip forcibly placed in their brain so they become controlled entirely by the Mainframe, outward contentedness ensured, and, given the lifetime of data the Mainframe has to work with, loved ones don't suspect a thing.

Then there's the Mavericks. Mindless machines trained for battle. But for what? What threat is King arming himself against? Surely not the surrounding nations. Airo-Aurora may be a pariah-state with its chip-system in place, but the viscount himself had said that we're left to our own devices, not in violation of any international law. So, the answer must come from within the nation-state itself. Dissatisfaction must be growing at a faster rate than I realize. King must be getting nervous of an uprising. A new dawn. An Airo-Aurora spring.

So. What can I do about any of it?

Despite regularly checking the stables, a new scroll hasn't shown itself since the one with the coordinates. I still don't know what role Timothee or Jill play in the whole thing, or which technician is my mystery caller.

I sit straighter on the sofa, the book splayed open on my lap toppling to the floor. Presumably I'll receive another scroll soon. After all, why should I stop receiving them now? And another scroll means another delivery. So, all I must do is wait in the stables and nab the person!

Of course, that may be easier said than done. Sitting in the stables all day during the current cold snap sounds less than pleasant, and surely suspicions would be aroused should I be stumbled upon by the servants or, god forbid, the viscount himself.

I drum my fingers. Well, if it is a technician, he or she would presumably be busy with work throughout the day. That leaves morning or evening, maybe even a lunch break. And I already know that the sender of the scrolls writes them in the dark to avoid a stain on his or her feed...so, presumably, delivery would be taken under darkness as well.

The evening then, right after the workday is complete. That's the most logical time for delivery, and so that's when I'll station myself inside the stables.

I stand from the sofa and draw up alongside the window in the middle of the room. I push back the satin curtains so I can survey the stables and the birch trees fighting for space behind it. And I smile.

The start of a plan.

———

IT'S LATE ENOUGH in the day now. As I slip from my quarters en route to the stables, a small squeal emanates from behind me. I turn and see Rebecca standing there, one of the maids. Kindly wouldn't quite be the word to describe her. In fact, the list of tricks she's played on me is long enough to take some recounting, and even though a truce had been negotiated between us, suspicion remains well and warranted.

Right now, she stands stalk still, holding a stack of

towels and a handful of soaps carved into swans. She stares at me with wide eyes.

"Am I blocking your path?" I finally ask, stepping to the side. The mirrors surrounding us catch my reflection, then drop it a second later.

Rebecca shakes her head hard enough that her ringlets smack her across the face. She grins mischievously. "Me, I was just restocking the essentials in your fiancé's quarters, like, and I heard something you wouldn't go on and believe."

"Oh?"

"Aye. You really wouldn't believe it, not in a million and one years."

"What is it?"

She blinks at me, looking horrified. "But I can't go on and tell yeh!"

"Let me get this straight," I say, as my patience runs thin. "You came to tell me that you have news that concerns me, but that the news can't be shared. Is that really necessary?"

"I didn't mean to offend yeh. We made a deal, fair and square, you and me. Don't think I've forgotten just how you got my back up against the wall, like. But go on. Just thought you'd like to know that change is afoot!" She winks, then darts around me and down the black and white checkerboard hall, finally disappearing under the rotunda.

A draft hits me along the back of the neck, making my hair stand on end, and I stare at the spot she occupied a moment earlier, wondering just what change she's privy to.

five

. . .

WITH A BRICK SET CAREFULLY along the doorjamb and a spare cloak pulled over my shoulders, I set out into the night. The slushy snow has hardened with the dropping mercury, and it crunches loudly underfoot—not exactly ideal for a secret mission. Every few steps I pause, I check over my shoulder, expecting to see the outline of a body blocking the sliver of light spilling out the back door.

It doesn't come, and I step inside the stables in a rush of relief. I should've brought a lantern—that's my first thought. Without the aid of the moonlight, the black is impenetrable. But after a few minutes, my vision adjusts, just as it did when I was here last with the man I'm obliged to wed. I shiver as I think about it, because it was here that he subjected me to those cruel curtailments to my freedom. It was here I glimpsed true emotion in him—anger, and frustration. To his credit, he had lifted those restrictions soon after, he had even uttered a nicety: *It was never my intention to hurt you like this.* He also shared with me pertinent details concerning the Mainframe—useful ones. Then, after all that, he shoved me heartlessly into the arms of Doctor Lebwitski.

Sedate her.

It's senseless. The man is impossible to understand, and frankly, I'm done trying.

Instead of wasting time standing around, I scour the stable as best I can in the darkness, stubbing my toe and bumping my nose in the process, checking obvious hiding places for any more scrolls. Nothing. Eventually, I shove my hands into the pockets of the cloak and bounce on the balls of my feet to stay warm. Following that, the pacing begins. Back and forth along the old barn boards. I trip over a loose plank, then a pail. I listen to the quickening of my chattering teeth and try to draw up the sound of approaching footsteps. Nothing but silence—even the horses have little to say.

Eventually, dinner hour arrives, the ending of the workday has come and gone, and I'm unable to bear the dampness, the dark, or the boredom for another second anyhow. Defeated, I push carefully into the night, then run as fast as my boots will allow, slipping and sliding across the hardened snow, all the way back to the palace. I can barely coax my fingers to move enough to lift the brick from the doorjamb, but once inside, the heat fills my insides and makes my extremities tingle. With my cheeks burning, I hang the cloak in the closet beside the backdoor where I found it, straighten my blazer, and head for Carnegie.

Best to make an appearance since I'm here anyhow, then back to my quarters for a long, lonely evening. I wonder what Aunt Jo is doing right now, or my best friend, Agnes. And Patrick, the boy all of Quire thought I'd be matched with, is he sitting down for dinner right now with his betrothed?

I turn the last corner before Carnegie and my sopping boots slow, because at the far end of the corridor, I spot the viscount and none other than Claudia, walking together in a slow, sauntering fashion. I suppose they've rekindled things after all, and I can't tell, with everything else going on in my life, if I feel apathy, or anger. If I feel jealous, or like joking.

Regardless of what I may feel, I take a closer look at her. She wears a short dress crafted in hot pink wool, and tonight, she's unfettered by her fiancé. Maybe it's for this reason that she walks so close to my own. As for Wolfe, he moves with his usual disinterest, engaging by the looks of it in polite conversation, his eyes fixed on the sparkling floor in front of him.

Finally, he lifts his gaze, and he frowns when he spots me down the hall. A second later, I slip inside Carnegie without a backward glance.

Tonight, red balloons by the thousands cling to the ceiling, they're tethered in giant bundles to the tables, and even to the trumpets. Morocco ties three bundles to Aubrey's wrist and shouts something about the baby's gender. James dances the jive with some girls from an east side estate, and Dear Matthew plays a card trick with King. At the table that I typically occupy sits Evie, staring at the debauchery, looking uncharacteristically melancholy.

"Is everything okay?" I ask, sliding into the seat next to her.

She seems to brighten at having company. "Splendid to see you, sister! It seems as though it has been absolute years since I last enjoyed your presence, you elusive bee, you!"

"I was...under the weather, I'm afraid," I reply, silently making a note not to skip these evenings in Carnegie after all. It appears my absence has been noticed, at least by her.

"The dreaded spring cold—a common malady at this time of year," she responds agreeably. "Where's my cherished big brother?"

"With Claudia," I reply evenly.

Evie shoots me a look, her brow knotted. "I'm sure it's nothi—"

"It doesn't matter." I take a moment to straighten my napkin. "So, tell me, how are things with Theodore?"

"Dead as a fish in the water. Is that how the saying goes? Oh, it doesn't matter. The point is, I don't have the foggiest who I'm going to be paired with during my Selection, and the very thought leaves me bothered."

"Don't you trust the Mainframe to pick the right fellow?" I ask quietly.

She pouts her lips. "You sound just like big brother. And of course I do—of course! But I thought there'd be a number of gentlemen near and dear to my heart, and the Mainframe would simply...oh, I don't know—help me make a difficult decision! Does that make any sense whatsoever, sister?"

"It does," I assure her as I squeeze her hand. "And maybe it will work out that way. Your Selection isn't exactly around the corner."

"But it's less than a year out! That doesn't give me much time to work with, I'm afraid. Not by my books. I simply don't know how you bear being selected to a perfect stranger. Well, I suppose he's not a stranger anymore, is he? I should get some solace from that."

I say nothing. Wolfe is more a stranger now than when I first met him, but I'm not about to take that bit of comfort from Evie. Instead, I motion to the crowd. "Looks like there are many potential suitors here tonight, doesn't there? Why not mingle?"

Her gaze sweeps across Carnegie and lands on Aubrey, who rubs a belly that looks no more pregnant than a month ago. "I shall, I shall," she murmurs, once again melancholy.

"Evie, aside from your concern about the Selection, what's wrong?"

"There's just so much change happening around here," she says with a sigh. "Sometimes I feel lost in the shuffle. Is that absolutely foolish?"

"Well, you're not lost to me. In fact, I think I'd lose my mind if it weren't for you."

She beams at me.

"Why is your face so flush?" comes the viscount's voice from way up high.

"I'm warm," I reply levelly.

"Sister's been sick, did you even know?" Evie deigns to add.

"Oh?"

I nod.

"Would that explain your absence from dinner the past few days?"

My body stiffens. Lying doesn't come naturally, but still I say, "It would."

His eyes narrow like he can see straight through me. "That seems satisfactory," he eventually grumbles. With that, he moves off to speak with his father.

"Evie, darling!" gushes a voice positively ringing with falsity. "However have you been? How I've missed our cherished sisterly chats." Claudia pulls out the chair next to Evie and, after kissing the girl on her head, seats herself with a dramatic toss of her hair.

"I've been keeping just fine," Evie replies, smiling. "Busy with my studies—you know how Mother and Father are. And yourself? Have you—"

"Why in the heavens aren't you on the dance floor?" Claudia interrupts, crossing her arms and pouting. "Has your tablemate been tethering you in place with her old-timey street knowledge?" She flutters her eyelashes innocently, and I'm reminded of King. I'm reminded of the entire aristocracy, actually.

"On the contrary!" Evie exclaims, good-natured as always. "Sister has been keeping me company as I simply don't feel like dancing—not yet, anyway. Say, have you met Alex?"

"I have had the dreaded misfortune, yes," she says glumly, without taking her heavily mascaraed eyes from Evie.

I roll my own. Clearly, Claudia doesn't realize I'm by now so accustomed to such barbs that I barely notice them.

"I can only imagine how strange it is to have the derelict dining right next to you, by god," Claudia adds.

Evie, for once, seems at a loss for words. For a second, I think she'll brush the remark aside. Then she sits straighter and says in a tight voice, "That isn't very nice."

It isn't often anyone stands up for me here at Strath Glen. Always the barbs are swept under the carpet. And so it's hard not to feel a rush of affection and warmth toward Evie, and it's all I can do not to hug her that very moment.

Claudia, too, looks shocked. Quickly she regains her composure and the false smile returns to her face. "Evie, darling...heavens. I was only joking, don't you know?"

Evie clears her throat and considers the red balloons overhead. They seem to sag a little lower than when I first arrived, I notice. Then Evie says pleasantly, "So, where is your charming fiancé tonight?"

"That lout? He has a match of some sort or another," Claudia replies, waving her well-manicured hand. "Boxing, or wrestling—rugby, that's it. Something absolutely vulgar and a complete disgrace to the Patel family name." She says all this in a bored tone as she scans the crowd.

"But you must have other things in common, given your pairing?" Evie presses, and I know that, once again, she thinks of her own impending Selection.

"A body to die for. It's mainly his pedigree that I object to. Of course his family is filthy rich, naturally, but they lack the touch of civilization one might expect from our crowd, *if* you know what I'm saying. Anyhow, I feel a fool complaining when there exist far more ill-matched pairings in the world," and her cool eyes finally acknowledge me.

Evie looks downright indignant. "Surely you aren't referencing Alex and my brother, because ill-matched pairings isn't the term I'd use—"

I pat her on the arm. "Don't trouble yourself, Evie, though I really do appreciate it." Then I push back my chair, ready to call it a night.

But Evie shouts, "Where are you going, sister? Don't tell me you're leaving?" and she says it so earnestly, with such round eyes, that I feel myself shaking my head.

"Uh, no. No, of course not. I'm going to get a drink, that's all."

"Oh, phew, sister. Promise me you won't leave until we speak again?"

"Certainly," I agree.

Claudia, for her part, has a sour look upon her face that brings me more joy than I care to admit. A moment later, I lift a flute of sparkling wine from a passing tray and head in the direction of the brass band.

"Hiya, doll. You been hiding on me, or something? Here I was, thinking we'd be two amigos."

I glance over my shoulder and see Dear Matthew raise a glass to me. "Good evening," I reply. Lifting my voice over the trumpets. "And no, I haven't been hiding from you in the slightest," I lie. Emboldened, I add, "I've just had a touch of a spring cold, that's all."

"You look healthy as a horse to me. But, who'd want to miss such festivities?" and he lifts his gaze to the tide of red balloons that now hang only a meter or two overhead.

"Your homecoming has certainly been well-received."

He puffs his chest and agrees.

"Amelia Bunny-Ears, is that really you?" calls King as he fights his way through a bundle of balloons. "Why, you've been missing the festivities!"

"That's precisely what I said!" exclaims Dear Matthew,

as my stomach sinks. "This little one hasn't been feeling well lately, the poor thing."

King gasps. "You mean to say you've been sick as a dog, trapped under a log?"

"No, no," I say quickly, trying to disperse of the unwanted attention. "Nothing serious. Just...a sore throat, that's all."

"Could it be you're being poisoned by the servant staff, dear one?"

I swallow as I turn to him. "I hope not, King."

"A rebellious cat will get broken like that," he says wisely.

"Good thing, then, that I'm no rebel," I reply.

"Ah, yes. And, has my nephew been taking good care of yours?" he continues, his brow drawing together in a show of concern.

"As well as he can," I say diplomatically, "considering all the other matters he has to tend to."

"Oh, most definitely. He's been helping me with a dossier or two of my own these past days, and I must say, his efficiency continues to please me. What an asset!"

"Really, Papa?" comes James's voice as he sidles up behind us. "And am I not an asset? Did I not renew the contract for snow removal just two weeks past?"

"It should've been done at the start of the snow season, you fool," King retorts. "Not the end."

"How unfair," James says, sulking. "Do you remember, Papa, who shall inherit the throne?"

King's face sours, much like Claudia's did a few minutes ago. "Yes, well." He coughs lightly into his fist. "That isn't for *many* years to come."

"On the contrary, I think retirement would suit you. Think of the time you'd have. Think of the billiard tournaments!"

King smiles falsely, then he pats the prince on the head.

"A run for the throne won't end well for you, my boy," he warns.

James flashes his own false smile. "Perhaps it will," he says, for once not conceding to his father.

Funny how quickly things change. People, too, and I suppose I can count myself among them. And then there's Wolfe. Helping King with a dossier or two. Why, I can think of a couple dossiers that I know King oversees—both the army of Mavericks and the rectifying of dissatisfied citizens —and once again, I find myself wondering where Wolfe's true loyalties lie.

Dear Matthew clears his throat, an attempt, perhaps, to dispel the growing tension between King and James. "So, the viscount has been leaving his fiancée high and dry on her sick bed?" Matthew interjects with a touch of shock. "I wouldn't dream of it with my darling Aubrey!" Yet another falsity, this one plain enough for all to see.

"Ah, but my nephew is an exceedingly busy man," King counters before I can say a word. "As am I, especially with a national address just a few weeks out! And that brings us back to you, dear boy. Should I clear out an office for you in Bishop's Aisle? Is there a portfolio you've been eyeing? A department that tickles your fancy?"

Dear Matthew's eyes round. "Sir?"

"Why, now that you reside at my humble abode, duties call, hmm?" I catch sight of the sneer curling King's mouth, and I'm not sure whether I feel badly for Dear Matthew or simply relief that I'm not the only one King clearly disdains.

Regardless, it's most welcome when King steers Matthew away from the band, listing off various aspects of governance to his listener's dissatisfaction. It would seem, at least for the time being, that King has other things to occupy his time besides me. All I must now do is do nothing to pique his interest all over again, and for the first time since that disastrous trip to Myopia, I feel calmer, like perhaps there isn't a giant bullseye painted on my back.

Then James, who I'd forgotten about, claps his hands together. He demands, "Why, girl from Quire, my adorable cousin Evie just shared with me the news. Tell me, am I the last to know?"

"News?"

He pats me on the top of the head. "Your wedding is just two shades away! It'll come and go long before the babe is due to arrive at Strath Glen, once again making you the most fascinating person in the room!"

"Hardly—"

"Soon to be a blushing bride!" he gushes, and he grabs me and spins me around under a ceiling of red balloons that hover just inches overhead. "That posits you at the very center of attention, don't you know? Here...allow me." He grabs a serving fork from a passing tray of appetizers and raps it smartly against his wine glass. Slowly the din of the crowd quiets to a smattering of voices, and when that doesn't cease, he uses the tines of the fork to pop several balloons lingering around his forehead. Now the hall is silent, all conversations blown into a hush.

"A travesty," he shouts. "A criminal outrage, a seismic failure with a hundred fault lines!"

The sinking feeling I'm beginning to know well—too well—returns. Slowly I shuffle backward, blending myself deeper and deeper into the crowd.

"Here we are celebrating the arrival of Dear Matthew, that and their most splendid little bundle of joy wrapped up like a caterpillar inside a chrysalis, tucked into my sister's womb, when there is other news worthy of celebration, hmm? That's right, ladies and gentlemen, our own Lord Viscount and his delightful little fiancée have set a date for their upcoming nuptials and, Christ on a cracker, is it soon! So, everyone, a hand please...to Viscount Wolfe Rocksavage of Airo-Aurora and the deeply appetizing, oh-so-fetching girl from Quire!"

Polite applause follows this rousing toast, even some cheers, a couple catcalls. Mostly confusion prevails. Then Aubrey's head swivels as though automated, her eyes pierce mine like daggers. Thunder stolen—and just like that, I feel the bullseye on my back emerge once more.

Deciding I'd better speak to Evie another time, I head at once for the door. At least, I try to, but the thousands of balloons lingering overhead begin to drop, and I'm lost— just as everyone is—in a sea of red latex.

"What the hell was that?" slices the viscount's voice somewhere far above me.

"A loving toast to the happy couple!" shouts James's voice in reply. "You can thank me later, dear cousin. Right now, I intend to take this lovely little lady for a dance!" and two hands reach through the wall of balloons and tug me deeper inside Carnegie. "Here," James calls, "you can have mine," and I spot Morocco's bulbous bosom through the balloons being propelled in the direction of Wolfe's voice.

Then James has my hand locked inside his, and we're on the dance floor before I can protest.

With his arms around me and the balloons now settling to the floor, he begins to dance, swaying sensually to the beat. With nothing else to do, I try to keep up while also maintaining a buffer of space between us. Eventually, I glimpse the towering frame of Wolfe near the edge of the dance floor, Morocco holding him by the lapels of his jacket as she dances like a snake.

"I was talking to my brother-in-law about the most fasci- nating of subjects recently," James says in my ear.

"Oh?"

"Any guesses?"

"None whatsoever."

He throws his head back in laughter, loud enough that

Wolfe turns his morose gaze our way, even as Morocco gyrates slowly alongside him. "That's one of the things I find so splendid about you. Never getting caught up in yourself, never thinking you're all that and a bag of potato chips. Does it come from being raised in a neighborhood that's nowhere? Don't answer that—it doesn't matter. The point is, you delight me. Me, a prince! A prince to be King! Now, back to Dear Matthew and our little chit-chat."

"Yes?"

"That most fascinating of subjects was *you*."

I say nothing. I'd been afraid of that.

"But not only that," he continues. "He confided in me the most delicious of secrets."

I eye him, my attention now his, even as I contend with the return of the sinking sensation in my stomach. Perhaps in order to survive life at Strath Glen, I should carry around a bottle of antacids in my pocket. Then I lift my voice above the horns and say as casually as possible, "I barely know the man. If the subject was me, I daresay the secret was nothing but illusionary."

"What, you wishing to live somewhere besides Strath Glen, you mean?"

My body tenses up, no matter how much I try to act nonchalant.

"Thought that nugget rang true!" James exclaims with triumph. "So, your too-tall, too-grumpy fiancé is sweetening on you like sugar, and you're having none of it—too funny! Of course, I don't hold you accountable for even a jiffy. He's a miserable old coot, don't you find?"

I draw away from him, or I would if he didn't hold onto me so firmly. "My feelings are nobody's business but my own," I say without a trace of amusement. Forceful words for me, though they don't seem to faze James in the slightest, so I add, "And as for the viscount, your suspicions couldn't be more wrong. Our feelings for each other are perfectly mutual, I can assure you."

"Forgive me for saying so," he says sensually, "but today, you strike me as being nearly as morose as he is! How I long to see you smile."

Once again, I eye him, more uncomfortable by the minute. Across the room comes the sound of balloons bursting, like rapid-fire gunshots, and the sound puts me on edge. Cautiously, I reply, "I'm perfectly content—"

"Nonsense! Can I let you in on a little secret? I intend to make the throne mine, and soon. And once I'm King, I shall make it my priority to make my little petal as happy as a minx! Why, anything in the world shall be yours!"

"Uh...really, that won't be nec—"

I stop short at the sight of Wolfe drawing up alongside us. Morocco follows after him looking put out. "My turn for a dance? Good." Swiftly Wolfe slides my hand into his and steps into James's place.

For a minute, I'm too stunned by the prince's words to pay attention. James really thinks he can steal the throne from his father? And why in heavens is he promising me the moon—

Morocco slaps James across the face, and I'm brought back to reality.

Or, at least to whatever this madhouse can be called. "Leaving me to dance with *him* while you trotted about with that underfed warthog—how *dare* you. Do you know the house from which I herald? It's the Moody House of Weaponry, James! Weaponry! Do you really want to cross someone with access to thousands—"

"Darling, darling," James coos, trying to placate her.

Meanwhile, Wolfe places his hand alongside my waist, holding me an arm-length's distance away while simultaneously ignoring the bickering at his shoulder. With nothing else to do, I reciprocate. Carefully I lay my hand on his shoulder, where the fabric is thickest. We look like two people trying very hard not to touch each other, I assume, and the sight amuses James, even as he cradles pink flesh and withstands a long string of insults thrown at him that range from *crotch-head* to a *sitting butthole*. And even though it's difficult picturing someone just called a crotch-head as ruler, I do my best to envision what that future may look like. Frankly, I'm not sure how much of an improvement it would be over the current ruler.

James isn't evil, though. Just woefully incompetent and reckless to the point of criminal. So, maybe it would be an improvement. Then, as Wolfe and I dance, avoiding each other's gaze, it strikes me that perhaps my greatest service to Airo-Aurora can come from helping to put James on the throne. Maybe, in that case, he would grant me the wish of disbanding the Selection process, and doing away with the override chip program. He had said he wanted to make me as happy as a minx, after all, although something tells me that comes with strings, and prostituting myself out isn't on my agenda.

Then James and Morocco move off the dance floor, still bickering, embalming Wolfe and I in relative silence, and a slow piece of jazz begins to play. We rock rhythmically back and forth, still avoiding looking at one another.

"Well, Alexandra?" he finally asks.

Now I can feel his eyes upon me, but still, I don't lift my gaze to his. I can't. Because whenever I look into his eyes, I'm reminded of that moment...*sedate her*. So instead, I stare to the side, past him and toward the burst balloon remnants scattered across the dancefloor. "Well, what?" I ask.

"You look less flushed than earlier. Are you sure that sickness claim wasn't a rouse?"

"Does it matter?"

"Of course it does. You remember my warning, don't you?"

"I'm here now," I mutter.

"You should be here far more often, or you will arouse suspicion."

"Fine."

"As for your flushed face, were you outside?"

"That sort of detail hardly seems important."

"On the contrary—"

"On the contrary, my foot," I counter boldly. "I don't appreciate people keeping tabs on me."

He's silent for a long time, and I wonder if I've made an impression on him. Then he sighs. "And what of the rest of it?" His voice becomes clipped.

"The rest?"

"Your private conversation a few days ago with Matthew. Your dance just now, with James. You don't think I deserve an explanation?"

The suggestion that he deserves anything after all he has put me through makes my insides pinch uncomfortably. "I'm afraid I don't follow," I reply, still not obliging him with my gaze.

"As my idiotic cousin so gracefully pointed out to the entire Reserve, you are to be my wife in two months' time. An explanation, Alex, right now."

Now I do look up at him. I stop swaying to the music, and my hands fall to my sides. He looks startled by this turn of affairs, but it pales in comparison to the look on his face when he spots the look upon mine. "You have never, not once, treated me as a fiancée or a soon-to-be spouse, and I have no intention of treating you like one. Just as you continually find explanations unnecessary to give to me, I intend to return the favor." With that, I depart the dance floor, kicking the remaining balloons aside until I'm out of Carnegie, not slowing my pace until I'm tucked mercifully inside my own quarters.

six

. . .

THE NEXT MORNING I'm once again awoken by a loud rapping at my door. I shove the covers down, push a handful of hair from my face, and consider it. First thing in the morning...the sun is barely up. I haven't bothered to fetch the viscount's breakfast for days, not since that disastrous flight to Myopia, and so surely it has nothing to do with that. And beyond that, frankly, the royals and servants alike want little to do with me.

Could it be Gerard with another message from the viscount? I doubt it. Things between the two of us hadn't exactly been warm and friendly last night. So, could it be someone from my own corner of life? My aunt? Agnes? Jill or Timothee? If it is, and considering the hour, they come bearing news, and so with that thought, I drop from the bed to the floor, landing on the core of a half-consumed apple.

I gaze down at it and frown. Again, with the apples in the middle of the night. Who keeps leaving them here, and why?

More rapping, this time louder, and by the time I toss the core in the garbage and swing open the black lacquered door, my mood has soured considerably.

"Gowns, toiletries—you name it!" Gerard is shouting over his shoulder to three other servants who nod in a focused way. When they notice the door pulled open, they immediately push it wide, paying me no attention whatsoever.

"Reading material on the nightstand!" one shouts.

"Check the far closet for overcoats—there's one cloak right there!"

"Papers and the sort from the desk!"

For a moment, I stand rooted to the spot, dumbfounded, watching the team of servants spread around my quarters, picking up each item they see, shoving garments under their arms, and yelling reminders to one another. Finally, I step forward and call to the butler through the mayhem: "Sir! Please, tell me...what's this?"

"Orders by the Lord Viscount, Miss Alex," says Gerard with a deep bow. Never has the head butler shown me such respect, and I lift an eyebrow, more disturbed by this small fact than the fact of my room being packed up around me. "Say goodbye," he adds, eyes twinkling.

My stomach lurches, stars pop through my vision. "Say *goodbye*? I...I'm *leaving* Strath Glen?"

The old man turns slowly. "Leaving?" he echoes. "Leaving the *guest quarters*, Miss Alex."

Suddenly there's activity in the House of Mirrors, and Monsieur Sawyer draws up alongside the open door. His mouth hangs open, aghast. "So, it's true? Heard the rumor myself down in the kitchens and had to see it for my own eyes. My oh my, Miss Alex. You really are a devilish little vixen, aren't you?"

"Please, Monsieur. Nobody has spoken a word to me about all this. What's happening? What is going on?"

"Why, you're being moved into the great Lord Viscount's private suite, of course!"

The news hits me like a powerful strike to the gut.

Breathless, I stutter something indecipherable, then Monsieur is shuffling me sideways, toward the bed which I drop upon. Good thing, too, as the room starts to spin around me.

Moved into his private suite. Moved into his *private* suite. Me. Now. Two months *shy* of the wedding. But...how? More pressing...*why*?

Finally, I lift my eyes to Monsieur, who now stands next to the bed, watching me with a hint of concern in his eye. "I don't understand," I say. "I don't understand why this is happening."

After an exaggerated shrug of his shoulders, he offers, "A smitten viscount, perhaps? One who can't resist having you close until the wedding is over with?"

"And me," I say hurriedly, not bothering to contradict him. "Do I have any say in all this?"

He smiles wryly. "None whatsoever. I daresay you keep on the same path you're on until he's wrapped right around that little finger, hmm? That's your surest way to get what you want. Until next time, Miss Alex," he adds before disappearing into the House of Mirrors.

"Time's now," Gerard announces, standing near the door and gesturing through it.

"Now?" I echo.

"Let's be on our way. The great Lord Viscount is awaiting our arrival."

Silently I slide off the bed, too stunned by the development to do anything but follow the butler's commands. So. This is what Rebecca must have overheard. Change a coming. Change indeed.

The checkerboard tiles are cold against my feet. A draft wraps around my ankles, but I barely notice any of it. Instead, I follow wordlessly behind the entourage burdened with my belongings, my head underwater, my thoughts spinning. As the doors to Wolfe's quarters are thrown open, I hear his ice-cold voice command, "Utilize the empty space in the closets."

Simple words. Nothing revolutionary. Yet they strike like a bludgeon, and I go still. Because this...this hullabaloo is not done in error. It's not a trick. I really must share a room with this man.

He sighs impatiently. "Where is she?"

One of the servants mutters something, and a moment later he comes marching around the corner, his grey suit pressed with precision, his tall figure seeming to extend itself to the ceiling.

When he catches sight of me, he comes to an abrupt halt, and our reflection is echoed throughout a dozen mirrors. His eyes cast quickly down, and I remember that I'm still wearing a nightgown, my legs and feet bare. The sight makes him turn to the side so I'm no longer in his field of vision, and some of his impatience ebbs. He clears his throat. "Yes, so...this. Perhaps I should have told you in advance—" He glances at me, then away again. "You didn't have time to throw on proper clothes?"

"Of course I didn't," I say, my voice barely louder than a whisper. I'm surprised I can string together a sentence, considering the circumstances. Too much shock for one person to withstand, surely, although it's not like I'm unpracticed in the area. I clear my throat and force myself to stand taller. I raise my voice and say, "As for the rest of it, advance warning would have been a start. So would've been asking me for my input on this move in the first place."

"Yes, well..." His voice drifts away. He says curtly, "What's done is done."

"You can have it undone," I press.

He shakes his head and reiterates, "What's done is done."

Suddenly the servants are filing past us, my few measly possessions already deposited in the viscount's quarters.

"Sir," Gerard says with a deep bow. He turns to me and, to my surprise, offers the same. A moment later, we're alone.

"You are doing this to punish me," I say in a voice that waivers. "Because I've been avoiding you and your family."

"Careful," he reminds me, turning his gaze to the ceiling, reminding me, perhaps, of King. "As for the rest of it, you couldn't be more wrong. I am not punishing you—that isn't my intention in the slightest."

The shock of the situation ebbs, and a wave of anger takes its place. I step forward. "I don't want this," I enunciate. "I don't want to share a bedroom with you. Not now and not ever."

He falters, and I see him swallow. But he recovers quickly, disregarding my words and my anger alike. He steps to the side and throws out an arm, ushering me inside.

I don't move.

He clears his throat, then straightens his already straight jacket. "Yes, well. I'll let you get accustomed on your own accord. I've work to do," he adds before brushing past me toward the rotunda.

I stare after him until he vanishes upstairs. Then, feeling ridiculous standing here in my nightgown and with nothing else to do, I inch forward. I step inside the entrance hall that's now my own. I close the door behind me, noting hazily that someone else has brought the viscount his breakfast, then walk silently to the threshold of his private quarters. My quarters.

Our quarters, actually, and the realization makes me crumble.

Strange. I've been here on a few occasions before, yet right now, in this dreaded context, the room looks completely unfamiliar. Totally foreign, and I feel like I'm staring at it for the first time. Sumptuous navy-blue velvet smothers the furniture, the towering bed way over there is fitted with impeccably dressed linens, and...ah. Someone has already set out my books on one of the nightstands.

No.

No, this simply won't do.

Sharing a bed with that man...that impossibly ruthless man who shoved me into Doctor Lebwitski's arms, who has known more darkness than anyone, who towers over me even while seated...there isn't any possible way sleep will ever come with him so near. There must be a mistake. There must be a *solution*.

Yet, haven't I been maintaining that very contention since the Mainframe placed me on the palace's doorstep? And where have my claims gotten me?

Right here.

Defeated, I head to the closet. It's more of a room, I find, lined with mahogany and with a velvet loveseat positioned in the middle, completely unlike anything I've seen before in the likes of Quire. Along the far wall is the assortment of gowns and riding gear that used to hang in the regular-sized closet of the guest room, and my stomach dives at the sight.

They take up only a fraction of the space, as do Wolfe's freshly pressed suit jackets. So... Did his first wife fill this space with her garments? I bite down hard on my lip. The answer, of course, is yes. Just as with the rest of the quarters. That bed, for instance. That bed used to be hers.

My skin prickles with unease as I continue with my self-guided tour.

The next room is a bathroom, one as spacious as the walk-in closet. I stare at my toiletries piled up beside the far sink, then pull out the drawer below and drop them inside. Next, I lift my gaze to my reflection, one bathed in generous lighting and surrounded by gold. My hair is disheveled, sticking up on one side from sleep, and with nothing else to do, I brush it out, then slowly plait it over my shoulder. After that, I familiarize myself with the rest of the bathroom. The drawers around the other sink I don't bother to open—undoubtedly, they hold Wolfe's personal items, and I have no interest or standing to see those. Instead, I open and close the assortment of doors around the room, finding each well-stocked with towels and other toiletries. The last door I try, however, holds far more than a towel closet.

I step into another room, this one dark and windowless. After groping around the walls, I flick a light switch and gasp.

A nursery.

Along the far wall sits a crib, its mattress dressed in a sheet with giraffes. A mobile with feathered owls hangs from the ceiling, and directly in front of me is a dresser. A change pad is fastened to the top, and beside it sits a neat stack of diapers. A teddy bear with a red bow is nestled on a rocking chair, and on the nightstand are a variety of picture books, some of which I recognize from my own youth.

I swallow so deeply that it burns the back of my throat.

Not just a nursery...one frozen in time. Waiting endlessly for a baby that will never return.

How often does Wolfe come in here? And, perhaps more pertinent, why? Surely most people would want those memories sealed tightly away, where they can't be reminded of such unspeakable pain. I stare at a lamp in the shape of an elephant, the same as the nightlight, and press my mouth firmly together in a bid to keep my composure. I might hate the idea of sharing a bed with the viscount, I might loathe the thought of being forced to wed the man who pushed me into Doctor Lebwitski's arms, but in this very moment, my heart cracks in two for him.

This side of him, the side I saw in the helicopter, *is* real. And that means at least part of him is, in fact, human. Right now, I can feel his pain almost as if it was my own, and it's so unbearable, so overwhelming, that I head for the far door, fling it open, and step into the walnut-lined entrance hall, coming full-circle.

I take a minute to catch my breath, I wait for my pulse to slow.

Eventually, back inside the bedroom suite, I move to the windows. By now, I'm used to staring at the howling birch forest that sits behind Strath Glen. So used to it, in fact, that every tree and arching branch are etched onto my brain, and so it's with fresh eyes that I gaze upon a vastly different view. Down below and stretching for as far as the eye can see, is my once-beloved city of Airo-Aurora.

The screens that line Central Boulevard flicker between news and ads, the lights that crisscross the streets lend themselves to the festivity, and headlights move slowly along slush-lined avenues. It's a beautiful sight.

But its beauty no longer rings true. It's a façade, just like life here at Strath Glen. Nothing more than that.

seven

. . .

IT DOESN'T TAKE LONG to pack a small bag.
Toothbrush, hairbrush, a change of clothes. The difficult part is
the mental burden, the knowledge of the nasty consequences
awaiting if I'm caught. It weighs heavily on me as I sling the
bag over my shoulder, as I pull open the door to Wolfe's chambers, but it doesn't stop me. Because staying here isn't an
option. Spending the night with that impossibly cold, too-tall
enigma isn't an option. Letting him control me isn't an option.

So, consequences be damned. I shiver just thinking
about it.

My bravado, however, doesn't mean that I'm not careful.
Indeed, it's several minutes before I move from my shadowy
spot surrounded by walnut. But when I'm sure that the
House of Mirrors is empty, when I'm positive all whispers of
life emanate from far off in the palace, I take my first step.

Immediately no less than fourteen pale faces stare at me,
all of them my own, bouncing from mirror to mirror like a
children's game. Directly above me comes the sound of
drilling, and drywall dust rains from the ceiling onto my
shoulders and the checkerboard floor.

Somehow I carry forward. Not for long, though, because as I pass by the placard announcing Evie's quarters, her door flies open, she bursts forward, grabbing me by the wrists and drawing me inside.

I try to resist...I don't want Evie to notice my overnight bag, after all, but there's no resisting—not right now.

"Oh, sister...heavens! I am so happy to have found you, my my my! Come, come, I absolutely do need to talk."

"But—" I clear my throat. "But, don't you have your studies?"

"I simply can't attend today...I can't! I've told Roberta I'm sick as a dog, absolutely I am, and I told Mother and Father that I caught your bug at dinner. Can you believe it? And perhaps I did, sister, because look at me," and she gestures to her outfit, a dressing robe, and then her hair.

Compared to how smartly she typically presents, I have to admit she doesn't look herself. "What's wrong?"

"Come, come," she mutters, drawing me across the entrance hall and throwing open the door to her bedroom.

I drop my bag discreetly in the hall and follow her into a room that is almost identical to Wolfe's, except instead of navy blue being smothered across every surface, it's a sumptuous rose hue.

Once we're seated on the sofa with our feet curled underneath us and the fireplace crackling, she exhales in a theatrical way. "I wanted to speak to you last night, sister, before you departed Carnegie—"

"I'm sorry—"

She waves aside my apology. "I really had a terrible time trying to fall asleep last night...I did. I just couldn't stop thinking about my upcoming Selection, sure, but also how rude Claudia was to you! And yet you didn't seem phased in the least. May I ask why, sister?"

"It's not exactly a new development," I respond. "It's no

different than the way Aubrey and Morocco have spoken to me for the past few months."

"And others you've met in your walk of life, others who don't herald from the aristocracy or its circles, are they equally as rude?"

"Oh. Well, no," I admit, not really knowing where Evie's going with this, and not wishing to offend her, either.

"So, my way of life, everything I've been taught is normal, is actually offensive to the great majority of Airo-Aurora's population?"

"Well, not—"

"I suppose it's possible I'll be slotted to marry into a family as rude as mine, isn't that true, sister? Or ruder? That they may fire barbs continually my way? It's simply not a way of life I think I could adjust to."

"I think your birthplace will preclude you from most barbs," I assure her, patting her knee. "As for the rest of it, well, I can assure you it doesn't take long to develop a thick skin."

"And so, what does that mean? That you simply can't be hurt, sister?"

"No," I admit. "No, that's not true. I can still be hurt. But over time, it's possible to be desensitized to things, that's all."

"So you've been desensitized to Strath Glen."

"That's right."

"And to all its cruel inhabitants."

"Evie, I'm not sure where this is going—"

"It isn't going anywhere, sister, I promise! I'm simply trying to grapple with my future and am having an enormously difficult time doing so. See, all my life, I've thought Strath Glen was the very best place in the world, and now that I'm seeing how cruel it can be, I'm not so sure. And then what of my Selection? Always, I wished my betrothed to move in here, but perhaps I've been misguided with that hope. Oh, what's the point of ruminating? The Mainframe is the decider, and...may I let you in on a little secret?"

I nod.

"I'm not terribly sure I *want* it to decide everything for me. Do you possibly know what I mean? Oh, you must, sister, absolutely, given your placement here."

"Evie," I say in a low voice, edging closer to her on the couch. My stomach aches with unease. "Evie, though I do know how you feel, and can empathize—you must keep in mind that airing such grievances isn't exactly looked upon fondly by your uncle."

"But my uncle isn't here, sister!"

"Yet it's all reviewable by him, isn't it?" and I tap my head.

"Uncle's a very busy man—I'm simply not worried," she insists.

Not wanting to reveal too much, I decide to switch course. "Regardless of what you want, or what you think you want," I add, "the Mainframe *is* the decider. And I don't think those advocating the merits of free choice are looked upon fondly, especially around here."

"Fair enough, sister," she says, sighing. "So, I suppose I must make peace with the inevitable, in other words."

I bow my head. "Don't forget that most Selection results are just what was predicted. Your betrothed could very well be Theodore or any other polite young suitor that tickles your fancy."

"And if it's not?"

"Then you'll learn to adjust, just as I have."

"I lack your strength, sister. You've an iron-clad constitution."

"You're underestimating yourself. Now, do try to stop worrying. I'd hate to see you waste this entire year fretting about something you have no control over."

"Wise words," agrees Evie as she walks me to the door.

Back in the House of Mirrors, with my bag slung over my shoulder, my ears swivel in an attempt to draw up sounds of danger. The singing of an aria. The clicking of well-polished shoes. The thud of a walking stick. But luck is on my side, and I make it to the rotunda without seeing a soul.

Laughter echoes from below. I freeze, ready to turn, prepared to run. Servants, I see next, and a minute later, they disappear into the parlor. A false alarm, but now the nerves are there, and my hands shake as I descend the stairs.

At the bottom, I nearly run headfirst into the Queen, but she holds a large hat box and I duck behind it without her being any the wiser.

There're royals in Devonshire Commons, though—I can hear their shrieks, I can smell the medley of cologne, body odor, and perfume leaching through the open door. But they're drinking, Aubrey and Dear Matthew are fighting, the parrot is screaming, so nobody notices me tiptoe along the corridor. A minute later, I swing open the front doors and Airo-Aurora spreads out before me.

"What are you doing, princess?" Jill asks. The other guard picks his fingernail, bored.

"Getting some much-needed space," I mutter to her.

"Aren't you always all by your lonesome in there?" she asks, looking puzzled.

I shake my head. "I've been moved into the viscount's room as of this morning."

"Really? Before the wedding? Isn't that kind of scandalous to you high-brow folks?"

"Not to this family," I reply swiftly. I don't bother to explain how little morals matter at Strath Glen. Or how far from high-brow I am.

"I'm guessing I never saw you?" she continues as she considers my bag.

"You didn't." Then I thank her, and I'm off, consequences be damned. I jog down the towering steps and into the bustling city, relishing the sensation of freedom and wishing it wasn't so very short-lived.

But, of course, at some point, I'm going to have to face up to reality. I'm sharing a room with Wolfe now, and that's that. For tonight, though…tonight, I'll sleep alone.

One person who will certainly notice my absence tonight is him, but it doesn't cause me concern. He'll be angry, sure, but navigating his temper is something I'm now practiced at. The important thing is that he doesn't tell his uncle, and I don't think he'll do that. I may not know where his true loyalties lie, but I *do* know he wants to avoid me upsetting his beloved King.

I plunge deeper into the city, avoiding Central Boulevard in case any of the aristocracy's well-heeled friends are out and about, shopping for fur coats or diamonds. They're sure to recognize me by this point.

I take a back street instead, one I've never been down. It's plain, almost grungy, peppered with garbage. Eventually, I pass by people sitting on the curb, looking as if they have nowhere to go. A few people are even rolled up in blankets, sleeping soundly.

"Spare a minute, love?" comes a voice from the shadows.

I jump, knocking into a lamp post. "Pardon?"

"Take this." A woman inches forward into the light, holding a pamphlet rolled up like a cigar. Her clothes are crusted with dirt, aside from a ribbon pinned to her overcoat that's as bright white as the paper.

Another hand reaches out of the shadows and swats the woman's hand away. "She's a rich 'un."

The woman pulls back the pamphlet and considers me. "That true?"

"Well, I mean, no, not me personally. But my fiancé's family—"

"Told you," says the voice from the shadows. "Why'd she want to join, hey? Use your head."

As the two argue, I hurry forward. One thing is clear—this isn't the Airo-Aurora I remember as a child, and I keep my gaze cast down.

After a while, though, I do lift my gaze. I look for signs that the city's disenfranchised have been tampered with, discontented as they are. White ribbons abound, and yet I see no glassy eyes, no false happiness.

It strikes me as strange that these people have been left to their own devices, and I wonder if they are more skilled at evading the Mainframe's bluecoats than most. If their natural suspicion of government makes them wary, vigilant. If they've so far been untouchable.

It would help to explain King's army of Mavericks, his 'insurance plan', if so.

I keep walking, eventually passing through the suburbs and into Quire, and once I'm in Quire, I pick my route carefully so that on my way to my aunt's house, I pass by the Quire nursery.

Visiting Agnes hadn't exactly been part of today's agenda, but right now, I turn up the walkway.

"Alex!" she shouts brightly, a few minutes later. She motions me inside. "Sorry, were you waiting long? I was just doing some cleaning," and she rolls her eyes. "You should see the mess that twenty kids make—unbelievable."

"Where are they?" I ask, looking around at a play space that's littered with toys, blankets, and building blocks, but no children.

"Out back with the other worker," she explains, pushing up her sleeves. She begins throwing dolls into a giant bin. "This is the closest thing to peace I have during the day," and she closes her eyes to underline how blissful it is. "What are you doing here? I thought you weren't allowed to leave the palace?"

"I'm not. But I couldn't take it anymore."

"What happened?"

"Wolfe moved me out of the guest room and into his own private quarters this morning," I explain, frowning. "I can't bear to spend the night with him—not yet anyways—so I'm spending the night at my aunt's."

"But if you're caught—"

"Yes. If I'm caught."

Her brow lifts. "Damn, girl. I'll cross my fingers for you. As for your fiancé, you realize you don't have to put out just because—"

"I know that," I say quickly, lifting my hand. "That's not remotely on the table, for either of us. Trust me. But even sleeping next to him..."

"Oh, it won't be that bad. Just pretend he's not there!" She glances at me and frowns. "Why'd he move you, anyway?"

"I have no idea. I've been skipping dinners lately, trying to avoid him and his family, so I'm guessing he wants to keep better tabs on me."

"That's seriously creepy. I mean, I'd kill Miller if he tried to keep tabs on me. Anyway, why've you been avoiding them all of a sudden?"

"It's a long story," I mutter, a half-hearted attempt to change the subject. But to delve into the rest of it—the flight to Myopia and all its ensuing drama—would be to say too much. Far too much, and the last thing in the world I want to do is implicate or endanger Agnes. I force myself to smile. "How are things going for you? How's things with Miller?"

"Things are fine. Today we're sending out invites for a wedding that's less than two weeks away."

"Two weeks away?" I cry.

"I know, I know—it's totally last-minute. I just want to get it out of the way, frankly. I sure hope you can come, though. I'm not sure I'll survive the whole afternoon on my own with Miller's family."

"I wouldn't miss it for the world," I assure her as I sort an alphabet puzzle.

"Will you bring that fiancé of yours?"

I snort. "I won't, no. Not that he'd agree to come, anyways."

"You realize, girl, he can't *hate* you if he moved you into his own room. It's kind of romantic, in a way—"

"It's not romantic," I proclaim, cutting her off mid-sentence. Once again, I change the subject. "So, has all your spare time been spent on wedding planning?"

"Not really," she says. "It'll be a pretty low-key affair, plus Miller's family actually enjoys this stuff, so they're arranging for the tents and chairs and all those boring details. I've been busy working on another project, actually, so I don't have time for wedding stuff."

I glance at her, noticing that her eyes are brighter than a minute ago. "What project?"

"Oh, I won't bore you with the details. Just an initiative I'm trying to get off the ground, that's all. Besides, I'm sure you've got enough on your mind with your crazy life way up there on the hill."

"It is crazy," I agree. "But I still want to hear what you're working on."

She takes a break from tidying and shifts her head back and forth, like she's trying to decide. "Another time," she finally says. "Like I said, I'm just getting things off the ground right now, and I don't want you talking any sense into me like you always do."

I grin. "Why, you're the most sensible person I know!"

She swats me. "I believe *impulsive* is a term you've used in the past. Plus, it's not the kind of project that Miller's family would approve of, so I'm being pretty quiet about the whole thing."

"Well, whatever impulsive project you're working on, I'm sure it's great. Plus, you seem happier than the last time I saw you, so I like it already. Or maybe it's your upcoming wedding doing it!"

She rolls her eyes. "I doubt that. And it's definitely not this place," she adds, gazing at the sea of toys surrounding us. "Kids are a grind."

"I believe you've mentioned that once or twice before."

"All I'm saying is that I'd think twice before having any kids of your own. Sounds like your fiancé isn't around much, which means you'll be doing the bulk of diaper changes, the late-night feedings, the—"

I hold up my hand. "There will be none of that, thank you."

"It's funny, sort of, isn't it?"

"What?"

"Well, I mean, when you were growing up, didn't you think the Mainframe would pick something that would actually make you happy?"

"You mean a job?"

"A life," she clarifies. "The Mainframe literally decides our entire lives. Isn't it kind of messed up we have no say in what we do eight hours a day? Or who we go home to after that?"

Before I can agree or warn her away from such talk, the back door flies open, and the harried woman I recognize from last time ushers inside a stream of young children, most of whom sport runny noses and filthy hands.

I hear Agnes groan next to me.

I pat her on the shoulder. "Good luck," I say before beelining for the door.

But even outside on the sidewalk, away from the shrieking children, peace doesn't settle over me like I thought it would. Instead, my brain lingers on Agnes and her comments.

She's dissatisfied. Dissatisfied with her Selection results. And if the bluecoats find out, Agnes's life will be effectively over, and I'll be without my closest friend.

———

THE STREET where my aunt lives is slumbering. Kids are at school, adults are at work, and I relish the quiet. The normalcy. I let myself into the place I called home until several months ago, when my unusual Selection results changed everything.

Aunt Jo's not home. She's probably out delivering post, and vaguely I think about visiting Patrick at the national gallery. Instead, I open the fridge, suddenly famished. Realizing I forgot to have breakfast and that it's now past lunchtime, I stick a homemade thyme and chicken pie into the microwave, just like old times, simpler times, and make myself comfortable.

After I'm finished eating, I wash up, then put another log into the woodstove to chase away the dampness of early spring. It's cathartic, this ritual, and all the tension from the visit with Agnes melts away. More content than I can remember, I shut my eyes, deciding to squeeze in a short nap before Aunt Jo returns home.

Suddenly I sit straight up and my eyes widen into dinner plates.

The stables. The cold, blustery stables. I can't risk abandoning my plan to catch the scroll writer, can I? Not when it's been so long since the last scroll was delivered. A new one is surely due any day now. I bite the inside of my cheek as I realize a long evening ahead beckons.

eight

. . .

"BUT WHAT ARE YOU DOING HERE?" Aunt Jo cries, looking pleased.

"I needed a break from palace life, that's all."

"But you're not allowed to leave."

"Uh, well, no. But I don't think they'll miss me for just one night."

"But if you're caught—"

"Please, Aunt. Don't worry yourself on my account."

"Will you visit Agnes since you're back? She's always asking after you."

I nod. "I stopped in at the nursery earlier," I explain. Then, deciding to fudge the truth in order to avoid more questions, add, "I'll be going out with her again tonight."

"Oh, how wonderful," she gushes. "And did you get something to eat?"

"A pie I found in the refrigerator. I hope—"

"Terrific, terrific." She rolls up her sleeves. "Let me get started on dinner."

"I'll help," I offer, and I follow her into the kitchen, chatting easily as we roll out the dough and make a lamb stew for the filling. Although she asks often about things with

Wolfe, I say little, not wanting to share with her that I've been moved into his private suite. I don't want to even think about it.

———

BY THE TIME we finish cooking and eating and I swing open the front door, darkness is rapidly descending. I run through the slushy streets, all the way to the towering palace.

Finally, I stand at the very edge of the property, scanning the windows for movement and keeping my eye on the greencoats working the front door. Jill is gone, done her shift, and the two men currently flanking the front doors are busy with a game of hacky-sack, though it's hard to tell from my vantage point way down here.

I wait a few minutes more for the darkness to thicken around me, for the drapes to be drawn throughout the palace, and then I step around trees as I climb the steep hill, using branches to keep my balance along the slippery patches. Finally, I'm walking the tree line around the back of the property, past the guest house, and up to the stables.

Tonight, though, is different. Tonight, there's a light on inside. I can see it spilling out around the doorway.

Once again, I scan the windows in the palace overhead. With no faces peering down at me, I wind my way around the structure toward the doors, more cautious than usual. It could be that the light was left on accidentally from hours before. Or, it could be that someone currently occupies the stables.

Not likely to be my messenger, though, considering the length he or she goes to write the scrolls in the dark. And nobody, aside from Wolfe, seems to do much riding. Of course, it could be a servant freshening the water trough—

Voices—that's the first thing my brain registers. The

wind carries them through the cracks in the wood siding, and immediately I backtrack, heart thumping. I place my ear over a hole in the wood siding left by a knot.

"And yet it was a rather enjoyable ride, my love, wasn't it?"

"It was freezing," snaps a female voice. "Another of your idiotic ideas, dragging me out before the snow has even melted. It's like you know absolutely *nothing*, James."

"Is there something on your mind? You seem even bitchier than usual, my dearest."

There's creaking wood, the sound of a smack along bare skin, an inhaled breath.

"Do mind your manners," the woman says in a prim voice. "And, if in case you couldn't tell, I do not appreciate being kept in the dark when it comes to your father's business dealings with my own. When will you finally make him retire and seize your rightful spot atop the throne?"

"In due time, my dear. And as far as Father's business dealings go, alas, for I too am in the dark, and really, it's not such a bad place to be. Perhaps if you try meditating—"

"The Moody House of Weaponry is a reputable and well-respected clan, and I will *not* stand for any shady business dealings that throw my family name into disrepute."

"I wouldn't dream of allowing such a thing to happen, my love. Do you really think so poorly of Papa? He would be devastated beyond compare."

"Of course I don't," the woman snaps, clearly Morocco. "But never before has such a large order of weapons been hushed up on purpose. It *is* suspicious, James, even you must recognize that."

"But, he has his reasons, I'm sure! Darling, you're worrying yourself to death over absolutely nothing."

"Perhaps so, and yet—"

"Did I tell you about the most exquisite dress I spotted in

the latest catalog? It's made entirely from endangered elephant tusks!"

There's a pause. And then, "Endangered, did you say? How deliciously unusual. And yet such a gown really ought to be paired with emeralds, and alas, my own have grown cloudy."

"Then a new set of emeralds shall be yours, my darling."

"And the dress," Morocco clarifies.

"Absolutely, yes. Now, shall we put this nasty business behind us and get ready for dinner? I'll tell you, riding certainly works up an appetite—I'm famished."

"Perhaps if it wouldn't take you twenty minutes to untack the filthy beast—"

"Dearest, you've simply been standing there, getting cold. God knows you could've lent a hand if you..."

Suddenly the voices grow dim, the light switches off, and the stable doors push open. Prince James and his wife Morocco stream into the night, still bickering, their embroidered riding cloaks billowing behind them.

My brain whirs with thought as I watch them from my shadowy spot behind the stable.

A secret order for arms placed by King himself. It's not exactly difficult to piece together—he's weaponizing his army of Mavericks—and the thought makes me feel like I'm teetering on the edge of a bottomless cliff. And what of James? Does he know the true purpose for those weapons?

If he does, then he's a skilled liar—not exactly a shocking contention. And even if he doesn't, his devotion to his father is more than enough to see King's mission through to its end.

If I had to guess, though, my guess is that James isn't privy to King's secret dossiers, and he's not privy to where the weapons in this recent order are destined to go. And then there's the chatter about him taking over the throne, and soon. Once again, I find myself wondering if this is the solution I've been waiting on. I wonder, too, if James has the constitution to make a serious run against his father.

But what I need to focus on right now is the arms deal. Putting a stop to it, more specifically. Because a weaponized, robotized army is a terrifying thought, and it hurts to think of my shimmering Airo-Aurora reduced to ashes, its residents who dare to dissent slaughtered.

And maybe that's why King is doing this. Because implanting the override chip is growing too risky, difficult, or time-consuming. Killing might be the best deterrent to stop the dissenters, and I shiver.

I wonder, too, if Wolfe knows of this plan. How nice it would be to work together to stop it from coming to fruition. But something tells me that Wolfe already knows, and for one reason or another, I'm alone on this quest.

What about Morocco? Maybe she's the key to stopping the deal, to halting the transfer of weapons. It certainly would bring her beloved House into disrepute should word get out, and yet...how much am I willing to risk? If I'm discovered to be involved, then my time's up. Besides, she wouldn't believe the likes of me, would she? And I can't exactly steal a helicopter and take her to see Ashville Range for herself, can I?

I sigh. No matter the scandal, Morocco's allegiance can be purchased—I must remember that.

Then the back door to the palace seals shut, blocking out the light that had been flooding the backyard, the royals tucked safely inside. Alone, I pick my way carefully across leftover snow, twigs, and slush, around the corner, and into the stable.

The horses grunt. I sniff the air, catching a whiff of Morocco's lingering perfume. I wait for my eyes to adjust to the velvety darkness, and when they do, I begin poking around the stables, looking for a scroll—a difficult feat without the aid of light. I break often to listen for the sound of approaching footsteps, but there comes none. Once I'm sure there's no hidden scrolls to be found, I pass my time waiting for my messenger by visiting with the horses.

The last one, tucked in the farthest stall, is the skeletal horse that Wolfe and I used to track down the Mavericks—the fastest rider, and the eeriest of the bunch.

Right now, he peers at me through the shadows, a knowing look in his eye. But what's there to know?

He knows Wolfe helped me deep inside the woods, and for a minute, I replay those moments in my mind, along with those startling words that I had uttered: *If you kill him, I will never love you.* And he had listened, he had turned his hand.

Several days after that, he had thrown me into the arms of Doctor Lebwitski, and I want to tell the horse that, I want to explain that I'm justified in my anger, but already he's lost interest. Eventually, when it's clear my messenger won't come, I walk the long route back to Quire, neither a scroll nor my messenger's identity in my back pocket. Instead, that overheard conversation about a weapons order spirals continuously through my head.

nine

. . .

FEELING both ludicrous and terrified at once is a strange sensation. But that's exactly how I feel as I gather paper and a pen, both as generic as I can find, both collected while wearing gloves and with a hat pulled down so low over my eyes that I can barely see where I'm going.

Safely back at the palace as of this morning, nobody had seen me return, a stroke of luck. But already here I am, breaking the rules all over again, and this time there's far more at risk than a lashing.

The conversation I overheard between James and Morocco had stuck with me, and I had tossed and turned all night long in my aunt's guest room, unable to sleep because of it. Morocco is not reliable. She is not driven by a sense of decency, she lacks integrity, she is not an ally. And yet I can't ignore what I heard. I must try to stop the arms deal from happening so all those innocent Mavericks don't become killing machines.

I need to protect them *and* Airo-Aurora.

The safest way to meddle, I decided during the early morning hours when sleep continued to elude me, is to use the same technique that I've been subjected to—notes, anonymous ones, written with extreme caution, and delivered with the same. And, so, here I am.

Of course, if anyone happens upon me right now, the game's up. But it's early afternoon, and most of the palace takes a siesta. Still, I take the servants' stairs, just to be safe, I lock the door behind me once I reach what are now my quarters.

The closet is dark, windowless, so I go there, closing the door behind me so I stand in the pitch black. I throw off my hat and sit on the floor, and, using touch, position the paper in front of me.

To Morocco,

I write. I flip the page over and continue:

King's arms deal is illegal. When foreign nations learn of it, it will collapse the Moody House of Weaponry. Contact your father immediately.

I wait a minute for the ink to dry, then fold it up with shaking hands. Delivering it will be tricky. I don't want it winding up in the garbage, not when there's so much on the line. And yet to do anything else, like slide it under her door, for instance, would be far too risky.

Dinner, in Carnegie—that's where I'll do it, and I tuck the note into my pocket. Nobody will see if I drop it on the floor in the midst of the festivities, and with any luck, another attendee or a servant will find and deliver it to its addressee.

Content with my plan, I stumble through the closet and into the bathroom, where I snap on the light. For a long time, once again, I stare at my reflection. I look different, I realize slowly, that's why I continue standing here, rooted in place. Less innocent, maybe. Older, definitely. Yet still small, still distinctly human, a small cog in a massive machine that is turning ever forward, at risk of crushing me with every rotation.

ten

. . .

THE HORSES ARE GETTING USED to me. It is, after all, the third evening in a row I've stood in the dark stables, teeth chattering, waiting fruitlessly for the writer of the scrolls. Perhaps whoever it is has abandoned the quest. Perhaps the meaning of Timothee and Jill's names being put to me is inconsequential, maybe I really have solved the mystery of the scrolls just as the viscount had said.

Well, if all this was put to me to take action, I really could do with a hand. Because despite wanting to affect change for Airo-Aurora, there's nothing a sole girl from Quire can do—that much is painfully obvious—and for the first time, a feeling of true hopelessness slips over me. I see a future here, isolated and alone, as Airo-Aurora is methodically stripped of its citizens.

Who am I, anyway, to go up against the likes of King? Who am I to bring down an entire system? I can't find a way out of wedding Wolfe, I can't find a way to affect change on a wider scale, period.

I stare at my watch, barely visible in the low light. As time ticks closer and closer to dinner hour, I admit defeat, again, swing open the stable door, and walk with a quick step back to the palace. It strikes me as I go that I haven't seen Wolfe at all since my unauthorized outing, and my stomach pinches at the prospect of the evening ahead.

A moment later, I freeze. Right now, I'm tucked into the shadows, where the spare cloaks hang. And around the corner, in the underused corridor leading to the back door, come a flurry of footsteps.

"Oh, Butch," a woman's voice suddenly moans, and I recognize it as belonging to Aubrey.

A man's voice grumbles something in reply, but it's too low, too muffled to understand.

Still, one thing is painfully evident: Dear Matthew, it is not.

And then their moans grow louder, nearer, and I sink behind the cloaks, seeing through the gaps in the fabric that they're currently undressing.

Inwardly I groan. Yes, I miss the normalcy of Quire, that's for sure.

Even though I should be pondering my escape from this uncomfortable situation, the sight of the two lovers reminds me that following the evening in Carnegie, both Wolfe and I will be retiring to our quarters—together—and nerves erupt in my stomach.

And then, as two naked bodies crush through the cloaks next to me, I leap forward, darting around the corner without a backward glance.

With one problem solved, onto the next. I pat my pocket, making sure Morocco's note is still tucked safely inside. Into Carnegie I go, finding there's less theater tonight, and a smaller crowd. The excitement from Dear Matthew's return has finally worn off, that, or James's speech that set to return attention to the wedding has caused revelers to flee. Whatever it is, the plenitude of chandeliers overhead shine more solemnly than usual, and aside from a string quartet, there're no performers whatsoever. It's the closest thing to a familial meal I've seen since arriving at Strath Glen, a time that now feels long past.

"Lovebirds!" booms a voice from behind me. I whirl around to see King standing in the doorframe wearing a red fur cloak and a wild grin. The Queen stands off to the side, smiling blithely, just like always. "Was the Mainframe right, or was the Mainframe right?" he continues, his beady eyes darting playfully between me and someone standing to my side. Angling sideways, I spot the tall, lithe figure of the viscount next to me, and there's a weightiness when his gaze fleetingly meets mine.

"Indeed," he murmurs, with a slight bow of his head, then he throws an elbow into my back.

Wincing, I say with as much enthusiasm as I can muster, "The Mainframe knows us better than we know ourselves, King." Sensing he's waiting for more, I sling my arm through Wolfe's and add, "For that, we will be eternally grateful."

King claps his hands together. He kisses both of us on the cheek, grabs the Queen, who continues to clap, and turns for his usual table. With those watchful eyes gone, I quickly fold my arm away, then brace myself for my first interaction with Wolfe since yesterday morning. Since me and my belongings were moved to his room without a moment's notice. Since sneaking out of the palace for an entire night.

"I guess this marks the start of you and me being...dare I say? *Family*," comes a voice over my shoulder, before I can even acknowledge Wolfe. Morocco inches closer and lifts her hands around my neck, and I think of that note in my pocket. She takes a steadying breath and leans forward, as if to kiss me.

I pull up my hand in the nick of time. "The wedding is still two months away," I remind her.

She yanks my hand down and kisses me anyway. "You're welcome," she says flatly. "How does my lipstick taste?"

"Like plastic," I reply truthfully.

She scowls, and James, who I hadn't noticed, howls with laughter. He steps seamlessly in front of Morocco. "My turn!" he says in a singsong voice.

Wolfe's hand lands on his chest. "I think not," he says darkly.

"On the contrary, as family members, we really must get to know each other *very* well, if you know what I mean," and once again, he steps forward.

"I think not," slices Wolfe's voice, more forceful than before.

James draws back, sulking. "A spoilsport if I ever met one," he pouts. "So, are the rumors true? The two of you sharing a bed?" He whistles through his teeth. "That's worth me thinking," he adds with a wink. "And yet, that means I won't again witness the delicate flower getting her beauty rest."

"That was you leaving apple cores in my room in the middle of the night?" I shout.

"He did what?" Wolfe queries, his brow furrowing as he rounds on James.

"Innocent, innocent—all of it!" James assures us.

"A disgusting invasion of privacy," Wolfe seethes, "is far from innocent."

"Miss Alex," comes a new voice, and this time it's Gerard who bows deeply before me. He raises a silver tray under my nose, empty aside from a small envelope.

"You have mail!" shouts Evie with glee. "Open it, sister! I absolutely adore getting post, don't you? I missed you dining with us last night...wherever did you scamper off to? Were you under the weather yet again? And after cousin's rousing speech, too! Hard to believe the wedding is so close, isn't it? We really have at least a thousand things to discuss, so come, sit, sit, and let us begin. But first, do open that envelope, the suspense is absolutely killing me!"

"Who would care to write to the Quire ditch-piggy?" Morocco exclaims, causing the Queen and Dear Matthew to turn my way. And with the attention of so many senior aristocrats upon me, the rest of the room follows suit.

Wolfe eyes me, his body rigid, and I know he's thinking the same thing that I am. Is it possible the mail is from the scroll-writer? That the entire room—including King—will learn that I'm receiving damning, incriminating clues?

I hesitate. The risk is real, and extremely pronounced. But as every last person in Carnegie waits for me to lift the envelope, I don't see any way around it, and I reach out my hand. Ignoring the way it shakes, I take the envelope with a slight bow.

Heavy, with creamy paper stock. My name is written in cursive—nothing like that near-illegible scratch along the scrolls. A good sign, I think, and I slip my finger under the flap.

Evie grabs the notecard from my hand before I can read it.

"A wedding invitation!" she declares. She pulls it to her chest and adds, "How romantic and exciting, sister! And the bride-to-be is none other than your friend Agnes...why, I know her! A charming girl, absolutely splendid. Are park weddings commonplace in your district, sister? The idea is so novel! And with only nine days' notice? Is that typical? Will you attend? Of course you will, she's a treasured friend. And look, plus one!"

"Evie," starts Wolfe, lifting his hand and fixing her with an icy look. "It's none—"

"You absolutely must attend, brother!" she cries, and several others around the room voice their agreement. "It's unheard of," she continues, "for a betrothed couple not to attend a wedding together. It would be a travesty, and if my Selected were to refuse, I would quite literally die from a broken heart. Will you go, brother? Will you?" She crosses her arms and stares sternly at Wolfe.

Everyone else stares at him as well. The quartet plays so softly that I can hear myself swallow. Wordlessly, and with bated breath, I oblige him to refuse.

But he sighs lugubriously, then nods.

Evie hollers and claps, and eventually, the rest of the room does, too. I can feel my face turn red; Wolfe's looks stormy.

"A date to your best friend's wedding, what could possibly be more romantic?" Evie cries. "And won't it set you in the spirit for your own upcoming nuptials? I'm absolutely resplendent over this most recent turn of affairs, aren't you? Oh, think of all the preparations we must make to get you ready for the occasion, and so soon! Let's schedule a dress fitting immediately—but don't forget, sister," and she looks suddenly serious, "you cannot wear white to someone else's wedding."

"I—"

"We'll also need to have you meet with a hairstylist so we can formulate a plan, along with a makeup artist—much the same steps we must take before your own big day! A trial run, that's what this amounts to, and nothing could bring me more joy. Do you feel the same, sister?"

"I think—"

"And, of course, you'll need to take a wedding gift to the happy couple, and it absolutely must be magical—don't forget you're representing the palace now!"

Instead of trying to fit a word in edgewise, I simply nod.

"You really are the most accommodating person I've ever met."

As the noise and bustle of the crowd returns, I attempt to sort out my thoughts. An invite to Agnes's wedding—that I'd been expecting. The attention of the entire dining hall on the event? Not so much. Wolfe attending as my date? Even less so. It's a shame, really. It would've been a wonderful afternoon in Quire all on my own. Then again, without Wolfe escorting me, I probably wouldn't be allowed to go in the first place.

Regardless, the preparations over the next couple days to ready myself for my friend's wedding—though completely unnecessary—will be something to fill my days. It will be something to distract from the disastrous state of affairs between Wolfe and me. And it will keep me out of King's crosshairs, too.

And yet, if I want to find a way out of my own nuptials, and I do want that, I can't exactly spare a whole week on something so frivolous. Besides, what of the Moody House of Weaponry and that large order of weapons placed by King? Silently I finger the note in my pocket, wondering when the best time would be to let it slip to the floor...

Suddenly Evie slaps a hand over her mouth. "Oh, sister, how could I have forgotten? You're no longer a resident of the guest quarters, are you? The buzz this has created throughout the palace, you haven't the foggiest. Can you believe it? Such levels of intimacy *before* the wedding are very unusual," she adds, her tone dripping with intrigue.

"It was pointless to take up the east wing's guest quarters for the next two months," Wolfe interjects with apathy. He examines his watch, looking bored.

"A sweet talker if I've ever met one," says James, who passes by with a puff pastry in his mouth. He pokes Wolfe between the ribs. "A morose old bore and a spry young thing undoubtedly unfamiliar with the logistics of passion, am I on the nose? A crying shame."

Evie swats him. "Away with that talk, cousin. Wherever are your manners? Come, sister, right this instant." She grabs my wrist and begins to pull me to our usual table as servants deliver steaming bowls of mussels. As we push through the crowd, I pull the letter to Morocco from my pocket using my knuckles and, swallowing a fresh eruption of nerves, let it drop to the floor.

"I've assembled a team for your wedding that we can use for Agnes's as well, isn't that aces?" Evie continues. "You'll be so familiar with these folks after Affair Minor that you'll be finishing each other's sentences by the time Affair Major rolls around in two months—"

"Affair who?"

"That's what I've just named them—Agnes's wedding is Affair Minor, and your wedding to my esteemed brother is hereby referred to as Affair Major. Do you love it? Isn't it dazzlingly official? Now, to the team—"

"A team that tackles what, exactly?" I interrupt.

"All manner of things, sister. There's Anne-Marie, the hairstylist. There's Mary-Kathryn, the makeup artist. There's Taylor-Mae, the seamstress, and there's Sue and Sue-Ellen, palace staff tasked with supporting you in preparations for both affairs...how grand! Then there are the designers, florists, and decorators for Affair Major. Now, I know exactly what you're thinking. What about food? What about music? Trust me, I, too, had those same thoughts. But the cooks downstairs will take care of whichever meal it is you choose, and I'll bring in specialty caterers for the hors d'oeuvres and dessert, not to fret. Does that sound divine? Do you know what you want to eat, or shall I create some sample menus? And you really must think on the music. The string quartet would be the perfect choice for the ceremony, though you'll really want something more upbeat for the dance—"

"More wedding talk?" Wolfe asks as he takes his seat. He exhales loudly.

"Don't be such a spoilsport, brother," she scolds. "It was you who insisted on the wedding date being so near, so naturally, preparations must get well underway. And don't forget your upcoming presence at—"

"Yes, yes. The wedding in Quire, I know. I believe most of Airo-Aurora knows at this point." Another heady exhale.

"Your first official outing as a couple isn't anything to sneeze at, brother," she reminds him. "All eyes will be upon you two, dare I remind you?"

His dark gaze swivels to me. "I need no reminding."

The implication, I suppose, is that I do. Yes, I have to play the role of happy fiancée. But I also must live up to my title as soon-to-be wife of an aristocrat. My stomach feels unwell just thinking about it, yet that's nothing compared to how I feel over the revelation that Wolfe is the one who insisted on the wedding date, one now less than two months away. Then there's the note left on the floor...

With a surge of adrenalin and my heart thumping in my ears, I chance a look over my shoulder at where the note had been left. Nothing but polished wood. Next, my gaze lands on the woman herself, and that's when my stomach drops. Stars dot my vision, and I feel faint.

Morocco has the note in hand, just as I wanted. What I hadn't counted on was her sharing its contents with all those around her, which includes not just James, but King himself. Somehow, I manage to turn away, determined not to let the panic show across my face. Determined not to watch what unfolds, even though every cell in my body screams to.

Conversation flits between Evie and Wolfe, Wolfe remarking about her studies mostly, and I try to nod along. But when a servant passes by, I turn and call out, asking when tea will be served in order to observe what's happening behind me. I don't hear the reply; I'm focused entirely on that far table, where Gerard now examines the piece of paper using a blue light and a magnifying glass. My stomach turns, and I think I might be sick.

But just before I look away, I see Gerard shake his head, I register a sagging in King's body that can only come from disappointment. No fingerprints, presumably, and I breathe a sigh of relief. Next, I think about my feed. I had been careful, yes, and I hadn't triggered any alarm bells. But I had also done a few things that would raise suspicion, too—walking around with a hat pulled over my eyes chief among them. Occupying a dark closet for several minutes on top of that. How to explain those things away? Of course, if King's going to review my entire feed, he's going to see plenty that will spell my demise. Not simply my outing to Quire, but the scrolls I've received, too, and my recent scouting of the stables.

But why would King go to that much trouble, anyhow? Why would he suspect me? It's people close to the arms deal that he'll be suspicious of, I remind myself. Deep breath. In, out, repeat. The real problem, I convince myself, is whether the note will have any effectiveness in swaying Morocco now that the entire royal family has seen it. I'm inclined to think not. I'm inclined to think that King will convince Morocco, if he hasn't already, that the note-writer is wrong, that the arms deal is above-board, and so on. Maybe there'll even be a pledge of diamonds to smooth things over.

"Are you feeling okay, sister?" Evie asks, interrupting my racing thoughts. "You look like you're about to pass out, my!"

"Tired, that's all," I assure her, wiping sweat from my brow.

But once the panic subsides, shame sets in. What was I thinking? Did I really think the note would work? This is the Rocksavage clan, after all. A tightly-knit group of savages.

———

AFTER DINNER and dessert is finished with, and the little drama behind me has quieted, a fresh set of nerves strikes. Blackness pushes against the windowpanes. There is no question the day is drawing to a close, that night is upon us. Normally I would slip upstairs right now to the respite of my own quarters—relieved to be away from the others, happy to have, at the very least, a space of my own. I would brush my teeth, perhaps take a book into the bath, then shiver my way to sleep deep under the covers.

Tonight, however, will be totally different. Tonight, I'll be returning to my shared quarters with Wolfe, not my own. And to make matters even worse, I've never retired to a room with a man before. I've never shared a bed with one, either.

It won't be so bad for him. It's nothing new, nothing foreign. He has known all kinds of intimacy. I throw a glance at him from across the table and, indeed, he reads the paper calmly. The thought of the night before him doesn't cause him any obvious distress.

Then there's the lecture I'm sure to get for sneaking out last night, to boot.

Maybe I'll slip upstairs first. That way, I'll have time to prepare myself for bed before he arrives. I can even pretend to be asleep when he does fold himself under the covers next to me. And, considering the width of the bed, there'll be such a gulf of space between us that it won't be noticeable anyhow.

With that settled, I lift my napkin from my lap and push back my seat.

"I'll come with you," Wolfe immediately barks from behind his paper. He tosses it to the table, stands, and strides toward me before I can compose myself enough to respond. With my legs shaking, I say goodnight to a grinning Evie, then do my best to ignore the catcalls and hollers that follow us out the door.

Outside Carnegie, neither one of us says a word. And even though the optics of us leaving together are favorable—

I can't help but wish he was still inside, reading his paper and forgetting entirely about my existence.

Between Wolfe, Morocco's letter, Agnes's wedding invitation, Aubrey and her mysterious lover, and the empty stables, well...It hasn't really been my night. The only thing that brings me any peace is the fact that Evie had been her normal cheerful self, which means the dread she has for her own impending Selection—still a year away—isn't weighing on her. For now, at least.

Wolfe sets off for the imperial staircase at breakneck speed. His footsteps click loudly along the polished floor, and when he's halfway up those stairs, he seems to remember my existence as he pauses, peering over the railing, waiting with obvious impatience. As for me, I lift my gaze to the storm grey suit, the cool eyes, the calculating face, but only for a second.

He looks away as quickly as I do.

When we reach our quarters, he clears his throat, then demonstrates several times how to turn the deadbolt to lock the front doors.

I give him a peculiar look. "I think I can figure that out, thanks."

"Always keep them locked," he advises.

I nod, hoping to keep our conversation to the bare minimum.

"Where is it you slept last night?" he queries.

"My aunt's house, in Quire."

"A risky and unwise endeavor."

"Perhaps," I oblige.

"I almost called the authorities."

I look at him, alarmed. The thought of that happening hadn't crossed my mind. Then I say tactfully, "Sometimes space is necessary, and I'd appreciate it if you didn't interfere with that."

"And if you're in danger, Alexandra? Should I refrain from interfering then?"

"I wasn't in danger."

"Yet how am I to know that."

I bow my head. "I will try to keep you better informed in the future."

"Of your rule-breaking, you mean?"

I turn to him, head-on. "Yes. Of my rule-breaking."

He holds my gaze, features stormy, and I anticipate his building wrath. Instead, he says in an impossibly crisp tone, "We'll take turns using the facilities, yes?" Before I can respond, he clicks the door shut behind him as he steps inside the closet.

Not exactly a scolding. I'd say I escaped last night's outing with barely more than a slap on the wrist. A small victory in an evening filled with anything but.

So, what will come of Morocco's note? How much danger have I placed myself in? How can I stop the arms deal from coming to fruition if I've failed to sway Morocco?

Then there's my messenger. Will I ever find the sender of the scrolls?

And last, but not least, Agnes's wedding. How in heavens will I survive an afternoon in Quire with the inscrutable viscount by my side? What will he think of Quire? What will Quire think of him?

I pace the room as I wait for my turn preparing for bed, my brain swirling with all these thoughts, all these worries, vaguely noticing as I do that during our absence at dinner, one of the servants has set a fire in the giant hearth. I stop in front of it and warm my hands, realizing that I'll see the viscount dressed in something other than a suit for once. Perhaps he'll even appear less menacing.

I'm surprised indeed when, a few minutes later, he returns to the bedroom wearing the same outfit as before. Only his suit jacket has been removed, leaving a crisp white button-up and dress pants. "Your turn," he says without looking at me.

Inside the closet, I hesitate. Does Wolfe intend to sleep in his workwear? Does that mean it would be inappropriate for me to change into a nightgown? I decide I don't care, and, ignoring the butterflies in my stomach, I get changed, then brush my teeth. Finally, shivering, I return to the fire. Wolfe is busy moving what looks like a massive animal pelt to the navy sofa. When he spots me standing there, he turns, and we stare at each other straight on.

A distinct look of discomfort passes over his features. His face looks touched with blood, he swipes repeatedly at his lip, then he turns for the nearest window. I consider his outline and the glittering lights that flicker off in the distance behind him, unsure of what to say, unsure of what to make of the silence, unsure, even, what I'd like him to say.

"I'll sleep on the couch," he announces after a while.

I swallow. The idea fills me with relief and, I suppose, something approaching guilt. "Uh, yes. Alright. Are you sure?"

"Sharing a bed with me, you've made it clear how little you wish to. So, I'll sleep here until you're comfortable with the notion."

"And if I never am?"

"Let's not discuss that," he mutters. "In the meantime, I sleep with the window open, something to fill the silence. It does make for a particularly cold night, so I suggest you wear more to bed than a nightgown." With that, he throws open the window, and a gust of icy air blown in from the north pushes into the room, along with an ear-splitting howl of the wind.

I don't move, aside from my hair that's pushed clear of my face and my nightgown that twists into a knot behind me. "Why am I here?" I ask, lifting my voice over the wind.

"Why couldn't I remain where I was, in the guest quarters?"

"You know why."

"Of course I don't. I wouldn't be asking if I did."

He turns to me, looking genuinely surprised. Then he speaks in a hushed voice: "These are dangerous times. The closer I can keep my eye on you, the safer you will be. Clear now?"

"Stop that."

He had begun to make up the couch with a blanket, but now he pauses, looking almost startled. "Stop what?"

"Stop pretending to care about me. And since we're on the subject, why did you choose a wedding date so near?"

"It's the latest date I could choose, rest assured."

"How's that?"

"It's the day of your eighteenth birthday, isn't it? The day that you will be subjected to far more oversight by the Mainframe, hmm? As I've explained before, your status as my wife will provide you with an added degree of safety."

There it is again, the guise of caring, and I shake my head. How can I rebuild even an ounce of trust in the man when he continues to play games? I stare at him, the words on the tip of my tongue.

But it's too much, all of it, and silently I go to the closet in search of more layers of clothing, closing the door behind me. I take a moment to lean against the wall, waiting for my pulse to slow, waiting for all those words on the tip of my tongue to dissolve. Only then do I fumble through a drawer until I find thick wool socks.

Without warning, the door behind me bangs open, and the viscount's tall figure fills the doorframe.

As we consider each other, it strikes me that he looks as confused as I feel, so I clear my throat and say, "Taking turns in the closet is rather pointless if you intend to barge in whenever you feel like it."

Grimacing deeply, he stalks over to me, bends his spine in half, and pushes his face so close to mine that I can smell his minty mouthwash. His eyes burn brightly, his mouth parts with words, but then he straightens himself, smooths his shirt, and turns on his heel. I grab a cardigan and follow him out.

He moves to the window, standing in front of it with his back to me, impervious to the bitter arctic air.

With nothing else to do, and with so much left unsaid between us, I walk to the towering bed where I make myself comfortable, exhausted after last night's sleeplessness and the excitement of the past few hours. Wolfe and his couch aren't visible from where I lie, and because of the howling wind, I can't hear his movements, either. I am, for all intents and purposes, alone.

With that wisp of reassurance, I slip into a fitful sleep.

eleven

. . .

LATER THAT NIGHT, when the palace slumbers, I wake.

I wake and remember where I am, remember that Wolfe shares the room at this very instant, and my eyes pop open. I peer through the darkness at unfamiliar shapes, the dying embers of the fireplace offering the only light.

It's funny—nothing is out of place. Wind whistles through the open window just like earlier; otherwise, there is nothing but silence. Yet something had woken me.

There it is—voices. Faint but undeniable, and I prop myself up on my elbow, more wakeful than before. Could it be Wolfe that I hear? I push the covers down and drop noiselessly to the floor. Without the thick eiderdown to cocoon under, however, I shiver—the room is downright glacial. Vaguely I wonder how Wolfe can stand it, especially lying right under the window. But as I tiptoe across the room, I see that the thick animal pelt covers him from head to toe— he looks like a slumbering bear.

So, the voices in the hall don't come from him.

I pull on a housecoat, then tiptoe out the door, into the walnut-lined entrance hall, where I pause. I press my ear to the door, thinking as I do that at least one voice sounds familiar. Now thoroughly perplexed, I step into the House of Mirrors and immediately stumble upon Monsieur Sawyer.

He whirls around and stares at me, his eyes wide with alarm. "Did we wake the viscount?" he whispers.

"No, Monsieur. Only me."

Monsieur and another woman, one of the oldest maids, exchange a look. "That's a relief."

"May I ask what it is you're doing?"

"Rosa here's talking my ear off about your old friend Worthers, that son of a bitch. If there was anyone crazy enough in this palace to take up a liking for him, it was this one. Well, how silly of me. You're no better, hmm, Miss Alex?"

"I meant, what are you doing up at this hour, in the middle of the night?"

"You got this covered, Sawyer? Good. I'm shoving off to bed," says Rosa. "Tip my hat to Dorothy." She disappears in the direction of the servants' stairs.

Monsieur moves wordlessly to the nearest window, places his hands around his eyes to block out the shadowy light offered by the torches, and stares earnestly at the city below. Only after that does he turn to me. "You wish to know why I play the watchman in the middle of the night, hmm? A curious cat, through and through. I'll indulge you yours if you explain something to me. Rumor is, the great Lord Viscount forgot you at the Sky Center after your international mission. True?"

I bow my head.

"Then, a few days later, he's moving you into his private quarters. So now. You can imagine how confused the rest of us are. A heart pushing one way, then another, and all that. A possible explanation that flitted through my mind...it was you, insisting upon the move...to make up for the slight at the Sky Center. Am I correct?"

"Surely you know me better than that, Monsieur."

"On the contrary, Miss Alex. Haven't you noticed the newfound respect you've garnered now that you reside here? You've pushed up the ranks in the eyes of the servants and royals alike, and overnight! A power play at its most profound, and if that doesn't stink of you, I don't know what does."

I chuckle. "Ingenuity has never been mine, nor has any sort of power grab. It was Wolfe's doing, and his motives leave me wondering as much as they do you. Now, your presence here, Monsieur?"

He returns his attention to the window, scanning the darkened grounds, then turns back to me. "It's Dorothy's turn for a night out, and it's my turn to play the watchman. How's that?"

"Not terribly clear, I'm afra—"

"It shouldn't be you blue-bloods having all the fun, don't you think?"

"I'm afraid I still don't follow."

"Must I spell it out for you?" He sighs theatrically. "Servants aren't permitted to just come and go from this fine institution. So, naturally, we go at night, taking turns slipping out the back door, down into the city for whatever our hearts desire. Of course, someone needs to open the door for us when we come back—it locks by itself, and we're not trusted with a key. Can't go through the greencoats at the front door either, isn't that so?" He peers once again out the window.

"Can't you stick a brick along the jamb?" I wonder, thinking of my own excursions to the stables.

He looks aghast by the suggestion. "Dumb as you look, and then some. Could you imagine the consequences should said brick be found, hmm? Imagine, endangering the most important lives in all of Airo-Aurora, all so a servant can slip off for a nightcap. Oh, look. There's Dorothy now," he adds, pointing to a figure way off to the side of the grounds, the same route I took when I was sneaking from Aunt Jo's to the stables.

"Can't let the guards at the front door see," Monsieur continues as he stifles a yawn. "Mind to keep this to your-self, Miss Alex?"

"Of course," I assure him, watching the servant known as Dorothy make her way up the hill, shrouded mostly by trees.

"I've got to go open the door, and that means this old chauffeur will be counting sheep well within the hour," he adds with a wink. A moment later, he departs for the servants' stairs, leaving me alone along the now-empty House of Mirrors, contemplating the darkened city, thinking about my own freedom.

———

"PATRICK."

I inhale the word. The concerto I'd been playing in the sunroom dissolves into the chords of light streaming through the windows. Outside, on the other side of the pane, the weather is changing. Today, spring is coming. Spring, and the boy I thought I would marry.

"One of the maids showed me in," he explains before I can ask.

"You're here for work?"

"Officially, I am, aye," he says, referring to his job at the national gallery. "But unofficially, I'm not. I told you I'd come back, Alex, don't you remember?"

I turn on the piano bench so that I face toward him, watching the way he scratches behind his ear, the way his gaze sweeps over the collection of plants that take up the bulk of the glass-walled room. "I remember," I say quietly. Of course I do. But I didn't know what it meant then, and I don't know what it means now. Carefully I slide to one end of the bench and gesture to the other. "Would you like to sit?"

He doesn't move with Wolfe's assuredness, but eventually, he positions himself tentatively next to me. "I'm guessing if you were working a librarian post you'd be stationed there right now, wouldn't you?"

I half shrug, half nod.

"What's going on with you?"

"You still haven't heard?"

He shakes his head.

"My Selection results were a bit of a surprise," I begin, clearing my throat. Then, hurriedly and without looking him in the eye, I mutter into my lap, "I've been betrothed to a viscount, and selected to serve as his handmaid."

Patrick doesn't move, but still, I can sense his shock. "A...viscount," he finally sputters. "And yet you're so thin, Alex. You look so miserable—today and last week in the library. Is it really as good a match as it sounds?"

I chance a look at him, and the tenderness in his eye is almost overwhelming. It's been ages since someone has looked at me like that. With feeling. With emotion and caring. I've grown accustomed to the coolness of Wolfe's gaze, I picture him staring down at me as a needle is rammed into my neck, and I shudder.

"Alex?"

"That isn't a question I can answer," I say tactfully, far more wary of the Mainframe than I used to be. Then I duck my head in his direction and say in an undertone: "It hasn't been easy."

Patrick nods. "I can see it written all over you. There must be something I can do?"

I shake my head. "You're too generous. You always have been."

"Alex, surely—"

"What about you? What were your results?" I interrupt. Because there's nothing he can do to help, that's the truth of it. I'm not sure I want him to know that though.

"I thought you would've heard by now."

"I don't get out much," I explain, then wait with bated breath. I'm curious, yes, but part of me doesn't want to know the answer, either.

"My results weren't nearly as interesting as yours," he says eventually. "You remember Annie?"

Instantly I feel light-headed. I can almost taste that secure, easy future that should've been mine, that now has become this girl's. Annie's. Somehow, though, I manage to nod. "Easy to get along with, from what I can remember," I say politely.

"Yeah." He turns and begins fingering the piano keys. "She's a nice girl. I can't complain, really."

"Well, that's something—"

"But she's not you," he adds, and he looks at me for a second, then back to the piano keys.

I try to ignore the way my heart pounds. "I guess we shouldn't have convinced ourselves we'd be matched in the first place," I add in a voice that sounds more strangled than I'd like.

"I guess you're right. Hard not to, though, when all of Quire is saying the same."

I agree.

"Do you miss it?"

"Miss what?"

"Quire," he clarifies. "I guess you probably don't, living here."

"I do miss it," I say quickly. "I miss it all the time. I mean, the palace is beautiful, but it's...I don't know. It's lonely." I say the last word quietly.

He gives me a look, one full of sympathy. "Do your handmaid duties keep you busy, at least?"

"Not at all."

"You could come hang out with me at the national gallery," he offers, his back straightening like he truly likes the idea. "There's—"

"I'm not allowed to leave palace grounds," I say softly. "But maybe one day, if I manage to sneak out, I'll come visit." Vaguely I think of my last outing, when I'd visited Agnes and my aunt. I had considered visiting him too, so what had stopped me?

Patrick is speaking. "...unfair to you, and does he even think of that?"

Wolfe—he must be talking about Wolfe. I take a sudden interest in the plant stationed next to the bench and say, "I suppose not."

"Have you tried talking to him about it?"

I nod, then add, "It's complicated."

"Love shouldn't be complicated."

I want to ask him if that's what he has with Annie, uncomplicated love, but I bite my tongue.

"Agnes' wedding. Will you be there, at least?"

"Yes—"

"Good. It will be nice to...you know. See you, again."

"It will be nice to see you too." I cough lightly into my fist.

"And if you manage to break free of this place for a day, you know where I work, right?"

"It's a deal," I say, smiling. "I'll walk you to the door, if you'd like."

He agrees, and we both stand at the same time. Our fingers brush. Then we're walking the corridors side-by-side, Patrick setting the lackadaisical pace. How many times we've walked together like this in the past, but here, now, it feels completely foreign.

"Should I be bowing to you or something?" he asks, nudging me.

I grin. "You'd better not."

"Who would've thought someone from Quire would wind up as royalty?"

"Certainly not me."

"Better you than anyone else."

"Why do you say that?"

"Because you're headstrong, more than anyone I know. How long have you been here, and still no tiara? I think that says a lot."

I look at him, flattered by the compliment. A moment later, my smile falters. It's because I spot Wolfe up ahead, speaking sternly with one of the servants, exchanging what look like keys. It's the last person I'd want to see me walking with Patrick frankly, considering his reaction last time Patrick was here. But when his gaze sweeps over us, I see no surprise cut across his features. Clearly, then, he'd been briefed about my visitor—and I'm reminded that he has many allies around here.

I watch him discreetly as we pass—I spot the way his jaw tightens, the way his long body hardens. In turn, he watches me coldly from the corner of his eye.

Even though the harsh cold of winter is over with, I still find myself shivering on the front stoop. Jill, who stands off to the side, raises an eyebrow at Patrick, even more so when he draws me into a hug. I watch him as he jogs down the steps and toward the nearest bus stop. It seems I'm watching that easy and comfortable life jog away with him. Delivered instead to *Annie*.

"Care to spill?" Jill asks, wiggling her eyebrows.

I make an exasperated face at her over my shoulder. "An old friend, that's all."

"An old friend with the hots for you. Don't let that boyfriend of yours see, or he'll have Sedaris back on your tail."

"I'd like to see him try," I mutter.

Jill spits over the banister, considering me. Finally, she lifts an eyebrow. "You've gotten feisty since I first met you."

"Have I?" but even I can see that it's true. Palace life hasn't simply been hard, it's been brutal, and I guess it really has changed me. Just not, I suppose, in the way most people would expect.

"Any new scrolls?" she asks, scratching her nose and scanning the grounds for intruders—more vigilant at her job than the other greencoats stationed here.

"Not so much," I say. But even as I speak those words, my mind churns through everything I've discovered. I owe it to her and Timothee to fill them in. And they'd want to know, I'm sure they would. And yet now that I know how deadly it is to wield such information, how can I?

"You okay, princess?" Jill waves her hand in front of my face.

"Tired, that's all." After a few more minutes of easy chatter, I wave goodbye, retracing my steps along the glittering black floor. However, I pause outside Counterdown, finally stepping across the threshold and gazing around at the towering shelves brimming with books, at the chords of dust illuminated by the sun pouring through the windows, at the furniture arranged so cozily around the fireplace. My favorite place in all of Strath Glen, indeed.

Patrick had deduced that a librarian I am not...and yet, why couldn't I be? Always I've maintained that someone ought to impose a cataloging system on these old books, haven't I? More to the point, my career as a pilot appears to have been short-lived. And since wallowing around the palace holds little appeal, as does partaking in wedding preparations, maybe I should carve out a niche while I still can.

Rebecca, holding a large duster, appears from behind a bookshelf. "What're you doin'?"

"I'm going to organize this library," I announce.

"Aye, miss?"

"First, I'll need supplies. Do you know where the palace keeps its office supplies and the sort? I'll need card stock, paper, tape, a typewriter, bins, and a filing cabinet," I rhyme off, counting each item on my finger. "I'll also need to take one of those desks as my own."

Rebecca stares at me. "Do you have permission for all that, miss?"

"I don't see why any should be needed, do you?"

She smiles wryly. "You're not nearly as kept as I'd thought yeh to be. Go on then. I can help you get set up."

Together we track down the various items, request that Gerard have an unused filing cabinet moved in, and set up a table at the back of the library where I'm sufficiently tucked away from those coming and going.

"You look happy, miss," Rebecca says as we set up the typewriter.

"Think what you want of me, but being betrothed to royalty with nothing to occupy my brain or time is in no way my calling."

"Aye, you're different than the rest of them then."

"Like Morocco and James, you mean? And Aubrey and Matthew?"

"All happy to do nothing, is my thinkin'. Don't go on and repeat it, mind."

"Without saying," I agree.

"And, you know. *Her*," she whispers.

I lift my gaze. "Her?"

"You know."

Slowly it dawns on me. "Wolfe's first wife, you mean."

"Go on."

I straighten my blazer and say carefully, "He told me what happened in the woods. To the infant, too."

"Aye, I figured, when I heard he was bringing you up in

his chambers. Not nobody's allowed to touch that nursery, see."

"I can't imagine the horror."

"None of us could, miss. That babe was a cute one, too."

I had promised Wolfe that I wouldn't go searching for information, a promise I remember keenly as I stare at Rebecca. But that was before. "And the woman?"

"Aye, her name was Maria. You know nothin' of her, like?"

"I know that she liked to drink," I say, shrugging.

"Oh, aye, she was a big drinker, that one. Crass as they come, too. The opposite of your viscount, aye. She was all too happy to put her feet up and let us servants pamper her head to foot. You think the princess likes her jewels, you gone and seen nothin'!"

"Was she well-liked around here?"

"Oh, aye, she was. Fit in with the other royals like a glove, don't you think?"

"And with the viscount?"

"Like oil and water."

I nod, having got that same impression from Wolfe himself. "I believe where the viscount is concerned, everyone is like oil and water."

"Maybe so, miss."

"Will you tell me more about this woman, Maria?"

"Not much to tell, miss. She didn't make chitchat with the servants. Besides, I only started here 'bout a year before the accident, aye. Pampered, just like I said. Big boned, too —'bout twice your size. Red hair, freckled, hot-tempered as I've seen."

I try to picture Wolfe with someone matching Maria's description, and her temperament, but come up short. Even without knowing the woman, I can tell it was a poor match —perhaps even more so than me and Wolfe. "When did the ordeal in the woods occur?" I ask next.

"Two years past."

"And during that time, the viscount dated Claudia?"

"Aye, for the past year, I'd say."

"They would've been ideally matched together, from what I can tell."

"Guess not, though, aye? Otherwise, they would've been, and you wouldn't be here talkin' to me and takin' over the library, like."

I laugh. "Life is strange, isn't it? And what about you? What's your story? You hardly look old enough to be working frankly, let alone for the past three years. And where's your betrothed, anyhow? I thought servants tend to get paired with other servants."

"I was born to servants, miss. They don't bother with Selections for people like me. Start me working as soon as they can, like. As for a mate, well, I'm what they call a servants' spare. New servant blood gets slotted in here, I'll be all his. He'll be all mine, I mean," she adds, winking.

I stop unwinding cellophane from a package of pens and look at her. "That doesn't seem fair. And what if your aptitude for a career is properly elsewhere?"

"Born a second-class citizen, miss. You might take a lot of flak for being the girl from Quire and all that, aye, but I'd take that head and shoulders over me and mine."

I nod. All this time, I assumed I'd gotten the short end of the stick, being stuck here at the palace, but all that's nothing next to Rebecca. A second-class citizen, indeed.

Yet another failure of the chip system, a seismic one, and this is what occupies me for the rest of the day, even as I begin the tedious task of pulling each book from the shelf to document it, categorize it, and find it a new and proper home.

twelve

. . .

THE NEXT DAY, as the afternoon shifts into evening, and just as I remove my gaze from glittering Airo-Aurora spread out down below with the intention of heading downstairs and out to the stables to wait for the scroll-writer, the door swings open, and Wolfe steps inside.

My body stiffens; I'm more guarded around him than I used to be.

Immediately his brow lowers, and he pauses ever so slightly, as if he noticed my reaction, but he says nothing of it. Instead, he removes his jacket and stokes the fire, paying me no mind. I set out from my spot near the window and am almost through the door when he speaks: "Early for dinner yet, isn't it?" My boots slow. "I—"

"You don't want my company," he interjects. "So I've noticed." Then he runs a hand through his hair, and I think he looks thinner than I remember. Dark lines ride under his eyes—not surprising, I realize with a pang of guilt, considering he sleeps on the couch. And then he says in a curt voice, "Isn't it time to put this behind us?"

"Put it behind us," I echo.

"Your attitude lately, it really is getting tiring."

Anger radiates through my veins at his words. *Me. My* attitude is getting tiring, and all of a sudden, I want to scream at him, tell him how much the sight of him staring down at me when the needle was plunged into my neck haunts me. Tell him how betrayed I felt when he did that, and when he left me at the bus stop without any explanation. How I don't know who to trust, who to turn to. But all I do is stride away, pulling the door closed behind me and walking quickly to the servants' stairs.

"Not a servant, tis," says Rebecca as I almost run into her. She carries a plate of cookies up to the third floor, probably for King.

"I wish I was," I mutter.

"Things not so well with the mister?" she calls over her shoulder.

There's no opportunity to respond as the stairs become crowded with servants all in the midst of their duties. A gust of wind whistles through my hair, but at the very least, three of the servants go out of their way to smile at me—a significant improvement from several months ago.

When I finally make it outside and am alone in the backyard surrounded by dusk, my muscles unclench, and I feel a surge of exhaustion, like I just ran a marathon. Because no, to answer Rebecca's question: things aren't well with the mister, and for some reason, it weighs on me. And so I don't notice anything different as I pull open the stable door and step inside—not until I slam headfirst into someone.

The person groans; I gasp.

My messenger, it's my messenger—I know it in an instant, in my gut. After all, his is an outline that doesn't reside in Strath Glen, I'm sure of it. And yet, as I peer at him through the near darkness, there's something familiar about his face. Then, as my eyes adjust to the low light, as the moon rises higher and slips through the barn boards, recognition dawns across his face. Recognition dawns across my face, too.

A shock of black hair, thick-framed glasses, a small build—the technician from the Mainframe, that's who. The very one I noticed that fateful morning when I tried in vain to have my Selection results changed. Yes, I'd noticed him through that window pane—I'd noticed him because he was the lone Mainframe employee unfazed by my sudden appearance in the heart of the building, a portion unwelcome and off-limits to visitors. Like he was expecting me...

"You're the sender of the scrolls," I say plainly.

He says nothing, yet I can sense his discomfort. Clearly, then, he hasn't been watching my feed lately, because he wasn't expecting this. He takes a step back, and I think he can sense my sudden anger, too. Anger I didn't know was there.

"You may as well grab whichever scroll you dropped and save me the trouble of searching. Or, maybe I won't bother at all. After all, they've almost killed me twice now."

Still nothing. No reaction whatsoever.

"Maybe I'll pass them to King," I continue. "He could launch a full investigation, and he and I both will find my messenger that way. Unless, of course, you're him?"

He hesitates, then turns to the saddles and pulls a familiar-looking scroll from underneath. He hands it to me.

I pocket it without bothering to open it. "Your name?"

"Neo," he whispers. Then he lifts his finger to his lips, imploring me to use discretion.

"Neo," I echo. "And you're a technician at the Mainframe, isn't that right?"

He nods.

"I noticed you when I was trying to have my results switched. I think you noticed me too."

"I expected you to make an appearance," he obliges after

a while. "Of course, I didn't expect the King to get wind of it. The last thing I wanted was to kick up suspicion."

"You expected me to make an appearance," I press. "You breach my privacy often, is that right?"

"By watching your feed? No, of course not."

"So then how did you know I'd make an appearance? What made you think that?"

He exhales noisily, then says in a voice so quiet I can barely decipher it over the whistling of the wind: "By the same reason that I placed you here, at Strath Glen."

Placed you here.

Now I'm the one who's silent. My heart thunders against my ribs, and vaguely I feel grateful that my eighteenth birthday hasn't yet arrived, that my vitals aren't yet being closely monitored. Because surely, right now, I'd be setting off all kinds of alarms at the Mainframe.

"*Placed* here," I finally stammer.

He nods. "Now that you've seen what our King is up to, can you blame me for taking action?"

"Taking action?" I snort. "How is ruining my life and sending me impossible-to-decipher scrolls taking action?"

"But you *have* been deciphering them."

I take a deep breath to steady myself. Finally...finally, I've found the sender of these blasted scrolls, but I'm too overcome with anger and shock to ask one of the thousand questions that have been plaguing me for months. "Why me?" I eventually think to ask.

"When the viscount's spouse Selection came up, I saw an opportunity. Place someone at the palace, with easy access to the King, who had yet to turn eighteen. Less surveillance that way," he adds as he pushes up his glasses. "I had it narrowed down to you three."

"You three?"

"You, Jill, and Timothee. Obviously, Timothee wasn't a possibility, given the fact that he's male, and—"

"Wait," I manage to say as my head spins. "There would've been hundreds of other still-seventeen-year-olds undergoing the Selection, so why—"

"Because only your three met my other criteria."

"Which was?"

"Someone strong-willed and clear on their passions. Someone who had been through hardship and who had a temperament that stops them from falling in line. One kind of informs the other, you might say," he adds in an elfin voice.

"I don't think I follow."

"I needed someone who wouldn't lie down and accept their Selection results. Someone who wouldn't lie down and accept results that didn't make sense. Someone who wouldn't swoon at the prospect of becoming royalty just because. Timothee, being a guy, was obviously eliminated, as I said, and Jill would have been too happy to move immediately out of her parents' place to make her a suitable candidate. You were the perfect choice."

So.

I'd been right, in a way. I wasn't suited to be a handmaid, or to marry a man such as the viscount. My results weren't exactly the result of a glitch, sure, and yet they weren't the result of a properly functioning Mainframe, either.

I think of my dream of becoming a pilot, a pianist, or a librarian. I think of Patrick, and that comfortable and easy life I had envisioned for myself, and I cross my arms. "Did you ever think of all you took away from me by playing God?"

"Nothing more than the Mainframe would have. Don't forget the Mainframe doesn't care about your own wants. It would've slotted you into the life it saw fit, which could've differed dramatically from what you desired."

"So, that's your end game, is it? A free Airo-Aurora?"

He nods. "The return of free choice."

I scoff, even though it's what I want, too. And Agnes, apparently. And even Evie. "And I'm supposed to help you make that happen?"

"Isn't it something you believe in?"

"Sure, I do," I say eventually. "But, obviously, I don't know how to do it."

He shrugs. "You've come this far."

"I can't go any farther without help," I whisper sternly.

"I'm a Mainframe technician, remember? I can tell you're the most qualified for the job, but I can't tell you how to do that job. Make sense?"

"I am not qualified for the job—"

"You are—"

"Having been through hardship does not make me qualified to dismantle an entire system of governance," I snap. "You may have been better suited to pick a person with a bit more sway than a girl from Quire."

"Listen," he says, yawning, and not looking at all concerned over whether or not I'm capable of tackling this impossible task, "I need to get going before my feed becomes questionable. It only takes fifteen minutes to walk home," he adds, pushing up his glasses, "and I've already prolonged it by ten minutes talking to you."

"Meet me again, then," I say, stepping across his path. "I'm tired of trying to decipher the scrolls. From now on, we meet, right here. If you expect me to affect change, I expect more help than what you're currently offering."

He lifts an eyebrow, caught off-guard by my assertiveness. I'm a little caught off-guard myself. "Yeah, I guess—I guess that sounds reasonable," he replies. "I'll return in five days then—it's too risky for me to come any sooner. Stay out of trouble and see you then, okay?"

I nod, then wave goodbye as he pushes out of the stables. A gust of wind catches the door as he goes, making it bang shut behind him. Several of the horses protest the loud noise, but I barely register it. In fact, I barely breathe. My head spins with this latest development. My messenger...I found him. *I found him.*

And, more important than that even—I found an ally. I may not know how to bring down King and his Mainframe and the Selection system, but at least I'm no longer alone in my quest.

———

I LEAVE the stables in a considerably brighter mood than when I arrived. Even the prospect of dinner with Wolfe and the royal family can't dim my spirits. And yet all that changes entirely when I'm halfway between the stables and the palace. For the back door is swung all the way open, and none other than the viscount leans against the doorframe, his silhouette illuminated by lamplight, his face covered in shadows.

Before I can react, before I can come up with a reason that I'm hanging out in the stables while the rest of the palace congregates in Carnegie, two things register at once. First is a dead fox laying across my path, its side split open and its innards half-removed. The other is rustling from behind me, the sudden crunching of snow, and over my shoulder, I spot movement through the darkness. Two beady eyes catch the light thrown by the open door.

"Don't move," Wolfe suddenly orders, then he grabs the brick I'd used to prop the door open and strides toward me.

The creature hisses, and every cell in my body goes rigid. I stare at the slain fox, its blood glinting silver under the moonlight. I think of Maria and the child, and it's everything I can do not to run. But I listen to Wolfe, I don't move —and then he is near, the hissing grows louder, and fast movement flashes through my peripheral. The brick smashes the creature to the ground.

Another strike, another, and under the dim light cast by the stars, I see fresh blood glinting across the weathered snow, I see lifeless claws the length of my face.

"Is that a wolverine or a wolf?" I ask.

Silence...and I realize it was probably a cross between the two. Interbreeding, Evie had told me, ever since the fence around Airo-Aurora's border had been erected.

"Do you think it would've attacked me?" I ask next.

Still no response. Instead, Wolfe wraps his fingers around my wrist, leading me past the stables, past the underground garage, and around to the front of the palace.

"You don't have a key?" I ask as I struggle to keep pace with his unnaturally long legs.

A cool glance over his shoulder at me is the only reply. He really is cantankerous tonight, although I suppose I'm partly to blame, walking out on him as I did in our quarters. Plus, the beast would've put him in a foul mood, although it's not like I entered the woods without him—a promise I intend to keep.

Up the stairs, past the greencoats that eye the blood splatter across his suit, and into the warmth of the palace we go. He stomps his shoes to remove the excess snow, pulls off my cloak, which is also stained with blood, then sticks his nose an inch from my own.

A moment later, he turns away, swallowing his words, taking the gilded staircase upstairs two at a time and leaving me to walk alone to Carnegie, feeling both rattled and excited.

ALL EVENING AT DINNER, he had glowered at me. I ignored it as best I could, instead chatting with Evie about wedding stationary and cursive, and about Agnes's upcoming wedding, now only a week away. I rearranged a bouquet of flowers with the Queen. I even danced a number with James, who spent the entire time giving me a surprisingly helpful rundown of all the guests in attendance, including their relative importance within Airo-Aurora's social circles, their marital status, their careers, and the dramas plaguing each.

And so by the time I excuse myself from the evening and go upstairs, my pulse is unsteady. Hiding from Wolfe isn't really possible now that we share a bedroom, and that means an uncomfortable conversation awaits like a ticking bomb on the horizon. I groan, or I start to, but then I remember something.

The *scroll.*

The one Neo had handed me in the stables. The one I had shoved into the pocket of the cloak I'd been wearing, that bloodied one that belongs to the palace, one that Wolfe had removed once we stepped through the front door. Too much had happened between my talk with Neo and that beast—I had completely forgotten about it, and now it's missing.

Shit.

How could I have been so stupid? God knows what the scroll said, a scroll that anyone could now read. So, how much danger have I put myself in? And what about Neo?

There's a chance Wolfe merely returned the cloak to the hook next to the back door, its regular spot. Yet he'd taken it upstairs with him, I saw that with my own eyes, plus it had been covered with blood splatter. Probably into the laundry chute, then, meaning I could go to the basement and root around for it in the laundry room. Simple. There's also the possibility that it's somewhere here, in these quarters. Or, the least appealing option—that Wolfe has already found the scroll, confiscated it, and read it.

I start the search here in the quarters. My hands run behind cushions, in drawers—I even poke my head into the nursery before thinking better of it and immediately retreating.

I search the closet thoroughly, checking between each garment for the missing cloak, examining every pocket for the missing scroll. Nothing. With no laundry bin, no pile of dirty clothes on the floor, I stick my arm into the laundry chute, grasping nothing but air. So. Down to the laundry room I shall go.

I take the servants' stairs to the basement, and right now, with most of the servants congregating in Carnegie, it's mercifully empty but for my elongated shadow that quivers under the torchlight. The damp corridors underground are likewise empty, although I do catch sight of Rebecca's backside, but quickly she turns out of sight at the end of the hall. I wonder, vaguely, why she isn't with the others.

Overhead comes the stomping feet of Carnegie's revelers, making the torches flicker, and when I swallow, I find my throat has gone dry. The reality is, I have no idea what the missing scroll says, and so I have no way of knowing what kind of danger I'm in. I have no idea who else I've put in danger, either.

Inside the laundry room, I take a deep breath. I'll find the missing cloak and its scroll. I'm worrying over nothing. But surrounding me is a sea of freshly pressed clothes, linens, and racks overflowing with plastic-covered gowns. I wade forward, pausing to examine a stack of impeccably folded cloaks, but none of them have a hiden scroll. Vaguely I wonder how quickly things are laundered—perhaps the blood-stained cloak is already in a machine, and I turn to a bank of them next. Two of the machines are running, but when I peer through the glass, I see both loads are white, and I continue my search of the room.

Finally, after pushing through the last rack of gowns and suits, I stand at the far end of the room where a large bin sits. No less than twelve chutes lead into it, and I feel my chest expand with hope.

I peer inside, and...jackpot. There's the cloak heaped at the top of the pile, the bloodspots matching the splatter across the suit next to it. I let out a long, slow exhale. Wolfe did throw it down the chute, just as I thought, and I lean my weight forward, snatching it up by the corner. I could practically kiss it—

My panic comes roaring back. Because each and every pocket is empty. I check once, twice, then I climb inside the bin, I scour the other dirty clothes and the bottom of the bin for the missing scroll.

Nothing.

Either Wolfe has it on his person, or...

No, *of course* Wolfe has it. He's been wanting to confiscate my scrolls for ages now, and he's finally done so. Sure, he'll never tell me what the message is, but at least I know it isn't floating around the palace, at risk of landing smack on King's lap.

A disappointment, this is—not a disaster. Besides, I'm meeting with Neo soon enough; he can tell me in person what the scroll had said. Case closed.

———

READY TO CALL IT A DAY, I throw open the bedroom door, then run headfirst into a tall and unforgiving frame.

"You have denied me an explanation all night," he says in a voice that vibrates. He is angry, very much so, probably on his way out to look for me, too, and I decide quickly not to bring up the scroll at all. "You wouldn't have done that in the past. You are taking liberties, Alexandra, and I don't think it wise."

"Uh, yes, well—"

"Tell me who you were meeting in the stables and why."

I freeze. It hadn't even crossed my mind that he may have seen Neo. Do I tell him the truth? Or do I make up some flimsy excuse?

"Why are you looking at me like that?" he presses.

"I'm trying to decide something," I answer truthfully. "If I tell you who I was meeting in the stables, will you pass along the information to your mentor?"

His gaze withers. "My mentor?" he echoes with a snort.

"Well? Will you tell King?"

"What do you think?" he snaps.

"If I knew the answer, I wouldn't be asking."

"No." He spits the word at me. "No, of course I won't, and for the love of god, do not call him my mentor."

"Fine," I agree, resigning myself to finally speaking frankly to my fiancé. Whether trusting him or not is the right choice will only become apparent with the passage of time, but for now I don't see a way around it. "Fine," I reiterate, and I walk past him and deeper into the room, warming my hands by the fire and wondering where precisely I should begin.

"So, it has to do with that, huh?" Wolfe calls as he follows me. "You haven't taken a lover?"

I stare at him over my shoulder. "Is that what you thought? How exactly do you think I would 'take a lover' when I'm not permitted to leave the palace, hmm? Where in your imagination do you think I would meet said lover?"

"I'll take that as a no," he says dryly, then points to the couch. He throws open the window, the whistling wind filling our quarters with its noise. I sit down and wait for him to drop his considerable frame next to mine.

"Warm enough?" he asks, without looking at me.

"I'm fine," I say between teeth that begin to chatter.

He makes an exasperated face, then places another log on the fire.

Once he sits next to me, I pull up my feet and turn so

that I can whisper directly into his ear, careful not to touch him. I draw back when I smell his aftershave and swallow. The little reminders that he's human are not welcome—not right now. Then I gather myself and say into his ear, "The young man in the stables that I was speaking to was the technician from the Mainframe, the one sending me the scrolls."

The news must catch him by surprise because he turns to look at me. Under his vociferous gaze and with every inch of his body taking up far more space than mine, I must force myself to hold his stare. "How did that come to be?" He speaks it plainly.

"I had the idea several days ago," I explain, "to wait in the stables, hoping to catch my messenger in the midst of a delivery. It worked."

"The stables?"

"That's where the other scrolls were left," I divulge. "And don't now try to block me from the stables, as I'll simply find another solution. You can't control me," I underline.

"I'm not trying to control you, I'm trying to keep you safe," he barks, indignant. "Did he pass you a scroll tonight?"

I almost fall off the couch, but immediately I mask my expression. He didn't find the scroll, then. Someone else in the palace has it tucked in their back pocket. Or is he bluffing? Testing me, trying to catch me in a lie...

I peer deeply into his eyes, searching for a shift, a tell, anything. Of course, there's nothing. His eyes are impenetrable slits, so whether he knows about the scroll or not leaves me guessing. Still, there was something earnest in that question, in the way he posed it...

"Alex?"

"No," I finally say. A gamble, but one with fewer possible questions. Besides, I don't think my ego could handle telling him the truth right now. That I've *lost* a scroll inside the palace.

"What was the point of him attending the stables, then, if not to deliver a scroll?"

I hesitate and inwardly sigh; the man is unquestionably astute. "Uh, well. His intention was to leave a scroll. Of course, when he ran headfirst into me, there really was no point."

"So then. What did you learn?"

"Not a lot," I reply, and I'm not being cagey. The only thing I did glean, frankly, was that I was placed at Strath Glen strategically and not because I was a good fit for the viscount. For some reason, though, I don't want to share with him that part. I don't want to share with him that Neo and I plan on working together to free Airo-Aurora, either.

"You won't tell me," he correctly surmises.

"Really, we didn't have much time to talk—"

He splays his hands open wide. "I told you to leave it to me, didn't I? Your involvement in these secret dossiers must now end."

"Pardon—"

"Tell me the name of this technician, please."

I stare at him. Surely, after all this time, after all we've been through, he doesn't expect me to hand him the technician and twiddle my thumbs.

"I'm quite serious," he continues as he watches me. "Don't you have enough to occupy your mind? I'd think between your friend's fast-approaching wedding, along with our own, you'd have tired of this ridiculous game."

"You really take me for the type to be caught up in wedding preparations?"

His brow sits low across his eyes, his full attention is mine. "Your recent activities in the library, then."

So, he knows I'm organizing the library. That's fine, it's no secret. Still, it doesn't sit well with me that he keeps such close tabs. Especially when I know so little about his day-to-day activities.

"Well, Alex?"

"You know what I saw during that helicopter ride," I say quietly, my voice barely audible over the whistling wind. "Do you really think I'll sit by as you continue to 'bide your time?' Besides, how am I to know now, where your loyalties truly lie."

"What a foolish thing to say."

"Is it?" I ask, thinking for the hundredth time of the moment he pushed me into Doctor Lebwitski's arms, the moment the needle pierced my neck as his ice-cold eyes gazed down at me. I snort, then add, "You must think me very stupid."

His gaze is unfathomably piercing. "What is that supposed to mean?"

I shake my head, determined not to say too much, determined not to open up to this man ever again.

"No, tell me," he insists.

"The hour is late. Sir." I turn away before he can say anymore, and, as I know he won't bother me once tucked between the sheets, I walk quickly to the far side of the room.

thirteen

. . .

THE NEXT EVENING, Carnegie Reserve twinkles. The chandeliers have been dimmed to their lowest setting, and a dozen candles have been added to each table. A lone soprano sings a tragedy in the far corner. I take a glass of wine from a passing waiter, and a meat-stuffed pastry after that, then retreat to the shadows. All the better to hide from King, James, Dear Matthew, and Wolfe.

I check my watch. I'm here too early, that's the problem. No longer busy stalking the stables, I should be using the social hour preceding dinner to do something useful, like search for the lost scroll. Then again, I'd spent the better part of the day looking, with no luck. I could continue my work in the library, I realize next, and as James looks to be trying to catch my eye, I drain my glass and head out the door.

"I forgot to ask," rings out a voice as I round the imperial staircase. "Was he impressed with your musical skills?"

I drop the remaining bite of my pastry. "You startled me," I say, gazing up into the rotunda.

Wolfe walks slowly down the steps, eyes on me. "We didn't have a chance to discuss it last night, seeing as how you went to bed in the middle of our conversation."

"I was tired."

"So. Was he impressed?"

"Was who—"

"That boy who visited you recently. The same one you reunited with in the library last week, of course. The one all of Quire expected you to be matched with. Isn't it nice, the two of you rekindling things," he adds in a voice laced with fire.

"Oh, yes. My old friend," I say pointedly. "I don't know whether or not he was impressed with my musical skills. He's heard me play before."

"Why are you punishing me?"

The question catches me off-guard and both arms drop to my sides. "Ex-cuse me?" I stutter as the soprano in Carnegie builds into a crescendo.

"They would have implanted a chip in your brain then and there," he says between clenched teeth, his voice barely audible. "The order had been placed. It was only my actions, Alexandra, that stopped that from happening. And yet, from that moment, you have been angry with me."

"How am I to know what happened?" I fire back, careful to keep my voice quiet. "I was left unconscious after you pushed me into Doctor Lebwitski's arms and ordered him to sedate me."

"It was a ruse—"

"That's all I see when I look at you now," I spit at him. "Do you realize that?"

Hurt cuts through his eyes.

"Then," I continue, in a rush of emotion—as if the words have been sitting balled up in my chest for ages, waiting to tumble out. "Then, I woke, alone in a bus stop. Your words to me there, before you deserted me, no less—do you think they brought me comfort? Did you think the disregard and callousness that you showed me would go unnoticed? Or letting me find my way home by myself, half-sedated?" I angle my body so that I'm square to him and add, "Is that truly how you'd treat someone you cared about, Viscount?"

He swipes at his mouth, then exhales with impatience. "I'm not great at expressing myself, I admit that. But there, in the bus stop, I was in a hurry, yes? So, enough with your behavior. It's due time to put all this behind us."

"Enough with my behavior," I repeat, slowly, deliberately.

He doesn't get the message. Instead, he continues, "I don't have time to deal with petty dramas. You wish to remain angry at me? Fine. But don't drag that boy into it and make me reciprocate." He and his towering height turn toward Carnegie.

I lift my voice over the aria that resonates through the old walls. "Make you reciprocate?" I echo, and I'm surprised to find that my voice shakes. "With Claudia, I presume?"

"Reciprocate with anger—"

"Ours will be a marriage by contract alone," I state, no longer interested in listening to him. "By all means, rekindle things with Claudia, if you haven't already. You have my blessing." With that, I stride toward the front door.

He calls my name, just once, and then Airo-Aurora spreads out beneath me like a woven tapestry of lights. I let the door swing shut behind me, give a curt nod to both greencoats on duty, then stride down the steps, following the winding road allowance until I stand on the threshold of palace grounds. Not allowed to take a step further, as ordered by King himself. Right now, though, I don't care, I don't even look over my shoulder to see if anyone peers from a window high above. I simply step forward, consequences be damned, and the further I walk, the better I feel. It's the sensation of being liberated, free, at least for now. It's the knowledge that I'm putting a great helping of space between me and the viscount.

The *viscount*.

Every time I think of him, I grow angrier. Never have I met someone so callous, so cold. Just as his mother had said, he isn't a man that a woman could love. His heart isn't cut from ice or stone—it quite simply doesn't exist. There is a void inside his chest, a hollow void encircled by tin—something I've long suspected, and now I know for certain. I kick myself for putting my faith in him, my trust, for even allowing myself to enjoy his company and companionship from time to time.

This rift between the two of us, the one that weighs so heavily on me, it's nothing but a *petty drama* to him. A minor inconvenience that he'd like to move past, the same way he cleans up all the little irritations in his life. Not only does he fail to understand my feelings—he doesn't *care* to understand in the first place.

With my head whirring with hurt and anger, I continue walking, deeper into the city, up the main drag known as Central Boulevard, unconcerned about who may see. Around me are the elbows of passersby, the horn blasts of drivers, the chaos of flashing screens and decorative lights. The downtown core is busy, unusually so, and for a minute, I feel lost at sea, unable to find my bearings. And then I run headfirst into the side of a horse.

A blackcoat stares sternly down at me, then carries forward, turning the horse down a boulevard that's been cleared of cars. I stare after it, I scan the street for bluecoat officers, shivering, and then I take another step, I bump into another horse. Twisting around, I see that I'm caught up in a team of them, all with unfriendly blackcoats sitting on top. I twist around once more, a full circle, fearful that the bluecoats might be close behind, but none catch my eye. No flash of white, either, to indicate Doctor Lebwitski.

Relax, Alex.

Once the horses pass by, there's a blast of a horn, and the glittering sky is clouded by confetti. I'm covered head to toe, and as I begin to clean myself off, the sound of circus music blares in my ear.

I move to the side, stepping on a sheet of paper in the process. A flyer, and the picture catches my eye. It's a drawing of a white ribbon, just like the ones I saw when I was headed to Aunt Jo's.

Disregarding the smudges of dirt and the boot print across it, I bend closer.

WHITE RIBBON CAMPAIGN, it reads in bold type. I squint at the small print as the circus music grows louder.

Feeling dissatisfied?
Fed up with having no say in your future?
Fight the power! Fight for a Free Airo-Aurora!

My brow lifts, my eyes grow wide, and the whirling music surrounding me seems to dim. *Fight for a Free Airo-Aurora.*

A plume of glitter shoots through the air, wedging between my eyelids, and when my vision finally returns, I re-read the flyer, assuring myself that I'm not mistaken, that I'm not dreaming. Assuring myself that someone else out there—maybe lots of someones—has the same vision for our nation-state that Neo and I do.

Neo, and I bend over to retrieve the flyer so I can show it to him, but I'm bumped to the side, more glitter wedges between my eyes, and when I finally clear them again, the flyer has fluttered away.

Someone knocks into me, and another, and I see a series of girls twirling sparklers waltz past. Following behind them is a self-automated float with a tiger on board, and slowly it dawns on me that I'm standing in the middle of a parade.

I side-step my way to the edge of the street. "What's going on?" I shout to an old woman cloaked in fur. All around us, the sidewalks swell with cheering.

"It's the Winter's End celebration, of course," replies the woman, as if it's the most obvious thing in the world. And maybe it is. Maybe if I were residing anywhere besides Strath Glen with its maddening occupants and its frenetic pace, I, too, would have some awareness of the shifting seasons.

A marching band materializes next, their blasts drowning out the carnival music. I wave my thanks to the woman and dart under a French horn, diving deep into the crowds where I can't be spotted...more cautious than before.

The Winter's End celebration, already, and this time a chill of foreboding rolls down my spine. Because with winter's end comes spring, and with spring comes my wedding to *him*. The dreadful viscount. And the hurt and anger come rushing back, dulling some of the excitement and intrigue created by that flyer.

The flyer. The White Ribbon Campaign. I must remember to ask Neo about it. Perhaps he, too, has stumbled upon it. Perhaps our next move should be to align ourselves with them. Power in numbers, after all.

The woman cloaked in fur is pushed back by a group of men in fedoras, and she ends up standing nearby, linking arms with a man in a bowler hat. At first, I don't notice it. But I do a double-take, I notice that the man in the bowler hat looks both content and bored all at once, and I recognize the expression for what it is.

"Is this your husband?" I ask the woman.

"Yes, it's my husband," she replies, looking indignant. "What's it to you?"

"It's nice to meet you, sir," I say, sidling closer to him and ignoring the woman.

The man tips his hat to me, his expression serene.

"Do you attend the parade every year?" I continue, undeterred by the way his wife crosses her arms.

"Oh, sure I do, miss," he says without taking his eyes off

the nearest float, one that features a towering ice sculpture in the shape of a dragon. He turns to me and smiles. "Why, you've forgotten your coat!"

I stare down at myself. Of course I have. I'd been so incensed with Wolfe that I had marched straight out the door, and until now, the anger coursing through my veins has provided me with more than enough heat. Now, though, as I forget what Wolfe and I were even fighting about, clouded as it is by my unusual outing, the parade, and the discovery of the White Ribbon Campaign, I begin to shiver.

"Allow me, allow me," says the man good-naturedly. He unwinds his scarf, then twists it mindlessly around my neck.

"You're very kind," I say to him. Then I turn to his wife. "Has your husband always been so gracious?"

Her face puckers, like she's suspicious of me and my questions, and before I can put her at ease, or try to, she grabs the man by the arm and pulls him away, ignoring my shouts that I have his scarf. They vanish through the crowd, and for a second, I consider chasing after them, keen to observe more of the man, but then I catch sight of the next float—the one approaching from up the street—and I go still.

My heart stops, I forget all about the man in the bowler hat.

Because there, on a throne built from tulips, sits none other than the princess of Airo-Aurora. Her husband, Dear Matthew, sits next to her, looking bored. Immediately I duck my head, sheltering behind a wide-shouldered man, and watch Aubrey and Dear Matthew from between a gap in the man's coat.

A wreath of roses in the shape of a heart hangs behind them. He strokes her belly as they wave to the crowd, and standing to the side, just like during the national addresses, is the Queen, waving and smiling as if completely automated. She clears her eyes, and just like that, a new commotion presents itself.

A large fellow, the size of a boulder, charging at the float. With the aid of momentum and determination, he clambers aboard, hollering, "My baby!"

Blackcoats burst onto the scene a second later, coaxing their horses alongside the float and shouting to the man to get down.

Meanwhile, I push through the crowd, barely managing to keep pace with the float, trying to get a closer look at the intruder. He's familiar, I know that.

I place him—the same man as the one trying to gain access to Strath Glen just a week or two prior, the one that Jill stopped with such remarkable efficiency. And that's not all, I realize next, I've seen the man naked...in the cloak closet at Strath Glen's rear.

Just as the blackcoats manage to jump from the horses to the float, Aubrey untangles herself from the tulips and Dear Matthew, and she rushes forward, grasping the man's fingers in her own. The blackcoats pull back their batons, looking vaguely confused and waiting to see what the princess commands. Matthew no longer smiles, he instead looks understandably disconcerted, rearranging himself in his seat and nodding smartly at the crowd. The Queen, meanwhile, doesn't seem to notice the commotion at all, she instead continues to wave blithely.

Carnival music plays louder now, drowning out the marching band, and Matthew, no longer content to wait out his wife's obvious interest in this man, gesticulates angrily. Two blackcoats grab the intruder by the arms, and as a thousand fireworks go off at that very moment, they wrench him free of Aubrey's grasp.

The circus music reaches its climax, and Aubrey's scream punctures the air and lifts over the banging fireworks. "BUTCH!"

He struggles against the two blackcoats, and then all three of them lose their balance, they topple to the slush-covered street and squash an acrobat juggling apricots. Aubrey rushes to the float's edge, Butch drags himself to his feet with blood trickling from his ear, and the two holler for each other as the float carries Aubrey away and the man's foot is stomped on by an irate blackcoat.

I can't see what happens next, the crowd grows too dense and too frenzied for me to follow the float any further, but I can still hear their cries as a slew of burlesque dancers traipse around the corner.

Too many times I've seen similar women in Bishop's Aisle, where King and Wolfe work, and the thought of them —the thought of the punishment waiting for me if I'm caught off palace grounds—makes me feel unwell, like my earlier bravado has trickled away. Besides, with the Queen, Aubrey, and Matthew here, my own absence from Carnegie will be more conspicuous.

It's time to return to the palace, and for once, the quiet of my new quarters, even if they are shared with Wolfe, appeals. But moving quickly through the streets is impossible. I have to fight my way to the far edge of the sidewalk, then tiptoe along the backstreets, winding my way around Airo-Aurora's downtown so that it takes close to an hour to finally reach Strath Glen. My clothes, by now, are soaked with dampness, and I'm chilled to the bone, but none of that compares with the sight awaiting at the top of the towering staircase.

Standing there, inside the doorframe and blocking my path, are none other than Wolfe and his uncle.

fourteen

. . .

"HO, HO, HO!" King bellows as goosebumps erupt across my skin. "Caught red-handed, you cotton-eyed innocent!"

Wolfe, meanwhile, has turned a dark shade of red. His lips are pressed into a thin, severe line.

King steps around me and taps his walking stick on my behind. "Forward, march, my dear," he says in a sing-song voice.

My feet shuffle forward, my brain swirls with dread, I feel like I could vomit. Inside the palace we go, and into Devonshire with Wolfe trailing silently behind. It shouldn't be guilt that I feel, and yet right now, I swear my stomach twists with it.

"Explain yourself, cutie! Kind old King told you not to wander off into that big old city, and did you listen?" He pulls his ear and makes a show of shaking his head theatrically back and forth, as though I'm a small child.

"Please," I say. "I just went for a walk."

"A walk!" he cackles. "Tell me the truth, now, and beware."

"The truth?"

"Make me wait a second longer, and you'll see."

"I'm sorry, but I don't—"

"I'll double your punishment!" Then he adds with less theater, "Do note that I saw you storm out of my palace with my own two eyes, wee one."

My breathing may be quick and shallow, my brain may be fixated on my looming punishment, yet still, I wonder how he saw me. And from where? Because now that I've discovered the White Ribbon Campaign, now that Neo and I committed to working together, something tells me this won't be the last time I sneak out into the city.

King stomps his walking stick. "Well?"

"Your nephew and I had a small upset," I acknowledge. "It was about nothing, really, but I truly did feel like taking a walk to clear my head. Before I knew it, I found myself in the middle of a parade, and it took quite a while to get around it and back here. It was a mistake to leave, I'll admit that, but it was stumbling upon the parade by accident that prolonged my outing."

"A mistake! An accident! You sorceress, you. Why, you'd better cast a spell on me if you think I'm going to fall for that malarky. There was defiance gleaming in your eye and quickening your pace. That's what drove you from the palace, little miss, hmm? Do you think I care for defiance? Do you think there's any room for defiance here at Strath Glen or in my magnificent nation-state?"

"No, King."

"What's that?"

I clear my throat and speak louder: "No, King."

"Daisies. Now, let's beat that rebellion from yours right this second." He stomps his walking stick loudly against the floor, and my entire body shudders. "Off with your riding jacket."

"Please—"

"Oh, I don't like begging, little Amelia Bunny-Nose. This

isn't Quire, and besides, it hurts my ears. Now, quick, quick...off with that blazer, or I'll strip it away myself."

"Once a killer, always a killer," chirps the parrot from the far corner.

I chance a fleeting look at Wolfe, but his gaze is on his watch. His mouth is still set at an unpleasant angle, but otherwise, he looks as disinterested as always. And so, with no other choice, I peel away the damp blazer.

"Good, good," he coos as he positions his walking stick along my neck, then drags it over my shoulder and down my side.

Every hair on my body stands on end with anticipation. Wolfe continues to stare at his watch, he won't intervene. And there is no place to run, no place to hide. The only thing I can control in this instant is my reaction, and so I think of my aunt, I think of all I've endured, I remember my strength.

I meet King's gaze with calm resolve.

For a fleeting second, he falters. I can see the surprise in his eyes, surprise that intermingles with alarm, and I'm reminded that fear really is King's most powerful weapon. I decide then and there to strip him of it.

"I think I'll flog your backside," he declares a moment later. "You, my dear," he continues largely, poking me in the stomach, "go lie on that daybed right there. Hurry up, dinner has surely been served, and I do not like my escargot cold."

"Nor do I," I reply in a level voice. "Let's get on with it," I agree, then I stride toward the daybed, certain in my peripheral vision I see Wolfe lift his gaze from his watch and consider me.

"Yes...let's!" King shouts after a beat of hesitation. His bombastic act, I think, is faltering.

I lie down, careful to tuck my trembling hands beneath me where they can't be spotted. And then I wait, every cell in my body not simply bracing for impact, but readying to stay cool. Calm. Nonchalant. Because reacting with tears and pain—that's what King wants.

That's not what he's going to get—not this time.

I wait, and I wait. Before, the punishments happened quickly, with little to no forewarning. Right now, King is playing with me, he is dragging this into an excruciating punishment in its own right. Breathe, Alex, I remind myself. Relax into it. Numb your brain, and the pain will be numbed, too. The anticipation will mellow.

King exclaims, "A perfect target!"

"Indeed!" I exclaim right back.

Breathe. Breathe. Breathe.

Nothing.

At first, I think it's part of the game. That he's drawing it out, building the anticipation of pain into an impossible crescendo. But too much time elapses, and finally, I chance a look at him.

A grin turns his mouth and he tosses the walking stick into the air, he catches it with gusto. Then he turns to Wolfe, who has resumed studying his watch. "You, dear nephew. It should be you to deliver the punishment. After all, it was your little fiancée here who defied you...storming away like that, and right under your nose! Now is the perfect time to teach her the ropes," he adds, knowledgeably.

Something shifts across Wolfe's face. He snaps the watch shut and turns to his uncle. "No."

"No?" King echoes.

"I don't believe in corporal punishment, something you know," Wolfe replies in an icy tone. "If you insist upon it, then be done with it and quick, otherwise, don't involve me."

"I insist that you do it, my dear boy! She is, after all, your fiancée."

"Indeed, she is," Wolfe says fiercely in a flash of temper.

"And I don't intend to poison our marriage before it begins by taking a stick to her. Frankly, I think you've already made her pay enough for her transgression, don't you?"

"You could've told me the party's in here, Papa!" James shouts from the hallway. He strides inside, looking put out, then notices me lying prone on the daybed. He stops abruptly, but understanding dawns slowly across his features. "Was your little fiancée naughty?" he asks Wolfe, clicking his tongue like a chicken.

Wolfe looks like he's swallowed something sour. He says nothing.

"Just about to offer up some punishment, huh, Papa?" James continues.

"I gave your dear cousin here the chance, and he flat-out refused. Count me *mystified*."

"A strange thing, indeed," remarks James with apathy. "And certainly an indication he's not fit for the throne," he adds pointedly. "You know, once you're ready to retire, Papa, and enjoy yourself."

King rolls his eyes. "I've told you a hundred times now—"

"Sometimes in life," begins James, wisely, "it takes someone else to show us the path—"

"For god's sake," King snaps. He stomps his walking stick, returning his attention to me and drawing the stick over his shoulder.

Breathe, breathe, breathe.

And then, "Might I, Papa?"

King looks at me, I look away. The request from James—it wasn't one I was anticipating, and so I have no counterplay, no recourse whatsoever. In my peripheral vision, I see King grin as he tosses James the stick.

James catches it with a flourish, then smiles down at me and strokes my cheek. "I wouldn't hurt you, flower," he whispers so the others can't hear. Then he stands upright and announces, "I want her standing. Over there, against the wall. Next to the portrait of the hunter in plaid."

"Up you get, little miss. You heard the man," commands King, his formidable voice filling every corner of Devonshire. Even the parrot, I notice, goes still. "Move to the wall this instant, you deceitful angel, you."

"I'm not deceiving you—"

"Now," King adds, tapping his wristwatch. "My escargot. Remember?"

"Then forget about the girl," Wolfe interjects. "Go, dine. I'll punish her for her disobedience in my own right."

"I believe James has called dibs," King points out.

Meanwhile, I walk across the room, completely unperturbed by the situation, or at least that's what I project. On the inside, though, I feel dangerously close to vomiting. *I wouldn't hurt you.* That's what James had said, and right now, that phrase echoes through my brain on repeat. I cling to it.

Then James is pacing behind me, back and forth, his chest thrown out, the walking stick dragging along the blood-red floor. "This will leave a bad bruise, is my thinking," he says wryly, and my stomach clenches. Then he's twirling the stick, much like the girls with the sparklers at the parade. He stares only at Wolfe, I notice, as he speaks. "Might even split the skin. I certainly hope she doesn't like to sleep on her back. Oh, silly me...were you hoping to have her on her back this evening?" He laughs. "I wouldn't count your lucky stars on that one, dear cousin!"

Wolfe grits his teeth but says nothing.

"Well, then," continues James. "No time like the present." He grips the stick in both his hands, like he's holding a baseball bat. He draws it behind him and over his shoulder—

"You're going to kill her," interjects Wolfe as I bite down hard on my tongue to stop myself from screaming.

"Oh, am I? Best to show some mercy, then," and with that, he drops the stick to the floor, twists me around so my back is flush with the wall, and kisses me on the mouth.

The taste of sherry and snails, and when I finally manage to extricate myself from James's embrace, I see that King has retrieved his stick, he currently pushes it into the viscount's chest.

"Delicious!" James exclaims, licking his lips. "Have you had the delight yet, my somber, boring old cousin? Or do I get first honors?"

I don't bother waiting for Wolfe's response, or to see what unfolds next. Instead, I turn for the exit, I run, sprinting as fast as I can from that room, away from those awful men, no longer concerned about putting on a show of bravery, taking away King's power, or whatever the hell I was playing back there. This is real life...not a game, and the whole business is so unjust, so nasty, that once again, I find myself intent on finding a way out from underneath my unfair—and fraudulent—Selection results.

The black and white Hall of Mirrors blurs through my peripheral in a streak of grey, and after that, I'm cocooned under the blankets in the sprawling bed that is now my own, teeth chattering with fright, heart thumping so fast, so heavily, I'm surprised it doesn't give out.

I could expose Neo for interfering with my Selection results. He would be sent to the gallows, undoubtedly—and yet that...that might be a way to free myself of the strings tethering me here and locking me in place.

I know, though, that I can't do that, and I cry slowly. I fall into a deep, dreamless slumber.

I WAKE the next morning to a stern face bearing down on me.

"Next time you are angry with me, find somewhere smarter to sulk, yes?"

Then he is gone, the door banging shut behind him. I rub my eyes and begin the dreary task of parsing out what happened the day before.

King had been cruel, no surprise there. Still, though, the enjoyment the game of cat and mouse brought him had been downright deranged. James, on the other hand, had been cruel to Wolfe, and Wolfe had been, well... He hadn't been helpful, that's for sure. Once again, he prioritized his position with King over my wellbeing. So, no surprise there, either.

But what *was* surprising, I suppose, was that he clearly didn't enjoy seeing me suffer. Last night was almost as painful for him as it was for me, I'm sure of it. And what about refusing to strike me himself? A small act of kindness from a man who is anything but. A risky move, too, to defy his uncle like that, but I suppose that was one red line he wasn't willing to cross.

Something to be appreciative of, I think grimly.

Next, I consider the day before me. Spending it locked away from everyone, in here, tucked under the covers, holds the most appeal. But not only would it allow King to win, it would mean the entire day is lost feeling sorry for myself.

I have other things to focus on. The White Ribbon Campaign that I've discovered, first of all. Agnes's upcoming wedding, now in just five days. My partnership with Neo, and once again, I think about turning him in to free myself.

I won't do it. Regardless of whether he deserves it or not for manipulating my Selection results, turning him in would help only myself. It would do nothing to help all the citizens of Airo-Aurora, and isn't that the ultimate goal?

So, after dressing and readying myself, I head down to the kitchen for a bacon roll, then to Counterdown Abbey to work on the cataloguing system, just like any other day.

"Miss likes to keep busy, yes?"

I glance up from my work to see Rosa standing there with a bucket of suds. "Yes, ma'am."

"Good on you. Aye, I heard you got the belt for leavin' the palace last night. That true?"

"Something like that," I say wearily, not having the energy to explain that it was rather James's mouth that I received—not exactly an improvement. "It's nothing new. Did you work the Rose Ceremony?"

"Aye, you took it right to the bare shoulders if memory serves." Then she grabs her mop and moves toward me. "Don't forget what you stumbled on a couple nights gone, aye. If you ever need a break from palace life, favors work in both directions."

I lift an eyebrow, intrigued. But a moment later, I shake my head. "I'm afraid I'm as unpopular with the servants as I am with the royals."

"Go on, Sawyer and I are happy to help. Speaking of, why'd Sawyer say you've got an interest in old Worthers, hey?"

"I saw his sacking when I first arrived at Strath Glen," I explain tactfully, "which sparked a natural curiosity, that's all."

"Aye."

"Did you know him well?"

"Aye, better than most. Not a popular man, but the two of us always had a special connection." The woman winks.

I lean forward with interest. "A romantic one?"

She grins slyly, then swats the air. "Hush up about it."

I drum my fingers on the table, intrigued. "One last question," I finally say. "Have you seen him since his departure from Strath Glen?"

Her face hardens. "Aye."

"Is he enjoying retirement?" I press.

"Oh, aye, I'd say as much. Bit more than that even," she

adds cryptically. Waving goodbye, she takes her suds and disappears around the corner.

I let out a long breath as something becomes clear.

All along, I'd assumed people weren't objecting to the mechanized version of their loved ones because they weren't noticing. Because the transition was so seamless, so well-informed by the Mainframe's extensive collection of data, it was simply seen as a dark cloud of anger and discontent lifting.

But that isn't remotely true. How could I not have seen that earlier? After all, I'd been suspicious of the Queen from the get-go. Even the short exchange with Worthers had left my blood running cold. And my aunt's neighbor, and the man at the parade...

Loved ones notice the change, of course, they do. Considering Rosa's tone just now, they suspect something sinister, too. And yet they remain silent, they say nothing.

Why?

Fear. It must be. Well-founded fear, too, because the Mainframe is always listening. It's always watching.

Once again, I think of the punishment the evening prior, I think of the effect it had on King when I showed no fear, no apprehension. *He* became the fearful one. In that instant, he was stripped of his power. So why can't I transfer the same principle, the same lesson, to the public at large?

Yet to spread awareness about the consequences of discontent will stoke fear even more, won't it? But there's a reason the override chip program is a secret. There's a reason King wants to keep his army of Mavericks secret, too...

Anger.

That's the key.

If people learn the truth, they will become angry, and angry people are far less susceptible to fear...

When I get up to retrieve another book, my fingers are

unsteady, and this time it isn't with dread or foreboding. This time they shake with excitement. Because if I can find a way to reach these people, to show them how deeply the injustice flows, to band them together—their anger might be enough to reach King. They may be able to compel him to abandon the override program, to abandon the insurance policy. Or, maybe, if I'm really lucky, the tide of anger and outrage will be enough to overthrow King completely.

My next meeting with Neo really can't come quick enough—three more days.

And then, as if on cue, I spot King through the bookshelves, walking the corridor outside the library, and a chill runs the length of my spine. His posture is upright, his eyes are slits that glint with arrogance, and his fur pelt trails with theater on the polished floor behind him. Like a spread in a magazine, his crown of rubies glints in the morning sun.

A formidable foe, by any extent, but I think...I think I'm beginning to see his weakness, too.

Next, my gaze snags on James, who trails after him. James, who kissed me yesterday without my consent. James, who spared me the stick. James, who currently sports an eye so deeply black and pinched shut it makes me gag.

fifteen

. . .

"AYE, I GOTS A LITTLE SECRET."

I turn to Rebecca, eyeing her under the dim parlor light, and sigh. "Another one? Please, I'm still recovering from the last one."

She grins. "Moving to the viscount's suite, that was an A-bomb. Nah, this secret's more of a question, like."

"A question for me?"

"Been meaning to track you down, too, but can't go knocking on the viscount's door at all hours. Lucky break to find yeh here, like."

"I'm looking for a stapler," I explain, perusing the drawers of the built-ins. Knick-knacks abound, including an extensive array of cigar-smoking paraphernalia, but so far, no stapler.

"For yer work in the library?"

"That's right."

"It's important to you...that."

"It is," I agree.

"Aye, well, I can help you find a stapler, miss."

"That's wonderful—"

"As soon as yeh explain a little something to me," she adds.

Eyeing her, I'm instantly wary. "Yes?"

"What truth are yeh lookin' to spread?"

My eyes narrow, I frown. What truth am I looking to spread? I'm looking to spread a lot of truth frankly—shocking, hard to digest truth. But how could she know that? "Uh..." I finally mutter. "Pardon?"

"Yeh didn't hear me?"

"I didn't understand the question."

"I'll spell it out for yeh, like. Me, I've got a keen eye. Not so surprising, then, that I found a note meant for your eyes only."

I go still. All the blood must drain to my feet, because suddenly I'm light-headed. Faint. Because...the scroll. She found the missing scroll.

"Know it's for you, like, since I delivered one to you before, rolled up just like this one in the shape of a ciggy. Chicken-scratch writing, too. So, who's the sweetheart?" Her eyes shine.

"It's not a sweetheart. I can assure you."

"Then who's writing to yours?"

"I don't know," I lie. "Whoever it is never signs their name."

"What's the truth you oughta be sharing, then?"

Funny that once I had her back up against a wall. Now the tables have turned, the tide has shifted, and I'm at a loss for words. I can't tell her the truth—not only is the girl far from trustworthy, but it's dangerous information to wield, and I must do it wisely. Not here and now—like this.

"I'm gettin' old here, miss."

"What exactly did it say?" I finally ask.

"To spread the truth, like. Told yeh already. Now, go on."

"Did it specify which truth he or she is talking about? Because I don't have any idea—how could I?"

Another lie. Because clearly, Neo had reached the same conclusion as me: spread the truth. The truth of Ashville Range, the Mavericks, and the override chip. Spread the truth and ignite anger. The question, of course, is how? How to spread the truth, how to do so reliably and efficiently, how to make sure people actually believe—

"It didn't specify, no," Rebecca says, interrupting my thoughts. "Sounds like maybe you know what truth it's talkin' of, though." She continues to watch me, waiting for an answer.

"I don't think that note has anything to do with me," I say eventually. "Sorry I couldn't be of help. And, I think I'll find that stapler on my own, thanks."

"I'll go straight to King if you don't tell me."

I freeze. Then, somehow, I manage a coy smile. "Be my guest. What do you expect him to do with a piece of paper addressed to no one with the words *Spread the truth* upon it, anyway? Besides lash you for wasting his time, that is."

Her lip curls, and a whisp of satisfaction surges through me. Because finally...finally, I am learning to play the game. Finally, I am finding my way at Strath Glen.

And yet...the worry doesn't dissipate as it should as I move about the day. Because already the chips are stacked against me, and one prod from the likes of Rebecca could be my undoing.

sixteen

. . .

FROM DEEP UNDER THE COVERS, after a bone-chilling night made far worse by the window thrown all the way open, I hear voices. Movement.

Is Wolfe hosting company? Did he forget about my presence in the giant bed tucked into the corner?

No, it isn't like him to forget. It must be Gerard and some other servants, perhaps delivering his breakfast, and I resign myself to returning to sleep. Then a weight drops onto the bed next to me. A woman clears her throat.

Reluctantly, I push down the covers, a small and hopeful part of me thinking perhaps it's my aunt here to visit.

Immediately I regret my hopefulness. But what's done is done, so I sit all the way up, staring at the Duchess of Airo-Aurora. In the far corner of the room, Wolfe and his father discuss tariffs.

"I would have prepared myself, madam, had I known to expect you," I say tactfully.

The woman smiles in a tight way. "We've just returned from an international endeavor. Stopping in to see our son is common practice. Surely you can understand that, girl from Quire?"

"Of course, madam."

"You can imagine my surprise, then, to see a slight figure buried under the blankets."

"Yes, well, your son decided—"

"Clearly, I now know what he has done," she says coldly. "Generously invited you into his personal chambers. And yet I fear that he is making more of an effort than are you," she adds.

I shake my head. "I assure you not, madam."

"Tell me, then," and her voice grows sugary sweet, yet sharp as a knife, "why my son is relegated to the sofa?"

I draw in a breath, understanding now where her anger stems from. "It was his decision," I insist, one word running into the next. "He wanted to sleep there—"

"I've never seen him look so tired and unwell. Imagine a man of his stature sleeping on the sofa like an animal."

"I understand your concern," I say, as sweat collects along my hairline, "it's just that we're not yet wed, and—"

"I'm not asking you to spread your legs for him," she hisses. "Your dress fitting for your wedding is to take place in a month's time, making a pregnancy a terrible inconvenience, but still. It is a wide bed, child."

"Ignore her," Wolfe commands. He moves in our direction, and though he had been speaking to me, now he turns purposefully to his mother. All he does, however, is lay his flashing eyes upon her.

"On the contrary to what you might think, son," she says at once, "I am not meddling. I am simply standing up for you, as I fear you are unable to."

"Her insolence is only made worse by thinly veiled threats and orders. I can assure you I know best how to deal with her."

"And yet I'm not convinced, my son. Indeed, your normally ironclad will seems to be shattering against this delicate little flower."

Wolfe exhales loudly but says nothing more about it.

The duchess turns to me. "I am supportive of the fresh blood you bring to the monarchy, my dear. But not if it negatively impacts my boy. Make him happy, fulfill your role, or I'll force that fresh blood of yours blue. In fact, is the butler still in the entrance hall? Bring him in."

The door swings open immediately, and Gerard bows. "Your service, my lady?"

"Find some gowns that fit this slip of a woman and deliver them at once," she orders. "And in the meantime, remove all riding apparel from the closet."

Before I can protest, the duchess turns her attention back to me and places both hands alongside my face. "If things for my son don't improve soon, that busywork I've heard you've been doing in the library will be next to go. Understood?"

I scarcely breathe. It's not fair that I'm expected to please her son—especially after the fiasco at the Sky Center and, frankly, his ill-handling of it ever since. It's not fair that she can strip me of the few measly things I have here at Strath Glen—my choice of palace wear, my work in the library... It stinks of blackmail, not to mention that it completely strips me of autonomy, of my own identity—

She clears her throat. "Understood?" she repeats.

I understand, all right. She has the power here, not me, and I nod, deflated. Wolfe, meanwhile, buries his nose in a brief handed to him by his disinterested father. A minute later, the duke and duchess head for the exit, followed by Gerard and several other servants carrying out my well-cut blazers and riding pants. Carrying out a part of me, in a way, and I cringe thinking of what my wardrobe will now look like.

As for Wolfe and I—we, the betrothed—are alone, and I turn to him, I look for, or rather hope for, a reaction. Empathy, platitudes, promises to speak to the woman...anything.

But he doesn't look at me, consumed by the brief as he is, no matter that I stare at him. The threats by the duchess echo loudly in my mind, and I clear my throat. Still, no reaction. Finally, I push off the covers and stride right up to him. He writes note after note in the margins of the brief he holds, still not noticing me in the slightest. I clear my throat a second time.

"Speak," he says gruffly from the corner of his mouth without shifting his gaze or ceasing his endless note-taking.

"I saw what you did to James."

He wasn't expecting that, I can see it in the way I've captured his attention. "Your point?"

"Choosing my own clothes and my own activities is very important to me. You didn't think to intervene just now?"

"What does one have to do with the other?"

"You're not completely unwilling to intervene on my behalf, Viscount," I say pointedly.

He snaps the brief shut and stares sternly down at me. "My cousin got exactly what he deserved. A man doesn't sit idly by while another man kisses his fiancée."

I snort.

"Something amusing?"

"I've never met someone guided only by rules and dictates from society," I respond, "You know, as opposed to true feelings."

He squints down at me. "That is ridiculous. I am a victim of my own feelings as much as the next person. As for you and my mother, your little squabbles don't concern me."

"But my riding—"

"It's just clothes, Alexandra."

"It is my freedom."

He gives me an exasperated look. Then he taps the brief. "I've work to do," he declares, just as Gerard enters the room carrying a handful of dresses.

"I'll sleep on the couch from now on," I say before he can go.

"That won't be necessary."

I stare at him resolutely. "I insist."

———

TWENTY MINUTES LATER, I stumble out the door wearing a gown too long, a cardigan too scratchy, and walking in high-heels that are far too big. Yet despite feeling like a child playing dress-up, I hold my head high.

One thing I refuse to do is stay cooped up in my room, cowering—the way I've done in the past. No, once again, I'll go to the library and complete my work just like any other day.

Maneuvering down the stairs, however, proves to be exceedingly difficult in high-heeled shoes several times too big, and after losing my balance twice and losing a shoe no less than three times, I kick both off, resolving to go sock-foot and to having perennially cold feet here at Strath Glen.

At the very least, I can now move with more agility, and I glide down the remaining stairs, noticing as I do Gerard at the front doors, checking, by the looks of it, someone's credentials. And when that person is approved, when that person steps around the old butler and into Strath Glen, I gasp. "Patrick!"

He smiles broadly, and quickly we close the space between us. I even think he's about to lean in for a hug. *I* even consider it, given the much-needed taste of home he brings, but at the last second he angles away, gesturing toward the library instead. "I'm here on official business," he announces, but I can tell by the way the corner of his mouth twitches that he's lying. I wonder if Gerard could tell, too.

"How lovely," I say politely.

"Perhaps you could give me a tour of the library's paintings on display?"

"It would be my honor," I say with a curtsy, pushing our game farther, and for a second, I feel like I'm back in Quire, my family whole, my dreams for the future yet to be shattered. I feel safe, in that second. Safe, secure, and content.

A heartbeat later, I remember my surroundings, my vulnerability, and that nothing around here goes unnoticed. "After me," I add with less humor in my tone. After all, this is how I must be if I wish to continue these visits with a dear friend, and I do want that.

But how much am I truly looking for? Is my chest bursting with happiness right now because of the taste of home that Patrick brings? The touch of familiarity that I so crave, especially after the past tumultuous few days?

Or is it something more? Something scandalous and...forbidden?

As we push through the doors and into the sunlight-streaked, wood-clad room dotted with overstuffed shelves, I realize I don't have the answer. At least not yet.

"That dress looks nice on you," Patrick comments. "Are your feet not cold?"

"Uh, yes. A bit." Then I add, "I'm running the library now," and I lead him toward the largest oil painting—a portrait of a plain blonde woman. "It's official as can be," I continue, though he didn't ask. "I'm even implementing a catalog system, and one day I hope to get approval to open the doors to the public."

"And you're very excited about it, too, I see," he says, smiling. His fingers brush against mine as he gestures to the portrait, as if it's something we are actually discussing. "I can't tell you what a relief that is. Have you been eating?"

"I...of course, yes."

"Good. It's important to get rest, too. Have they set you up with a nice room, at least?"

I think of the fact that I no longer have my own room

and inwardly cringe. But I nod to Patrick, because no matter how much I want his company, I don't want his pity, and already he's too concerned over me. "A nice painting, isn't it?"

"Beautifully executed. One day I hope the national gallery won't have to borrow it to put her on display. Hopefully, people enjoy her right here, where she ought to be enjoyed. Once you turn this into a functional library for all of Airo-Aurora, I mean."

My chest swells. Patrick has always had the knack of making people feel good about themselves.

"Have you been able to do any flying?" he asks next.

"A bit," I say, once again, tight-lipped, considering how disastrous my sole flight was. It's hard not to feel dismayed, too. So many secrets. So much I don't dare divulge. And even if I did, where to begin?

I think of what Rebecca said, what was written on that missing scroll about spreading the truth, and my own conclusion on the same—and I realize what a tall task it will be.

Then Patrick is stepping closer, and he lowers his voice. "Why is it," he begins, "that I get the feeling you're keeping things from me?"

"Sometimes the truth is complicated," I reply, my voice as quiet as his.

"Alex, we've known each other for years. Try me."

I look into his eyes and see myself doing it. Every shocking and miserable detail of my own life and the secrets I've uncovered falling from my mouth and into his lap, I see him comforting me, that sturdy rock that he's always been. But that would just make it harder. It would just make *this* harder. I shake my head. "Sometimes it's so complicated," I explain, "it would take too much time to recount. Ages."

He stares at me for a while, then nods. "It's just..." He takes a deep breath, and his blue eyes cast down. "It's just that my truth is quite simple. I didn't want to be paired with Annie. I wanted to be paired with...well, with you."

My breath hitches. I don't know what to do, say, or which way to turn. Of course, I suspected as much, but voicing it...this is unchartered territory. What to make of it? Where to go from here? Then, seeing that he watches me, waiting for a response, I decide to be honest: "I...I wanted that, too," I admit.

He steps closer, and this time, his fingers brush deliberately against mine, and a profound sadness washes unexpectedly over me.

For a while, we just stand there, sharing the tight pocket of space. Yes, I wanted to be matched with him. It would have been easy. It would've been familiar. It would've made sense, whereas nothing with the viscount—not one fraction of a second passed with that man—has ever made sense.

But in the absence of computer chips and Mainframes playing cupid, what brings two people together? A mutual quest for something comfortable? Or something with 'energy,' as Agnes had put it?

"I should go, Alex," Patrick murmurs, interrupting my thoughts. He squeezes my hand, and, a moment later, with one last look over his shoulder—a look full of concern and warmth and, I suppose, something even more—he walks out the door, and I'm left pondering my situation, the Mainframe, and the meaning of love.

———

LATER THAT DAY, after several hours of cataloging behind me, after a few friendly conversations with the servants tidying the library, and with more thought given to the hazy outline of a plan developing in the back of my mind to ignite an uprising against King, I receive an unexpected visitor in the library.

"Smart dress," comes the viscount's churlish voice.

"What is it?" I ask, without looking up from my work.

I can sense his displeasure with being ignored, but he says nothing of it. "I came to inquire about the details of your friend's upcoming wedding in just four days' time. Monsieur Sawyer, in particular, would like to know when he is to take us."

"I'll leave the invitation on the entrance hall for you to peruse. All details are listed there." Still, I don't acknowledge him with a glance.

He hesitates, then says, "That seems acceptable." Another pause, followed by a sigh. "I also came to apologize."

At this, I do lift my head. I stare way up high as the afternoon sun funnels joyfully through the windows. "For what, precisely?"

"For not adequately explaining to you what transpired after you were sedated at the Sky Center. For leaving you alone in the bus stop. For not being able to stop King from punishing you for leaving the palace grounds. For not persuading my mother to show you more grace."

For a minute, I'm stunned, and a wellspring of emotion stirs unexpectedly in my chest—even more so than during my conversation with Patrick. I push it down and say curtly, "That's quite a laundry list."

The rigidness of his body seems to intensify. Then he lowers his voice and leans forward so that his hands rest on the desk. "But I *am* sorry."

I know intuitively that he speaks the truth. It's how vulnerable he is making himself right now, how still his body is. And then there are those lines that ride under his eyes, the brow that lately is ever low, the thinness that is sculpting his face—they are not there by coincidence. He really has been suffering.

Whether I can forgive him for all that, though, is another

matter. Or maybe the question isn't whether I can forgive him...it's whether I want to. After all, I have been suffering, too. And, as Neo said, I was placed at Strath Glen with an express purpose. Wolfe and I are not ideally suited to one another, not in the slightest, and so, do I really need to make an effort to set aside all that hurt?

Then again, even though we're not true matches, even though ours will be a marriage by contract alone, we must at some point learn to peacefully coexist. Plus, part of me—a small, infinitesimal part of me—wants less hostility with this man and perhaps even something more than that.

With those last thoughts in mind, I sit up straighter. "Very well."

The words have no discernable impact. He doesn't move a muscle; he simply squints down at me as if he didn't hear a thing. Then he stands quickly to his full height, jams those bony hands into his pockets, and sweeps his gaze along the desk. "Tell me, precisely, what you're doing here and why, please."

"I thought you—"

"I know only that you're organizing the library, but by the looks of it, you're doing more than that."

"Since the library lacks any sort of organizational scheme whatsoever, I'm designing and implementing a catalog system so that books can be easily retrieved."

He nods, then scratches behind his ear. "Why, exactly?"

"I believe I already explained why."

He exhales, sounding more exasperated by the second. "Why are you bothering with this when you don't need to?"

"Perhaps you haven't noticed, sir, but I do like to keep busy. Sitting around the palace with no interesting work to do, well...I can think of nothing more tedious than that."

"Many would say otherwise."

"I am not many," I remind him, meeting his gaze.

"Don't I well know. You realize, of course, that not many

aside from the two of us actually make use of the books in here?"

"Which is why I was thinking Strath Glen should open the library up to the public."

He stares at me as if it's the most outlandish idea in the world.

"At the very least, to the schoolchildren," I continue.

"We have no children's books here."

"Not yet, we don't. But we could bring some in for the youngest readers. And the older and more agile students would find the current selection to be a tremendous resource. The atlas collection alone is far superior to any in Quire—I can speak from experience."

"Yes, well." He continues to stare at me out of the corner of his eye. Clearly unable to think of any response, he stalks between the nearest row of books and out of sight.

I hold my hand over my mouth as I smile. I hadn't really expected to make that proposal, not in reality. And all in all, it had gone over quite well—better than I'd dare expect. The apology he'd proffered, too, had been a pleasant surprise, and a future of peaceful civility with Wolfe and a career as a librarian flashes momentarily before my eyes.

And yet, what of the rest of it? King, the Mainframe, the Mavericks, and the override chips? I can't carve out a comfortable life here at Strath Glen *and* attempt to overthrow King at the same time, can I? No, it's one future or the other. I need to commit to one path, and that's to rectify all that's wrong with Airo-Aurora.

Then I stare around a library I've come to love and sigh. Well. In the meantime, I may as well continue to pass my free time here, surrounded by books.

And, who knows... Perhaps I can have my cake and eat it, too.

seventeen

. . .

THE NEXT DAY, as I'm working in the library, methodically taking down details of each book and assigning it a number, something strange happens.

I can hear Gerard speaking to the servants dusting the sitting area, but I don't pay it any attention until Rebecca says loudly, "Right now, like?"

"Yes, right now. Straight to Carnegie," comes the old butler's voice, and it has an unbending quality to it that makes me nervous. Like something's afoot, something that makes the seasoned veteran of Strath Glen straight as an arrow.

I tidy up my desk, more a nervous habit than anything else, and just as I stand to see why the servants are being rounded up and sent to the dinner hall in the middle of the day, a rickety shadow crosses my desk. "Miss Alex."

"Yes?"

Gerard bows to me before speaking, a habit that only began when I was moved into Wolfe's quarters, and I think I understand Wolfe's contention that I'll have an added layer of protection once I'm his wife. Room location alone has added greatly to the level of decorum and the helping of respect I get around here, though neither matter very much compared to my safety.

And then he says, "To Carnegie, Miss Alex," and I freeze.

"But for what reason?"

"King has summoned you and the others."

"Servants and royals alike?"

"Even those hovering somewhere in between," he replies, and his gaze sweeps over my well-organized cataloging desk.

"But why?"

"I believe he'll explain once the occupants of the palace are sufficiently rounded up."

"I'm sure," I say hurriedly, "but in the meantime—"

"Miss Alex," he interrupts. "Carnegie."

"Yes...yes, of course," I stutter as I edge sideways out from behind the desk. Clearly, Gerard won't give me anything, not even a scrap or a morsel, and the rush of nerves at whatever awaits makes me feel unwell.

By the time I reach the main corridor though, the sheer number of others heading toward Carnegie distracts me from my nerves. Surely, with this many people, I have nothing to worry about. Surely, with this many people, the spur-of-the-moment meeting will have nothing whatsoever to do with me.

Entering Carnegie Reserve in the middle of the day, however, without the pomp that dinner-hour brings, is more disconcerting than I would've thought. I swallow, then follow a servant named Ray to the back of the room where the others congregate. I make a point to stand at the back of the crowd, intending to remain as inconspicuous as possible.

Nobody, it seems, knows precisely why we've been summoned, but the mood is light, laughter rises here and there, and I let myself relax, at least somewhat.

Next, I scan the crowd for Wolfe, but he's nowhere to be seen. The only royals here, in fact, are Aubrey and Dear

Matthew, and they sit at a table while the rest of us stand. I wonder what, if anything, came of the fiasco with Butch at the parade.

Five minutes pass, then ten. No longer does the door swing open and closed...all those living in the palace are here, save for a few senior members of the aristocracy.

Once again, the nerves set in.

I take to the window, staring out at the birch forest that used to occupy so much of my time when I resided in the guest room. I watch the limbs sway in the wind, a dreary sight compared to the dead of winter when each branch was blanketed with freshly fallen snow.

And then the door swings open, and Evie and Wolfe walk in, followed by their parents. James and the Queen are next. The only people missing now, I realize with a sinking feeling, are Morocco and King.

Morocco and King. *Morocco and King.*

Instantly I know precisely why we've been summoned, or at least I have a theory—an informed one.

That note. That blasted note I wrote in the darkened closet that I deposited in this very room when nobody was looking. Somehow in the commotion of the past couple of days, I'd forgotten all about it—and the arms deal, too. Clearly, though, King has not forgotten.

It was foolish to write it, and it was foolish to forget about it, assuming, I suppose, that it would simply be swept under the rug. As far as King can tell, after all, he has a mole under his roof—a serious concern. And it just so happens that mole is me.

Presumably, other methods of finding the note writer have turned up nothing. No fingerprints, no useful fibers, no distinguishing letter stock, and that realization brings me a whisp of relief. My only vulnerability, I suppose, was when I discreetly dropped the note to the floor.

Maybe it wasn't as discrete as I had imagined. Maybe

154 · Jerri Chisholm

someone *was* looking. Maybe the person who can implicate me, who can end my life, so to speak, is in this very room right *now*.

My heart thumps as I gaze around. Is Doctor Lebwitski on the premises? Is he waiting in the wings? Will I be thrown heartlessly into his arms before the meeting is through?

With no other real options, I set my sights on Wolfe. But he speaks with James on the far side of the room, standing near the table occupied by Aubrey and Dear Matthew.

I bite my thumb.

Do I go to him this very moment? Do I confess what I've done? I decide that I'd better, that the situation really is dire enough that I must, no matter how much I'd rather avoid the subject or, frankly, turn to him for help in the first place.

But just as I start to push my way through the crowd, the door to Carnegie Reserve swings open once again. A stern-looking Morocco fills the door frame in a tight green dress accented with velvet stripes meant to resemble the markings of a snake, and a hush falls over the crowd. In the silence comes the sound of soft thuds.

King, and his walking stick.

I can barely breathe as he strides into the hall, his Cheshire smile looking downright sinister, his dark gaze sweeping the entire room and all its occupants, his fur robes doubling his size and making him look that much more foreboding.

That gaze, though...it doesn't linger on me, and my sense of hopefulness surges. Doctor Lebwitski, too, is nowhere to be seen—another good sign.

But still, my body trembles. I feel like my legs could give out, and, most distressing of all, I crave the company of one individual. One man, one I've been angry at; my trust weakened but clearly not shattered.

Wolfe.

As I stare at him from across the room, I realize how deeply I count on him, and just as I digest how surprising this development is, his head tilts, his eyes find mine.

He stares steadily at me, and I think he can read the fear radiating from mine. It's the way his brow narrows, alongside the tightening of his body. Ever so slightly, I nod...as if to say, *Yes. Yes, I did this. I did this, and now I need you.*

And then King stomps his walking stick—three sharp raps against the floor—the room grows silent, and everyone, even Wolfe and I, stare at the man of the house. The most powerful man in all of Airo-Aurora.

He spreads his arms, his Cheshire grin growing. "Ladies and gentlemen gathered before me, we are here today to put our heads together, to collectively fetch some answers old kind King is hungry for. Hungry...hungry like a mad dog," and he claws at the air, then throws his head back in false laughter.

Across the room, several servants look at one another. Most, however, are used to King's antics, myself among them. We wait with bated breath for whatever comes next.

"Let me explain, let me explain," King calls, his voice suddenly strained and wheezing, as if he's aged fifty years in the past five seconds. A playact, one I'm now painfully familiar with, and I grow more nervous than before. The more agitated King is, I think, the more alarming his behavior is. The more dire are the consequences.

And then the act of aging is gone, and he pulls from his breast pocket a square of white—a square of white I instantly recognize.

It's the note I wrote to Morocco, of course.

He parades it back and forth, holding it high above his head. Finally, in the middle of the room, he stops. Three more loud stomps of the walking stick, silencing the crowd that had begun to murmur. "This is a letter," he begins, unfolding the paper and waving it through the air for all to see. "A letter addressed to none other than our dazzling Morocco Moody, a direct descendent of the Moody House of Weaponry."

Immediately I catch sight of a swiveling head in my peripheral vision, tossing ringlets, wide eyes. Rebecca stares straight at me, no doubt recognizing the chicken scratch writing and connecting it with the scrolls addressed to me.

My throat goes dry.

Then King clears his throat dramatically and begins to read. "*King's arms deal is illegal,*" he begins, pausing on each syllable, lingering on each note. "*When foreign nations learn of it, it will collapse the Moody House of Weaponry.*" Once again, he pauses, until every occupant of the room, even the senior members of the aristocracy, wait on the edge of their seats for him to finish. I wonder, vaguely, if they can hear the hammering of my heart the way I can. "*Contact your father immediately,*" King finishes.

Then, he releases his walking stick in a rush of anger, its echoing crack so loud that everyone stands straighter, everyone goes still as a statue. The laughter and lightness from earlier are long gone.

"Someone here thinks poorly of good old King," he says in a simpering voice as he tucks away the note and steeples his fingers. "Somebody thinks my motives lack purity and principle."

"Where was the note found, Papa?" James calls as he rises from his seat, striding toward Morocco, who continues to look put out. I can't tell who precisely she's unhappy with, but when she swats away James' hand, I realize the promise of an elephant tusk dress and new emeralds are, this time, insufficient. I wonder, too, if she did, in fact, tell her father about the letter, whether a hold has been placed on the arms deal, as I'd hoped.

"It was found in this very room," responds King, "which

is why I know the indecent person who authored it stands here amongst us today."

"What about a guest, Papa?" James thinks to counter as he takes his place next to King. But the look given to him by his father is enough to make him falter, and a moment later, he returns to his seat.

If James wants the throne, I think to myself, it will be an uphill battle.

King clears his throat. "I don't believe many people know about the arms deal this note references. In fact, the only people who *do* know of it reside here, in the very palace I call home, the very one in which I'm known as master of the house. And yet somebody has set about on a smear campaign. Somebody challenges my authority." His beady eyes land on me. "You, Girl from Quire, do you challenge my authority?"

All eyes in Carnegie swivel to me. But I don't withdraw into the shadows, instead, I remind myself that the palace is theater, and I step forward and lift my voice. "I don't challenge your authority in the slightest, King," I say with a curtsy. "In fact, I don't have a clue which arm problem you're referring to."

Just like that, he swishes his hand, casting me back in line. My relief is temporary, however, as I see Rebecca staring my way, her eyes sparkling under the midday light that funnels inside.

She steps forward and calls King's name, and I feel close to fainting.

"My dear," coos King.

"Most of us aren't privy to your secret keeping, like, so could you let those of us get goin'? Hard to manage a castle, see, when we're all holed up in here."

I exhale with relief. Rebecca, for now at least, isn't looking to throw me under the bus. It's bothersome, however, if not downright disturbing, that she could, and I think right now she's reminding me of that fact.

"Indeed it is, young ginger flower, indeed it is," booms King. "Yet I'm inclined to keep all of you here until I find my culprit—"

"Papa, I'm bored," complains Aubrey. "I'm *hungry*."

King does a double-take at the interruption, then flicks away her words. "Somebody knows something, I'm sure of it," he continues. "And with time, with the lack of necessities such as food, drink, sleep, the toilet—dare I go on? Without all that, somebody is bound to crack," and he rubs his hands together with glee.

Wolfe and I exchange a look, a weighted one, and I know that he knows of my guilt. If nothing else, the two of us can communicate practically by code at this point.

It's funny. We know each other not at all, and yet exceedingly well.

And here I am, in trouble yet again.

But in the silence the threat has cast, a new sound emerges, one distant and vague yet undeniable.

King hears it, too. I can tell by the turn of his shoulder, the cocking of his head. He turns toward Wolfe and the duke with an inquisitory lift of his chin but receives shaking heads in return. Nobody, it seems, knows what causes the racket.

"Gerard, go out front and see," he orders a moment later.

The old butler bows deeply, King's loyal servant through and through, and the rest of us stare at his backside as he crosses the floor, his perfectly polished loafers clicking softly with every measured step.

I think King will address us again, returning immediately to his intimidation and threats, but instead, he positions the walking stick between his legs and leans his weight on it, waiting. Listening.

Even from my spot all the way over here, I can see the

crease between his brow, the way his frown bends at the corners.

What's the source of the noise, and why does it bother him so?

Geese, perhaps, and someone nearby mutters the same thing.

And then Gerard must reach the front door because the sound amplifies, the volume quadruples in the span of a second, and it isn't geese, I realize. It's people.

People make all that sound.

All at once, King turns on his heel, he strides with angry intention as fast as his legs will go out the door.

It takes virtually no time for the rest of us to decide unanimously to follow after him.

Somewhere amongst the stampede winding toward Strath Glen's entrance, Wolfe finds me. He positions a hand firmly over my shoulder and murmurs in my ear, "How did you find out?"

"Now is not really the time," I call, as I'm shoved from behind, as every occupant of the palace pushes harder to see what precisely creates the sea of sound, what causes the ruler to freeze in the door frame as he currently does.

And then we shore up beside him, somebody thinks to throw open the other door, and all of Airo-Aurora spreads out before us.

Down below, flooding the street that runs in front of the palace and the Mainframe, is a pack of hollering protestors.

Protestors.

It's not something I've ever seen before—not in this nation-state. That's the kind of thing that happens in other countries, countries where free-choice rules, where people's lives aren't controlled by artificial intelligence that eliminates the calamity caused by human error.

And yet, here we are.

Many of the protestors carry signs, but they're too far

away to read. A few of them, however, feature a drawing of a white ribbon, and that...that I can see. That I can understand, and my stomach flips. The White Ribbon Campaign —this protest is for a free Airo-Aurora.

Something resembling hope...or pride...or maybe both, floods my insides. Just as quickly, I remember the arms deal, and King's determination to find the note writer, and I feel nauseated instead.

Beside me, Wolfe's hand continues to rest on my shoulder, and it feels so calming, so reassuring to have that slip of human contact right now that, against all odds, I don't want him to remove it. When I finally chance a look at him, I see that his lips are pressed firmly together, he looks stern and contemplative, and I long to speak freely with him, to ask him what he makes of this, to ask which thought currently occupies his formidable brain.

But I can't do that, at least not here, and I turn back to the protestors, admiring their strength, wishing silently I was amongst them.

Then King stirs, he turns to James, who stands at his elbow. "Put blackcoats on the scene," he says in a voice devoid of its usual dark humor. "Let's break it up. And some bluecoats, too, to get some footage of my naysayers. For reference purposes," he adds.

The balloon of hope in my belly pops completely. The footage won't be for reference purposes in the slightest. It will be used to round people up, so override chips ensuring compliance can be implanted in their brains.

I feel like crumpling to the floor. Because with the tools that King has at his disposal, it will be all too easy to crush the White Ribbon Campaign before it can really get started. How powerless the people of Airo-Aurora truly are.

And then James has vanished from view, King is shuffling backward, and the towering doors are closing.

"Bring me my cigars," King says to Gerard as he sweeps

past the rest of us. He begins climbing the staircase without a backward glance, and me and the others realize we're no longer being held hostage in Carnegie, that King is distracted, for now, at least, and I'm lost in a sea of relief, confusion, and dread.

———

"CARE FOR A RIDE through the woods, Alexandra?" Wolfe announces a moment later.

"Sir," says Gerard, and he bows deeply to Wolfe as he scurries around him, following King up the stairs.

"Save yourself and decline," Morocco advises me before she, too, sweeps toward the stairs.

"Darling," James calls after her, following in her footsteps. "If that letter continues to cause upset, might I recommend a day at the spa..."

"Who were those protestors, sister?" Evie asks me. "Do you know?"

"Why in heavens does Papa care so much about that silly note, my god!" shouts Aubrey, fanning herself. "I've never had such a dull morning..."

"They're members of the White Ribbon Camp—" I start to explain to Evie.

"Alexandra," Wolfe intones, his leaden tone cutting through the racket. "Shall we?"

eighteen

. . .

I GLANCE AT WOLFE, and the look in his eye leaves me with no doubt that the invitation is not optional. I bow my head and promise Evie we'll discuss it later. Next, I follow Wolfe through the rest of the servants still milling between the ming vases.

Normally, it would perturb me that Wolfe strides so far ahead without bothering to wait, but right now, I welcome it. A few minutes to collect my thoughts, and that's precisely what I need.

Protests. Ones that had perturbed King, and not in a little way. Protests for a free Airo-Aurora, courtesy of the White Ribbon Campaign. Protests that have little chance of succeeding now that King's blackcoats and bluecoats have been sent to the scene, and I shiver thinking about the future that awaits them.

But there's anger there, too. The injustice runs deep—the cruelty does, too.

Then there's the note I wrote and left for Morocco, one that's now in King's hands. One that makes my situation here at Strath Glen more tenuous. Because he now knows that he has enemies not simply outside of the palace walls but inside, too. His grip on power is being challenged, and as much joy as that brings me, as much satisfaction it sends coursing through my veins, I know it puts me and every other citizen in a more precarious position, and I can't begin to think what King may be capable of with his back against the wall.

Then there's Wolfe. How much does he know? How much does he suspect? And, assuming he knows it was me who wrote that letter, how much trouble am I in?

"Do hurry," he calls at that very moment. "I'm in the midst of several important work projects."

"Perhaps our ride should be delayed—" I start, but immediately he shakes his head.

Wordlessly he hands me a cloak at the back door and draws on another, then we're pushing into the midday sun with the scent of spring firmly in the air. Our boots squelch against the wet ground, yet the dampness is biting. Still, the promise of warm weather ahead hangs in the air, along with the sound of songbirds echoing from the birch trees.

It's difficult to hear them over the sound of the protestors.

"Has it ever happened before?" I ask as we walk toward the stables, and I gesture in the direction of the protest.

"Never," he replies heavily, and he gives me a stern look as he pulls open the stable door.

"What?"

He leans toward me and speaks quietly. "You tell me."

"Tell you what, precisely?"

He sighs as though I really do tire him. "Did you have a role in orchestrating this protest?"

I draw back with surprise. "Not in the slightest. I believe there's something called the White Ribbon Campaign behind it, not that I want you mentioning that to King."

"What makes you think I would?" he queries as his eyes narrow.

"I'm just saying—"

"It should go *without* saying," he replies tersely, then he ushers me inside. The horses bray softly at our arrival.

"Have you heard of the White Ribbon Campaign?"

"I have not," he replies as he leads a large horse from its stall, pausing next to me. "How is it," he begins quietly, "that you came to learn of the arm's deal between my uncle and the Moody House of Weaponry?"

I say tactfully, "You mean the one to arm the Mavericks?"

"Precisely."

"So," I say, turning to him, "you did know about it."

"Naturally, *I* did. I work closely with my uncle, as you well know. What I fail to understand is how a slight, bookish girl from Quire manages to keep pace with developments that have nothing to do with her. I, too, am curious how she can exhibit such arrogance that she deigns to intervene."

"Arrogance?" I echo, but already he's gone, leading the towering creature outside. "It isn't arrogance," I call after him. "It's called *caring*, and it's more than—"

"Keep your voice down," he reminds me with a stern look. "Do you really think you're the only one bothered by this development? Do—"

"Perhaps you share my feelings," I interrupt. "But change won't come from sitting idly by."

"It won't come from behaving in a rash manner, either. You and I both know what the consequences of that are."

I have to admit, he has a point. "Do you think King will reconvene the meeting in Carnegie?"

He snorts. "Coining it a meeting is rather generous, isn't it? A hostage scenario might be more fitting." He scans the tree line and sighs. "It's my hope that, given the protests, my uncle loses interest in the arms scandal. If he doesn't, you must not waiver in proclaiming your innocence."

He gestures to the massive beast stomping its hooves

next to me. I edge closer, and he positions his hands like a step, allowing me to lift myself and swing my leg over the horse. A moment later, he maneuvers himself into position behind me.

"I thought you insisted on entering these woods armed," I point out, clutching the horse's mane with both hands as it starts forward in the direction of the trees.

"I am armed," he replies curtly.

When I chance a look over my shoulder, I see the arc of a bow fitted to his back, a weapon he must've picked up in the stables.

"Is that thing able to kill a—"

"Indeed."

"Do you intend to hunt?"

"Not unless you care to hold the meat."

"I don't," I say hurriedly, and I think, in my peripheral, I see a hint of a smile.

All in all, this journey already feels dramatically different than the last time we entered the woods together. Not only was it dark, then, but fiercely cold. We were also on a mission—searching for Mavericks—and so we moved at full speed through the trees. Right now, however, Wolfe keeps the horse moving slowly, a lackadaisical pace that allows me to appreciate the beauty of the crisscrossing branches overhead and the pockets of moss on the forest floor, now visible thanks to the retreating snow.

In time, the shouting and chanting of Airo-Aurora's protestors fade away, and the sound of songbirds fills its place. "This is quite relaxing," I say after a while.

"Certainly, compared to Strath Glen," Wolfe agrees.

"Is that why you come here, then?" I ask.

"In part, yes. Solitude is difficult to come by, otherwise."

I say nothing, but I wonder to myself: why, if he's after solitude, did he bring me along?

As we move deeper into the woods, the cawing and the

chirping is replaced by silence, and the treetops overhead block out the sunlight, so it's dark and far cooler. I shiver.

Wolfe draws me closer and clears his throat. "Were you mindful of your feed when you wrote that note?" he murmurs into my ear.

"Yes," and as I say the word, I turn my head, unaware that his own still lingers there, and our faces bump together. Immediately I straighten myself with my heart hammering, I feel blood blush color my cheeks.

"I have been in touch with Mr. Moody, Morocco's father," he continues after a while, and my embarrassment is forgotten about as my ears strain to hear him. "As my uncle didn't specify the type of assault rifle he wants to arm the Mavericks with, I took the liberty of choosing the model with parts in short supply. That should delay the order and buy us some time."

For a moment, I'm speechless, and not simply because of his cleverness. It's because of his choice of words. *Us.* He had really said that—it wasn't the woods playing tricks on me. *It should buy* us *some time.*

Right now, Wolfe and I feel like allies, working together, and if that's the case, there must be implied trust between the two of us. Things aren't as estranged as I had feared, and I allow myself to relax into the curve of his large body. "That's wonderful news."

"Indeed," he says as he clears his throat. "So, tell me more about the White Ribbon Campaign." He leads the horse across a narrow stream as he waits for my response.

"I don't know much about it or who's behind it—"

"Tell me, then, what you do know."

"I know that it's a movement in support of a free Airo-Aurora."

"Free as in—"

"Free as in free choice and self-determination."

"And how did you come to learn of this campaign?"

"I saw a flyer that time I left the palace—"

"Which time, precisely, was that?"

"When you and King caught me. When James kissed me—"

"Continue," he orders.

"Well, that's the first time I heard of the movement, at least by name."

"At least by name?" he echoes.

I nod. "I'd noticed people wearing the white ribbons on a previous excursion."

"*Wearing* them? Do these people not realize they are marking themselves as easy targets for both the blackcoats and the bluecoats?"

"I suppose not. Before coming to Strath Glen and learning all I did, I'm not sure I'd appreciate the danger, either...particularly from the bluecoats. Nobody would."

"That must be rectified. You must discreetly let those in charge of the movement know of the danger they are placing themselves in—and their supporters."

"But I don't know who's in charge of the movement—"

"Find out. You clearly are skilled at digging into matters that have nothing to do with you."

"Do you think the movement originated from inside Strath Glen?"

He looks at me sharply out of the corner of his eye—I can see it in my peripheral. "Hardly. What would make you ask such a foolish question?"

"I'm simply trying to ascertain how to investigate," I respond pointedly. "Given that I'm not permitted to leave palace grounds."

He sighs. "And yet that hasn't prevented you from making headway in the past."

I agree, frustrated with my lack of mobility, yet unabashedly pleased that he is entrusting something so important to me. And, frankly, finding out who is behind the

White Ribbon Campaign sounds like something I should've had on my to-do list, anyway. After all, it may well be another ally for Neo and me.

And then, I almost do it. I almost tell Wolfe about the plan I'm hatching with Neo and my upcoming meeting with him tomorrow night—but I stop myself at the last second. After all, even though Wolfe and I may very well be on the same team, we prefer to go about business in different fashions. Besides, for one reason or the other, he is exceptionally risk-averse when it comes to me...

"How is it you came to know of the arms deal?" he prods.

"I was in the right place at the right time," I reply, then he's pulling at the reigns, and the next time I look over my shoulder, I see that the bow is held in front of him, an arrow is swiftly pulled from the quiver.

When I follow that stern, hard gaze of his, I notice movement in a bush fifty yards away. Then, before the full wave of fear can hit me, the bush tremors, and a deer steps into the clearing.

"It's a gentle creature, Wolfe," I say when I notice that the bow and arrow remain in the same position—cocked and ready to kill. "One of my favorites," I add, and only then does he lower the weapon.

I hear him swallow. Then he says in a distant voice, "Best to get back to work," and he steers the horse around, leaving the deer to silently watch over us.

nineteen

. . .

THE NEXT DAY, I'm once again summoned away from the library and its unending stack of books. Just as well, too, since with every day, every development, it becomes harder and harder to concentrate.

Right now, Gerard stands over me, the summons still stuck between my fingers. A dress fitting for Agnes's wedding, a wedding now only two days away. I know from chatting to Evie though, that the fitting won't be a simple affair. No, my 'team' is supposed to be there, the group of individuals tasked with making me picture-perfect for my upcoming wedding to Wolfe Rocksavage, and my chest constricts at the thought.

One thing at a time, I remind myself.

I shift my cataloging cards to the side and push back from the desk. "Have you heard anything following yesterday's protest?" I think to ask as I follow the butler out the library doors.

He glances at me. "Such as?"

"Such as who was responsible for it? Or what it was for?"

Once again, he peers at me, and I do my best to act

nonchalant. "Radicals were behind it, naturally," the old man says, sounding unperturbed.

"And do you know what the radicals were protesting?"

"No," he says plainly, but I know he's lying.

"What was King's reaction?"

"I believe you were in attendance, Miss Alex."

"He didn't seem pleased," I admit. "Though I don't see why it would bother him."

"Is that a question?" His eyes narrow.

"No," I say quickly. Silently I follow him up the stairs, passing out of the rotunda and along the east wing. We careen by the guest chambers that used to be my own, through a world of black and white, until he stops before a plain door, one I had assumed opened to a linen closet.

He bows, then throws it open, and I'm pushed forcefully inside.

But it's not the old man that pushes me, it's a stick, and over my shoulder, I spot the Cheshire grin of King before the door snaps shut behind me.

I turn, rattled, and see that a linen closet it's definitely not. Clearly designed for this specific purpose, the large room boasts a three-sided mirror that surrounds a pedestal positioned in the middle, with plush velvet furniture taking up the rest of the space. A team of servants move through the crowd, passing out breakfast burritos and mimosas. And, in addition to my so-called team, the female royals are all in attendance. Morocco, Aubrey, the duchess, even the Queen, who sits placidly on a loveseat, sipping orange juice and mindlessly flipping through a bridal magazine.

"Aren't you excited, sister?" Evie gushes, rushing forward and taking my hands.

"Uh, yes. Yes, I'm...that." I clear my throat. "Is this all for the dress fitting?"

"But of course...my! Whyever would you ask such a question?"

"It's just...well, there're so many people here, Evie," I say quietly, so the others can't hear.

"Oh, nobody at Strath Glen would *dream* of missing a fitting," she declares. "A riotous good time for all, don't you find? Just wait until it's your own wedding we're fitting you for," she adds, her eyes gleaming. "It will make today's affair appear downright dull, sister!"

And then I'm propelled forward, past dissecting eyes, and onto the pedestal as a flock of women with blunt haircuts begin circling me. They pinch at my current oversized ensemble, they make comments on the width of my hips. Finally, the tallest of the bunch steps forward. "Please. Step behind the mirror, mademoiselle, and pull on gown numero uno."

"Gown numero uno," I echo.

She nods curtly, then, when I don't move, taps her watch.

So, I do as she says, ignoring the way Morocco sneers in my direction. I pull the dressing curtain shut and flip through a rack of gowns until I locate a sequined one marked with the number one.

As I pull off my clothes though, my mind wanders back to yesterday, to the ride with Wolfe through the woods. I think of his use of 'us,' how it feels like we are finally on the same team, even as we keep certain things to ourselves, like my upcoming meeting with Neo, for instance. I think, too, of the protest, and how urgent it is that I find out who's behind it, that I warn them of the need to remain anonymous. I barely notice the sound of approaching footsteps, or the curtain fluttering open. Finally, though, I whirl around, covering myself as best I can as Aubrey steps inside.

"Don't play the innocent birdie with me," she snaps, wrestling my arms to my sides and looking me up and down.

I pull myself free of her grasp and cover myself again. "Excuse me?"

"You know precisely what it is I speak of. Pre-cisely."

"I'm afraid I don't—"

"I know you saw me in the cloak closet at the back door, you dirty-birdie-peeping-Tom. You've seen me naked, and now I've seen you—cha!"

"Fine," I say through my teeth. "We're even," and I gesture for her to go.

She doesn't move. "I must be assured of your..." and she coughs delicately into a tiny fist, "...discretion."

Ah. So that is what she's after, and I sigh. "If you're concerned, why didn't you corner me right away?"

She gasps. "Do you have any idea how busy I am? Do you have any clue about the toll a pregnancy takes on a woman? It's truly exhausting, and it's not like my social calendar can simply be cast aside. Besides, it's only Papa who would care about my Butch in the first place."

"Well, I haven't repeated to anyone what I saw, and I can assure you I have no intention of even thinking about it ever again."

She flutters her eyelashes at me and coos, "You really are the accommodating doll Evie pledges you are."

I'm not fooled, but I carry on with the act, bowing my head agreeably. From the other side of the room, people begin to shout for me, but I ignore them, instead setting my gaze on the princess. "You two love each other, don't you." I state it like a fact, and frankly, I'm confident that it is. After all, I had seen the emotion on her face that evening at the parade. I had seen it on both of them.

For a second, she looks shocked by the declaration, then her features shift, and she vanishes, leaving me to pull on the sequined dress and return to the pedestal.

"What took you so long?" shouts an old woman lounging on a daybed.

"She's from Quire," Morocco responds, mouthing the word Quire as though it's covered in filth.

"It's very festive, sister," says Evie as she gazes at my reflection.

"It looks more fit for a funeral," the duchess remarks, and the hardness in her eyes tells me that she hasn't forgiven me for the arrangement that left Wolfe sleeping on the couch. After that, I'm shuttled behind the mirror again with orders to try on the second dress.

"What do you know about love?" Aubrey hisses, drawing back the curtain once again.

"Nothing," I assure her. I don't bother to cover myself this time, I just continue to get changed, determined to wrap up the fitting as quickly as possible. Really, I need to figure out who's behind the White Ribbon Campaign, and I can't do that with distractions like this.

"Well, me oh my! I never thought Miss Perfect would admit something like that—"

"Coming through, coming through!" A woman with bluntly-cut hair shoves past Aubrey, grabs me by the wrist, and pulls me from the change area.

I clamor the rest of the way into the gown, this one made with silk and elasticized at the waist, just as I'm shoved around the mirror.

"Doesn't accentuate her figure," shouts another blunt-haired woman, and I'm turned around on the spot, not even making it to the pedestal.

"Time for Dress Numero Tres!"

"Who picked these hideous things?" shouts Morocco as I emerge a third time.

I spot the hurt across Evie's face and say loudly, "I love them all so far. Any one will do just fine."

"And there's still several more to try on, sister," Evie reminds me, more upbeat than a moment ago.

Once again, in the midst of getting changed, the curtain swings open, and Aubrey steps inside. "Maybe it is love, so?"

I shrug. "So, nothing."

"So, something," she snaps. "Or you wouldn't have brought it up in the first place."

I resolve to give Aubrey my full attention in the hope that she'll stop with these constant interruptions. I cross my arms and consider her. "So, what are you going to do about it?"

"What in god's name is that supposed to mean?"

"It means," I begin, lowering my voice and speaking gently, "are you going to leave Dear Matthew?"

"Divorce isn't allowed, you stupid toad."

"I thought perhaps your father would make an exception—"

"Not in a million years."

I nod. Then, out of the blue, Aubrey leans toward me, grabbing my wrist so we're pulled together—close enough that I can see every speck of glitter in her shimmering eyeshadow. "I've hired him to build a playhouse for the angel," and she pats her belly. "That way, he'll at least be close."

I stare at her as the crowd once again grows agitated. "The baby is his, I assume?" I ask over their shouting.

"But, of course."

"I assume, also, that Dear Matthew knows, so why did he move back to the palace?"

"Papa put his foot down," she says glumly.

"Ah."

"Love ruins everything," she adds with a sigh. "If you think you'll find true love in whatever derelict district you're from, don't bother."

I'm about to ask her why she thinks I'd find love there, instead of with my fiancé, but already she's vanished, and the chant of the group on the other side of the mirror grows louder.

A minute later, I'm spun on the pedestal, I'm poked and prodded and finally handed a fur bolero to pull over the gown to account for the weather. More spinning, prodding, but even I can tell that I'm wearing the winner. The crowd claps politely. The duchess congratulates Evie. The blunt-haired ladies speak feverishly to each other, then come at me with pincushions. Twice the pins catch my skin, but I barely notice. I'm too busy thinking about my conversation with Aubrey.

It's hard not to relate it back to Patrick, even if I'm not sure how fitting the comparison really is. Perhaps it's a good reminder, though, to not go down that path, not now and not ever, just like she advised, and I wonder how painful it would be to love someone so much you'd rather live a lie than lose their touch...

It's hard, too, not to feel badly for Aubrey, at least a smidge. It humanizes her, this development—as much as she can be humanized. But it also vilifies her, and I wonder what the public would think should they find out the very family we put our trust in, the very family that mandates the Mainframe and the chip system and enforces our compliance, doesn't abide by it themselves.

And what should happen to Aubrey if King finds out about Butch? After all, he's as worried about the family image as anyone. And if he's not afraid to implant the override chip in his own wife, who's to say he wouldn't do it with his daughter?

twenty

. . .

ONCE THE DRESS fitting is declared over and the room clears out, I thank Evie for organizing the whole thing.

"My absolute pleasure. And do you love the dress to bits, sister?"

"Er, yes," I assure her.

"Oh, me too, me too! I especially love the delicate beadwork, don't you?"

"Absolutely," I agree, even though I don't recall noticing any beads in the first place.

Thankful to have the fitting behind me, I prepare to return to the library. Not only do I have cataloging work and investigative work on the mysterious White Ribbon Campaign, I have this evening to ready for, as well. Another meeting with Neo, and I feel a rush of excitement.

Perhaps *he* knows who's behind the White Ribbon Campaign...

"But sister," Evie cries as I head for the door, "don't you remember?"

"Remember what?"

"Why, your dear friend's wedding gift, of course. I told

you earlier this week we'd be fetching it today. Did you really forget?"

"No, of course not," I lie upon seeing how crestfallen she looks. "Thank you once again for helping me find something," and as I speak, I rack my brain, trying to recall what it is Evie had planned. Fine China...that had been it. Or emeralds...

"It's my absolute pleasure, sister! Now, Roberta won't be happy that I'm missing my studies today for two reasons, but alas, duty calls! Are you thrilled? Let's go round up Monsieur, shall we?"

So I follow Evie downstairs, clueless as to where we could be going and, frankly, confused why we must retrieve it ourselves when things are delivered to Strath Glen on the regular. Then again, she saved me the trouble of finding the newlyweds a gift, so I'm not about to complain. I smile graciously at her as we enter Devonshire.

Her idea of rounding up Monsieur, I soon see, is tasking the butler with finding him, and in the meantime, she motions for me to have a seat next to her.

"Iced tea, please!" she calls, and a servant that I hadn't noticed standing along the far wall promptly disappears. "Is there a drink you'd like, sister? Are you excited for your friend's gift?"

"I'm fine, thank you, and yes, of course I'm excited," I say, with as much enthusiasm as I can muster. Inwardly, though, I kick myself. Evie is my closest friend around here, and without her support, I really don't know what I'd do. So, how come I didn't pay attention to what she had said about the gift in the first place? How come I didn't notice the servant tucked along the wall?

Is it possible that in learning to play the game of Strath Glen, my crimson Quire blood has turned a shade of blue? The thought is frightening. After all, I've always maintained that palace life has not and will not change me, and I set the intention right then and there to be a better friend, and to stay true to my roots as well.

"Evie, why is it you're not taking your studies?" a familiar voice demands.

Wolfe, I can tell, not just by the frigidness of his voice or his halting way of speaking, but by the clicking of his shoes as he rounds into the sitting room.

He pauses, staring at me. "What's this?"

"Official palace business," Evie replies promptly. "Roberta will simply have to wait."

"Does Mother know of this?"

"I was just with Mother during your fiancée's dress fitting, so I'd say as much. She really was impressed with the selection of gowns I chose for sister to wear this weekend, did you hear?"

Wolfe once again glances at me. His eyes have the uncanny ability to flicker with every movement, and it's hard, if not impossible, to ignore them. He falters for a second as we consider each other, but then he smooths his jacket and stands taller. "Now that the dress fitting is finished with—"

"We're waiting for Monsieur Sawyer, brother! Don't be such a boorish lout…heavens!"

"I'm not…that." He goes back to straightening his impossibly straight jacket. "Where are you having Monsieur take you?"

"Why, your darling fiancée and I are picking up the wedding gift I've arranged for Agnes and Miller. Isn't that divine? Don't you remember me mentioning it a moon past?"

I can see by the look on his face that he, too, missed that bit of information.

"Iced tea for the lady," announces the servant, bowing deeply in front of Evie.

"Splendid!"

"Duty calls, hmm?" shouts Monsieur as he turns the corner with Gerard following after him. Both men dive nose-first into a bow upon spotting the viscount. "Will you be joining the young ladies on today's outing, sir?" asks Monsieur in a show of politeness.

"It wasn't my intention," he replies, still staring between Evie and me as if we're in the midst of hatching a devious plan. "Where is your destination?"

"McGonery Farms," Evie replies. "Do you know the place, Monsieur?"

"Uh, yes. Although, I can't imagine any sort of palace business taking us there—"

"Well, indeed it does," Evie insists, draining her glass of iced tea and dusting off her hands. "We're ready now," she adds.

Monsieur bows agreeably.

"Ensure you take up your studies once you return, Evie," mutters Wolfe, striding swiftly out the door. He pauses in the hallway though, and turns on his heel. "Enjoy your trip to the farm."

He vanishes, and Evie, Gerard, and Monsieur all exchange looks. I feel myself blush. Because Wolfe, just then, he'd only been addressing me.

"To the garage," Monsieur announces.

"Oh, I'm excited, sister, aren't you?"

I nod, yet just what kind of wedding gift is available from a farm, anyhow? But I don't dare question Evie, not after all she's done, and instead, I follow silently behind her and Monsieur down the stairs and into the underground parking garage.

Evie grabs my hand. "Brother is absolutely besotted by you!"

I snort. "Because he wished me well on today's excursion? Hardly."

"On the contrary, such niceties are *completely* foreign to

him. I myself have never heard him utter something so pedestrian and kindly in all my life. Why, you really must have captured his heart."

I say nothing, not wishing to argue. Still, the suggestion that I've *captured his heart* simply because he told me to have a good time is so outlandish and overdone it's almost comical, and vaguely I wonder just how rude Wolfe typically is for those simple words to have such an impact.

"After you, my ladies," says Monsieur as he holds open the door to the behemoth. We climb inside, and a moment later, we're off, the garage door opening seamlessly and unleashing us into the early days of spring.

All the farms in the nation-state sit to the west of the city, but before the snout of the limousine can even turn in that direction, Evie claps her hands together. "Now, Monsieur, now! I can't wait another second!"

I watch with interest as Monsieur slides a disc—a relic from the past—into the vehicle's console. A second later, a woman's voice fills the behemoth, the beat fast, the tune catchy.

"What is this?" I shout over both the music and the singing of Evie and Monsieur.

"Music, sister! The greatest music in all the world!"

"It's certainly unlike anything I've heard before."

"Oh, sister, it's pop music from the United States! Isn't it lively?"

"It is that," I admit. "How did you ever find it?"

She laughs gaily. "Why, someone doesn't simply *find* music like this, not remotely! Uncle doesn't allow such things into our beautiful nation-state, can you believe it? And me? Why, I fell in love ages ago when I was traveling with Mother and Father—I was just wee, do you remember, Monsieur Sawyer?"

"With the largest brown eyes I've ever seen," agrees the chauffeur.

"But then, how did you get this disc?" I press as Monsieur winks jovially at her.

"A secret present from Auntie a few years back...shhh. Isn't that grand?"

"A secret present from the Queen? Under King's nose?"

"Oh, sister, she is tremendously cool, didn't you know? And she's so—I don't know—feisty! Well, perhaps not so much these days—I think she must have an awful lot on her mind," she adds solemnly.

Quite the opposite problem, I think to myself. But Monsieur watches us closely in the rear-view mirror, so I say tactfully, "Perhaps so."

"Turn it up, Monsieur!" Evie cries, and for the rest of the drive, it's impossible to converse over the blaring music.

Once we arrive at the farm, however, Monsieur switches off the music, and Evie squeals with delight. "Are you excited, sister? I must say, this is all *quite* unfamiliar to me."

"You mean the farm?" I ask, feigning surprise.

"And the wedding gift, even more so."

I stare at her, more perplexed by the second.

"I'll go track down Farmer," she continues.

"Is that his name?" I shout as she swings open the door.

"I haven't the foggiest," she calls over her shoulder. A moment later, Monsieur and I watch her maneuver through haystacks and around puddles, still wearing the bedazzled gown she wore during this morning's fitting.

"What in holy hell is this wedding gift, anyhow?" Monsieur asks.

"I don't have a clue," I admit, snorting with laughter when one of Evie's shoes gets stuck in a pile of manure.

He glances at me with a wry look. "Are you quite enjoying yourself, Miss Alex?"

"Any outing from the palace I enjoy, Monsieur. Surely, by now, you know that."

"I don't care for farm life personally, but I suppose this is better than the wild goose chase you planted me on not so long ago."

"Wild goose chase?"

"After the blasted Monsieur Worthers, of course."

"How could I forget... Since we're on the subject, have you seen him lately?"

I expect a snarky reply, but instead, Monsieur shakes his head in earnest. "I still have damn goosebumps from last time," he replies. "Doesn't mean I don't still think about it, though."

I lean forward with interest. "You were that bothered by your encounter with him?"

He makes a show of rolling his eyes. "I've worked with that man for decades, and there's no convincing me that the fellow we spoke with was one and the same. Either that man is seriously ill in the head, or something fishy is afoot."

A chill runs the length of my spine, along with a whisper of excitement, but before I can even consider whether to share the truth with Monsieur, there's a flurry of activity outside the window, feathers fly through the air, and Evie is banging on the windshield. Monsieur jumps into action and throws open the door.

"In, in, in!" Evie's shouting, and it takes a minute to realize that she's corralling half a dozen chickens into the seat beside me.

"What..." I begin, "Evie, what...what is this? What's going on?"

She doesn't respond. I don't think she even heard me over the commotion. Finally, though, she's buckled next to me, a giant feedbag is placed at our feet by the man Evie calls Farmer, and the door is slammed shut.

Monsieur Sawyer lays on the gas a second after that, kicking up a plume of dust along the dirt drive, speeding toward the palace as if the car is on fire. I don't really blame him, and judging by the roundness of Evie's eyes as she surveys what I suppose is the wedding gift, neither can she.

The chickens, for their part, seem completely unbothered by their change in scenery. They peck at our feet, they cluck loudly, and every time they ruffle their feathers, a waft of them float around the behemoth, which grows louder and dirtier by the minute.

"Evie?" I finally call over the mayhem.

"Sister?"

"The chickens?"

"They're not what you expected?"

"No," I admit. "As grateful as I am that you decided to undertake all this, I don't remember discussing chickens at all. I'm sorry."

She scratches her chin. "Perhaps I never did mention it, now that I think about it. Anyhoo, aren't they a perfect gift for your friend?" she queries, but even I can see the uncertainty across her face.

"Yes, well...why, exactly?"

"Don't Agnes and her fiancé hail from Quire quite like you?"

"They do. And?"

"And I thought that, well, that coming from such a poor district, egg-bearing chickens would be most useful. Am I terribly wrong, sister?"

I stare at her, dumbstruck, then cough into my fist, or attempt to, but immediately it devolves into a fit of unabashed laughter. For a second, Evie looks horrified, then faintly bemused, and then she too, is laughing.

"Truly, I never thought they'd take up so much space or be quite so...messy!" she shouts.

"It's a lovely idea," I assure her, patting her knee, "although I don't think Quire is quite as impoverished as your cousins have made it out to be—certainly, there's no shortage of food. That being said, I have a feeling that Agnes will really get a kick out of this gift!"

"Then my job is done!" she shouts gaily. Her smile falters, however, when a chicken lands on her lap, and we spend the rest of the drive trying to keep the chickens on the floor. That, and plucking feathers from our cloaks.

As soon as the behemoth comes to a stop in the underground parking garage, Evie shouts something about her studies, leaving Monsieur and me alone with the chickens.

"At least I now know how to keep Evie focused on her schooling," I mutter.

"Raid the farm? Indeed," sighs Monsieur. "In the meantime, what in holy hell do we do with this mess? The wedding's not for two blasted days, and I'm not having a flock of filthy chickens making themselves at home in my limousine."

"What if we keep them in the stables?"

He lifts an eyebrow. "Now there's a solution, Miss Alex. I see you're as sharp as ever."

"If I were that sharp, I wouldn't be stuck carting around barn animals," I grumble as I hike up my gown and tie the fabric in a knot. "Tripping hazard," I add when I see the way Monsieur stares.

"A true lady," and he bows his head. "I'll return in a jiffy with a wheelbarrow."

But the wheelbarrow proves too small to transport six hens and a feed bag, so I wind up carrying two of the chickens under my arm. Monsieur, however, has it even worse than I do, as the chickens keep jumping from the wheelbarrow, particularly as he pushes it up the steep incline leading to the rear of the property.

By the time we reach the stables, both of us are covered in sweat, which has the unintended effect of making the feathers stick to us like glue. The laughter from earlier is gone, and I begin to bemoan Evie's unconventional gift idea.

A stack of China plates, after all, would've been far less bother.

"Grab that one," Monsieur is shouting as I kick open the stable door. Together we manage to steer the runaway chicken inside, sealing the doors shut behind us. Monsieur fills an empty bowl with feed, spilling half of the bag's contents along the stable floor. He snaps, "Is that everything, then?"

"I suppose they can drink the horses' water?"

"Damn straight they can," and he turns on his heel. "You've quite exhausted me for one day, Miss Alex."

"I believe that in today's case, it was Evie who did the exhausting," I call after him as he swings open the door.

"What in god's name are you two doing?" comes a cold voice, and when I lift my head, I see Wolfe's towering figure taking up the bulk of the doorway. Monsieur dives into a bow at once, then, unable to stand the stables for another second no matter the need for decorum, vanishes around the corner.

"Evie secured some chickens for Agnes and Miller," I explain, "as a wedding gift. We've just brought them up from the limousine."

"Who in god's name gifts someone chickens?" he demands, sounding incredulous.

I stifle a laugh. "Given all the chatter about Quire around here, she was led to believe that the district is so impoverished that food is in short supply. It was actually quite a thoughtful gift."

His dissecting gaze zigzags down my body, and I glance down, too. My dress is still tied at my knees, and I'm covered in feathers, and what I hope, frankly, is mud.

"Thoughtful, yet messy," I add.

"Can they be secured in a stall so they don't escape when the door is opened?" he asks, and I notice for the first time that Wolfe holds the lead of a horse which stands behind him.

"You'll have to bunk up two of the horses for the next couple of nights if I do that."

His gaze narrows ever so slightly, but he nods, and several minutes later, Agnes' chickens are locked away with feed and water.

"Thank you," says Wolfe as he leads the horse forward.

I watch him out of the corner of my eye. I'm not sure he's ever thanked me for anything before. "You're welcome."

Forced politeness, nothing revolutionary. But for us? It feels seismic.

Once the horse is put away and the saddle removed, Wolfe strides over to me and laces his hands behind his back. "Are you looking forward to your friend's wedding, since we're on the subject?" At that moment, a plume of feathers is sent into the air from the chickens' stall, and he sighs. "You'll have to forgive my sister for such an outlandish idea."

I smile. "I am looking forward to the wedding, yes. As far as the chickens go, I think Agnes will find it quite humorous. And I know I'd enjoy this type of project. Besides, who doesn't like fresh eggs? Perhaps even Strath Glen should consider building its own personal coop."

The corner of Wolfe's mouth twitches—an attempt, perhaps, at a smile—and I realize he really is trying. He turns toward the doors. "Evie's right, you really are accommodating," he says before leaving me amongst the barn animals.

twenty-one

. . .

SCRUBBED OF CHICKEN FEATHERS, I pass the rest of the afternoon in the library. Finally, though, with my meeting with Neo only an hour away, I tidy up my things, leaving Counterdown in a wave of satisfaction with my work on the catalog system. Yet I'm alarmed, too. Because rebels aren't content—they can't be—and once again, I find myself musing over whether I can work to overthrow King and his regime while also enjoying my newfound job and, to some extent, my new home here at Strath Glen.

Things have certainly changed for the better since I first moved in, but what this means for—

"Papa, you scared me!" shouts a voice from Devonshire —Aubrey, by the sounds of it—and I go still.

"Perhaps a good scaring is what you need if your recent behavior is any indication," replies King, and I can tell from his tone that, for once, he isn't playacting.

"Recent behavior?" she echoes as I tiptoe closer.

"I heard all about what happened at the Winter's End parade. It isn't a good look, having you step out on your husband, especially when you are, ahem, with child."

"Nonsense. Besides, I can do whatever I like, Papa," she trills. "I am a princess!"

"If that's what you believe, perhaps it should be your lover—a commoner, of all things—that I set my sights on. Shall I have him thrown to the gallows, hmm?"

"Oh, please. We all know how much James sleeps around. You wouldn't dare—"

"Indeed I would," interrupts King, his walking stick thudding against the floor menacingly. "And you? It simply won't do to have you stepping out with *that boy*—especially when you're married to Dear Matthew and pregnant to boot. It's time, my dear, for you to learn there are consequences to your actions," and he stomps the walking stick again.

While my mouth goes dry and I feel suddenly unwell, Aubrey has the opposite reaction. She bursts into laughter and calls, "Surely you jest, Papa!"

"Indeed I—" he begins, but his voice is cut off abruptly by the sound of skin hitting skin. When I edge closer to Devonshire and peer around the doorframe, I see the King of Airo-Aurora cradling his face—one side considerably redder than the other.

"Threaten me and my Butch again, and see," she hisses. "And care not to forget that I am your daughter. Mother's, too," and with that, she turns on her icepick stilettos and bustles out of Devonshire in a cloud of taffeta, mercifully not noticing that I'm glued to the wall outside the door.

I have to hand it to her, I think, as I watch her disappear around the corner. The woman has claws. Sharp ones.

Before I can go, King's voice rings through the silence, and I think he must be speaking on the phone. "Put me through to Lebwitski," he commands. "I need a favor."

"Always a killer," shouts the parrot.

———

THE DAY WASN'T SUPPOSED to go like this: not the dress fitting, not the chickens, and certainly not this. Yet here I am, climbing the stairs, my pulse unsteady, my hairline touched with sweat, risking being late for my meeting with Neo. But focusing on what's on the line, I force my socked feet to point in the wrong direction along the House of Mirrors.

It's only been the one time I've ventured down here, in search of the Queen, but between the beehive in the ceiling and Morocco vomiting Jell-o shooters across my path, I hadn't exactly made it very far.

Today, however, all is quiet and still, except for the drilling in the wall along Bishop's Aisle upstairs. The princess's quarters are marked as such, and when I rap my knuckles on the door, I hear laughter alongside a man's voice inside.

Dear Matthew I realize as I pull at my lip.

Perhaps I'll ask to speak with Aubrey in private, or maybe—

The door flies open, and a man in his underwear the size of a boulder fills the doorframe. Definitely not Dear Matthew. "You look familiar," he says as he squints at me.

"You do, too," I say, coughing lightly. "Is Aubrey home?"

"Who's asking?"

"My name is Alex."

"Hold on." He shuts the door, and a minute later, it opens again, this time with Aubrey standing there, her hair that's usually piled on top of her head flowing to her waist. Instead of the elaborate taffeta gown I spotted her wearing a few minutes ago, she now wears a housecoat.

"What do you want, you darling little mouse, you?" and she pokes me on the nose.

"I wanted... Are you not going to dinner?"

"Why do you want to know?"

"I don't," I assure her. "I've simply never seen you look so—"

"Do *not* say ordinary."

"Casual," I say instead.

"I was up all matters of the night, *mon petite* ditch-piggy. The whisky sours simply wouldn't quit," she adds with a yawn. "Besides, I have other plans this evening," and her yawn turns into a wink.

"Is Dear Matthew away?"

"He is, but what business is it of yours? Is this a Quire inquisition?"

I wave away the question. Then I step toward the princess, ignoring the look of alarm passing over her face, and say in a low voice, "I'd like to have a word with you and, er, Butch, but it's imperative we're discrete."

For a second I think she's going to burst into laughter, but perhaps she catches sight of how drawn my face is because her own straightens. She steps to the side. "Come in, and let's get this over with. Do you not own shoes?" she adds, as she looks at my sock feet with disgust.

"None that fit."

"I think I preferred you in the riding ensemble."

"You and me both," I mutter.

"Your confidence has grown," she remarks as she leads me through a door and into a vast living room, her quarters even larger than Wolfe's. "Put a robe on, my love," she advises Butch, "before this junkyard Susan begins to salivate."

"Oh, I really—"

"Let me remind you, doll, that I could eat you up and spit you back out in less time than it takes you to drag a comb through that rat's nest you call hair."

"I believe you," I assure her, thinking of King clutching his bruised cheek.

"Then what in heaven's name brings you to my quarters?"

Instead of answering, I walk toward the record player that sits along the far wall, between the windows. "May I?" Without waiting for an answer, I move the needle into position, and a moment later, the room is full of the same music Evie had listened to in the behemoth.

I chuckle to myself. Acts of rebellion run rampant here at Strath Glen.

When I turn to the others, I see they don't smile as I do. In fact, Aubrey stares at me like I've lost my mind. And maybe I have. Maybe what I'm about to do is far too reckless, far too risky. Yet as I spot the subtle outline of a burgeoning baby bump along Aubrey's midsection, I know deep down that I'm doing the right thing, so I'm prepared to take the risk.

"It's important to speak with a backdrop of music," I begin, "so the Mainframe has no record of our conversation." I turn to Aubrey and get straight to the point. "I believe you're in grave danger—"

"I can't. I just can't," she interrupts. She shuts off the music. "To have someone here of her lowly rank, heralding from Quire and speaking to me like an equal..." She fans her face. "It's causing my vertigo to act up."

"But you don't mind *me* being here," declares Butch, looking concerned. "I have no rank, and if she says you're in dang—"

"Oh, it's different with you, darling—everything is! Please, Butch, darling, see this turd out."

"You," he says, pointing at me. "You heard the woman."

"But I'm only trying to h—"

"Now," he reiterates, looking more menacing than before. "You're not upsetting my baby. Or my other baby," he adds, winking at Aubrey, who now languishes across a daybed.

Defeated, I trail after him toward the door, out into the House of Mirrors. At the very least, the abrupt end to my conversation with Aubrey means I won't be late for my meeting with Neo.

But Butch follows me out the door and grabs me by the arm. "What kind of danger is she in?" he asks in an undertone.

I look at him and see clearly his devotion to Aubrey. I see, too, someone whose childhood wasn't clouded by tiaras and silver spoons, someone who will listen to reason. "I overheard her father just now," I explain, "give instructions to a man named Doctor Lebwitski. He specializes in implanting override chips into the brain to correct improper or rebellious behavior. I believe Doctor Lebwitski will be arriving at the palace imminently, likely with some blue-coats in tow, with the intention of performing the procedure on Aubrey."

He blinks, frowns, and blinks some more. "Why Aubrey?"

"Among other reasons, her affair with you."

"And how does it...how does it correct behavior?" he continues, his brow contorting as he struggles to follow along.

"It turns off her brain completely," I explain. "The Main-frame and the data it collected from Aubrey over the years will fill the void."

"Like some sort of robot?"

"Precisely."

"You're not shitting me?"

"Uh, no, I'm not...shitting you. And if you don't mind," I add, "you didn't hear it from me."

He grunts. "What should I do, then? Break things off with her?" He swipes at his mouth, looking suddenly agitated. "That's my baby—"

"I believe it's too late for that," I interrupt.

"So then what?"

"Be by her side. Constantly. Don't let Lebwitski or the bluecoats near her."

He rolls up his sleeves. "I won't let them within a mile of her, how's that," he says roughly, turning for the door. But he pauses before he disappears. "Thanks," he adds over his shoulder.

twenty-two

. . .

AS DARKNESS FALLS, fatigue following the eventful day settles in. But eventually, even that is replaced with excitement.

Back to the stables I go. This time, however, it's not because of chickens. It's to meet Neo to discuss ways to overthrow King's regime, and my skin prickles at the thought.

I pause outside Carnegie Reserve as I pass, listening to the voice reverberating from inside. It belongs to none other than King himself, and right now, he sings an aria for the crowd. Ghostly, that voice, and it echoes in my brain as I draw on a cloak and boots and position a brick along the doorjamb.

It echoes in my brain, haunting me.

Outside, the wind has picked up since earlier, the unimpeded gusts knotting my hair and, fortuitously, eliminating any possibility of others eavesdropping on our conversation. I stick close to the palace this time, more mindful of beasts than before, then run as quickly as I can under a tapestry of stars to the stables.

Funny how foreign this place felt at one time. Now, I squeeze through the doors, knowing precisely which angle to use so they don't squeak. Seeing as how I'm the first to arrive, I greet the horses and the hens. And then, before I can grow impatient or even bored, I hear a familiar groan, and a gust of wind fills the stable.

"Hi," Neo whispers as I stride toward him.

"Hi. Did you hear about the recent protest by the White Ribbon Campaign? Do you know who's behind it?"

"I heard the protest from my workstation," he explains. "It was the talk of the office for the whole day. Did it ruffle some feathers here?"

"It did," I confirm, thinking of King's reaction. "So, do you know who's behind it? Or the campaign in general?"

"I don't. Certainly nobody on my radar, if that's what you mean. But there's plenty of outliers in the population, so don't count me surprised."

"There are? So why did you only pick from me, Timothee, and Jill?"

"Because you three were the most obvious choices from your year. Don't forget I was looking specifically for someone about to undergo their Selection."

"Right," I mutter, my voice barely audible over the whistling wind.

"And I'm sure there are others I missed. A wizard I'm not. You probably realize by now that the blackcoats and the bluecoats were sent to the protest?"

"Meaning a bunch of those protestors are now either in jail or have an override chip implanted in their brain?"

"Precisely. Too bad. We could've used those dissenters on our side."

I nod, and even though I was already aware of that, I still feel glum. "Your last scroll advised me to spread the truth. Do you have any idea how I can do that? Without getting killed, I mean?"

"Straight to the point, you are."

"Last time, you said you can't spare much time here," I remind him.

He nods. "Okay, word of mouth is one way that's safe, so long as you're discrete."

"Safe for me, maybe," I reply. "But telling others would mean endangering them, wouldn't it?"

I can see under the glimmer of moonlight peeking through the old barn wood that he shrugs, essentially confirming my worst fear. "At some point, Alex, you have to roll the dice. Fear is what the King wants."

Yes. Fear is what King wants—I know that from experience. It's the best weapon that he has. But that doesn't mean I'll ever feel okay with putting my friends and family in danger. "There must be a better way. Something more efficient, where the truth is spread widely, all at once, so nobody's in danger. I mean, he wouldn't want the entire population run by override chips, would he?"

"There's power in numbers, too," Neo adds as he agrees with me. "But aside from dropping pamphlets from the sky...wait. You can fly a helicopter, right?"

I think about the lawn-green beast at the Sky Center. I can fly a helicopter. I have a license to fly, too. But do I have the authority? Not remotely. "I'm not sure that would work," I say tactfully.

"Why not?"

"Well, ignoring for a second the repercussions I'd face and assuming I could find a way to use a helicopter in the first place, would anyone even believe a pamphlet dropped from the sky? Don't forget we'd be making some huge accusations."

"It's the only real option we have. Tell people the truth and hope enough believe us to demand change." Though he speaks quietly, always cautious, I can hear the excitement in his voice.

"Maybe..." I say slowly, suddenly lost in thought, "...maybe we *don't* tell people. Maybe we *show* them."

He hesitates. "What do you mean?"

"I mean, we have to show them what King's doing. Just like you did with me. It's too risky to go to the trouble of telling people and hope they choose to believe us. If I'm going to risk everything, I want people to see the truth for what it is. I want it to be completely unavoidable."

"How do we do that? Deliver secret scrolls to the entire population?"

"No. I think...I think the answer is...the Queen."

"The Queen?"

"She's a public figure that everyone knows, and I think in the right scenario, it's obvious that something's not right—"

"Just because she's a public figure doesn't mean the whole country has access to her. Besides, she was on a float at the Winter's End celebration, and nobody noticed a thing."

"Neo," I whisper, my voice hoarse from the effort needed to keep it level and restrained. Because, I've got it. I've got the answer. "The national address."

He registers no reaction, none that I can see, then his face breaks into a grin—his white teeth sparkling even through the darkness. "Alex, that's brilliant. When is the next one?"

"Soon, it has to be. King's been talking about it for the past two weeks now."

"I can look up the date tomorrow at work."

"I can ask around the palace, too. Usually, during these addresses, the Queen just stands behind King as he speaks, so how can we—"

"I know precisely how," he interrupts.

"You know precisely how to make it clear to all of Airo-Aurora that the Queen has an override chip illegally planted in her brain?" I ask, sounding both doubtful and hopeful at once.

"Yep. We manipulate her override chip, that's how. Make it obvious during the address that she isn't controlling herself."

I consider it. From all angles, it seems to be the perfect way to simultaneously show the entire population of Airo-Aurora that something fishy is happening and that King needs to be held to account. "Is there any way to actually put it in motion?"

"It shouldn't be difficult to access her override chip from my work computer. I'd need help though, writing a program that interrupts her 'normal' behavior and controls her new behavior."

"Wait." I look at him through the darkness and swallow. "The Mainframe technicians will be the first people to be scrutinized if it works. If they review your feed—"

"It's risky," he agrees, and I hear the trepidation in his voice. "But it might be the only shot we have to spread the truth to everyone. Have you told Timothee and Jill yet?"

I shake my head. "They're my friends. I haven't wanted to put them in danger."

"You have to tell them. All three of you are outliers, remember? They're going to want to help, I know they will. Besides, I'll need Timothee's help writing that computer program for the Queen."

He's right, the time has come. "I'll talk to them tomorrow," I agree.

"Under the cover of darkness," he reminds me. "And don't forget to whisper."

I nod. Then, out of the blue, I ask, "Do you think Wolfe is trustworthy?"

Under the moonlight, I see Neo do a doubletake. Then he sighs. "He's very skilled at hiding his emotions, so he's difficult for me to read. But, based on the rare time he does register emotion worth reviewing, I'm inclined to believe he's opposed to King and his agenda, making him ultimately trustworthy."

Opposed to King. Trustworthy. Not a total confirmation, as I was hoping, but at least it's something. I thank Neo for his input.

"Plus," he continues, "I don't think you two would've made such a good match if he wasn't somewhat of an outlier himself."

For a moment I'm silent, confused. Then I remind him, "I was placed here at Strath Glen by you. Wolfe and I weren't put together because we're a good fit."

"You weren't placed together because you're a good fit, but you still are. Don't forget you never would've been paired up by the Mainframe given your different stations in life, but aside from that, you two could realistically have been a legitimate match."

I feel light-headed all of a sudden, and the excitement at having a real and tangible plan to dethrone King becomes somewhat muted.

"It might be helpful if the four of us meet," continues Neo.

"Huh?" I stare at him blankly.

"You and I, Timothee and Jill."

"Oh. I mean, yes...sure. I can set that up."

"Meeting here is too risky. Too many sets of footprints coming and going. Besides, if anyone finds you meeting in secret with a Mainframe technician and a greencoat, they'll be rightly suspicious. Can you swing something in town, late day?"

I start to shake my head but then catch myself. "That might work," I realize, "if it's late enough." I think of the servants coming and going all hours of the night.

"How about this...I'll meet you here in three days. How

does that sound? Can you chat with Timothee and Jill by then and arrange a meeting for all of us?"

"Sure."

"I'll see you Sunday then. Same time," he adds, and he draws away through the darkness. There comes another high-pitched squeal from the stable door, another gust of wind, and then I'm alone.

Alone, except for my racing thoughts and my thumping heart.

A plan—a real one—and after all this time. I feel like I could do backflips and scream for joy. A *plan*. One to induce real, tangible change—a plan that could potentially change everything. And then there's the news that Wolfe and I are a good match, after all...

I give myself a shake. Why should I care about that, anyhow? What difference does what the Mainframe thinks make? This is the very system I'm trying to dismantle, after all.

Human choice is what should bring two people together, and the fact is, Wolfe and I simply don't choose each other.

twenty-three

. . .

THE NEXT MORNING, when I finally pry open my eyes, I see that brightness floods the quarters. I curse myself for waking late, not that it's exactly surprising—not after all that happened yesterday. Still, though, today I have a mission, and that's to track down Timothee and Jill.

I need to arrange a meeting for us to talk with Neo, to fill them in on all that's happening, and with that thought, I throw off the covers, determined not to waste another second.

Wolfe, fortunately, has already gone to work, as he does every morning. I head to the closet to root around for the least flashy gown, developing a plan for the day as I do. Sneaking out of the palace to track down Timothee will be risky, but if I use the back exit and take the woods to street level, there's far less chance King will notice. And frankly, even before I do that, I must corner Monsieur Sawyer to see which evening would work for me to slip out. *If* he and the other servants are willing to help, that is.

But as soon as I step into the House of Mirrors, I notice something that makes my carefully laid plans slip from mind. It's a printout pasted to the window, and as I walk closer, I see that it's a picture of a white ribbon with an X placed over it.

> The organizers of the White Ribbon Campaign and its associated protests are declared enemies of the state. Any information you have concerning this terrorist organization and/or its act of terror, including but not limited to protests against the royal family and its Mainframe, must be passed to appropriate authorities. All members of said organization, as well as those participating in protests, will be prosecuted as being complicit to a terrorist organization.

My brow lifts, and a push-pull sensation fills my insides. On the one hand, there's no doubt these posters have been plastered across the nation-state, spelling the likely end of the White Ribbon Campaign and its protests—a shame for the country, and a shame for me and Neo too. We could've used more people willing to collude against King. On the other hand, these posters are proof of something—something that has never happened before in Airo-Aurora.

That *King* is scared.

"They've been pasted absolutely everywhere, sister," comes a voice directly over my shoulder.

I jump. "Evie, you frightened me," I exclaim. "Everywhere?"

"Sorry, sister," she says, and her voice sounds melancholy. "And yes, everywhere. The front door, the breakfast nook, Devonshire—need I go on? I must admit, I'm a tad disappointed."

"By what?" I ask, genuinely confused. "King's attempt to quell civil unrest?"

"Why, yes, precisely. The protest the other day certainly added a touch of drama, didn't it?"

"There's plenty of excitement around Strath Glen now that spring is in the—"

"It's not simply about the excitement though, is it?"

"No?"

She shakes her head fiercely, then sighs. "I'm worried to bits about my Selection, sister. You know that."

"I do," I say slowly. "But I'm not entirely sure what one has to do with the other."

She leans toward me, surveying the hallway to ensure we're alone. "Why, if the Mainframe system is dismantled, if free choice is the determinant of our future, then I can avoid my Selection all together!" She claps happily. "Now, I simply need a way to cajole these daring rebels before Uncle completely snuffs them out!"

"A risky endeavor," I remind her. "Even discussing it—"

"There's nobody around, sister—"

"Except for the Mainframe," I remind her. "The Mainframe is *always* around. It creates a record of everything we do and say. And, by openly supporting the White Ribbon Campaign, you're aligning yourself with what King has declared a terrorist organization," and I gesture to the poster.

She sighs glumly. "You're an ambitious young woman. You truly believe in the Selection system after it destined you to be a handmaid to my brother? After it paired you with a perfect stranger, one who no woman would characterize as a sweet and fitting mate?"

I may be able to do it, to lie, if it weren't for her eyes. Rounded with innocence, burning with earnestness. And so now, I'm the one to sigh. "I may not be a proponent of the system," I say quietly, my voice hidden, mostly, by the drilling overhead. "But I do know that the consequences of having that opinion are severe."

"So you choose to stay silent?"

"I choose to be careful," I clarify. "As should you."

"But if you believe something in your heart of hearts,

you owe it to yourself to be loyal to that vision, don't you agree?"

"Loyal, perhaps—"

"You must fearlessly fight for what is just—"

"Evie," I interrupt, lifting my palms. "When the danger is great, being reckless won't advance your cause—"

"And yet this woman did," and she taps the poster.

"Wait, did you say *woman*?"

"But of course, sister. You don't seriously believe a man would think to name a political movement after a piece of ribbon, do you? Oh no, this has womanly handprints all over it. I'm certain."

"Wherever is Rosetta?'" a new voice echoes, and when I turn, I see the duchess exiting her quarters. Her red and orange gown cascades after her as she joins us, and though her eyes linger on the poster, she says nothing about it. Instead, she turns to Evie. "Have you not begun your lessons for the day?"

"I haven't yet made my way downstairs," explains Evie, yawning. "I was simply chatting with—"

"Go now," the duchess orders, patting Evie gently on the head, a gesture that contrasts with the steely look in her eye. It's a look I know well, her son having inherited the same uncanny trait of communicating volumes without the opening of the mouth.

When the two of us are alone, the duchess turns to me. "Evie's studies are very important," she states, her tone scolding.

"Indeed," I agree. "We bumped into each other by happenstance and got to chatting, just as she said."

"And what were you two chatting about?"

"Oh, uh, these posters," I sputter. "I take it there are quite a few pasted around the palace?"

"Around the nation-state, too, I should think."

"Yes. Yes, of course."

She gives me a peculiar look. "Given your unexpected Selection results and your love for your hometown of Quire, I take it you sympathize with the White Ribboners, hmm?"

"On the contrary, madam," I say swiftly, not missing a beat. "I can think of nothing more venomous than to support a terrorist organization."

"What about to instigate it?"

I almost choke on my own saliva. "You think I...you think *I* started the White Ribbon Campaign?" I ask, shocked by the accusation.

"It's just a question, child."

"Hardly a fair one—"

"Indeed, a fair one, given your circumstances, given your gumption, given the fact that the campaign is clearly run by a woman."

"Run by a woman?" I echo. "Because of the ribbon?"

"I've seen the flyers," she snaps. "All that talk of a brighter future, the emphasis on our children—those are a woman's concerns."

"Perhaps," I say carefully. "Although, with all due respect, madam, I'd think many fathers would likewise want a brighter future for their children."

"So you admit that without the Selection, the future would be brighter?"

"I admit nothing," I retort, as goosebumps slip over my skin. "I'm commenting only on your claim that the movement was started by a female."

"You miss my point. Of course, a father would want a brighter future for their children. But only a woman would think to use that to appeal to the masses. A man would never attempt to appeal to a woman's senses, surely you recognize that."

I don't completely disagree. Woman, after all, are largely invisible here in King's realm. I bow my head. "You make a fair point, madam."

Her eyes narrow, as if she's trying to see deep into the recesses of my brain, but I give away nothing. Finally, her weight shifts back, as if she's satisfied, at least somewhat, and a moment later, she carries on through the House of Mirrors, sweeping into the distance and leaving me mercifully alone.

Right now, two things trouble me. The first is how easily it can be assumed that I'd align myself with the White Ribbon Campaign—something that's in fact true, but not something I can afford to be associated with. The second is that Evie, of all people, is not just aligning herself with the movement, but doing so openly too.

At least I had warned her of the danger, all I can do now is hope that she heeds my advice.

Just as I decide to return to my search for Monsieur, however, I spot none other than Aubrey and Butch on the far end of the House of Mirrors. I frown because...yes, my eyes aren't playing tricks on me. They currently walk *hand-in-hand* along the corridor, brazenly flouting the rules, not even attempting to keep their relationship a secret.

My stomach drops. If King sees this...

At the very least though, Butch is following through on his word to be glued to Aubrey's side. And I did all I could yesterday to warn Aubrey. With any luck, King will be so preoccupied with the White Ribbon Campaign that he won't even bother to follow up with Doctor Lebwitski.

Silently I descend the imperial staircase in my sock feet, my head spinning. And then, I freeze, because who do I see? None other than the man himself.

Lebwitski.

Carefully, I take a step backward and then another, disappearing into the shadows behind the staircase before I can be noticed.

Gerard ushers him inside, past the towering ming vases, toward Devonshire. It's impossible, when confronted with the man in the flesh, not to let the old memories rear their head, along with all the attached feelings, and in my mind's eye, I see Wolfe peering down at me, I feel the syringe pierce my skin.

Focus, Alex.

That was in the past, nothing lasting or terrible came of it, and this? This is happening *now*.

"Greetings, old friend!" comes King's voice, and I see him stride out of Devonshire with that Cheshire grin plastered to his face. As ever, the smile doesn't reach his eyes. "An absolute pleasure to see you again."

"A shame that it's in these circumstances. A special favor can mean only one thing I take it?"

"The final solution," agrees King, and I see him hang his head in a show of dejection. I almost laugh at the falsity of it all.

"Who in your beautiful residence is causing you grief?"

"It's Aubrey, I'm afraid," laments King as he ushers Lebwitski inside Devonshire and instructs Gerard to bring them a fresh box of cigars. "She's simply out of control. Her mother's child, indeed."

"Speaking of child, isn't she with one?" asks Lebwitski as they round the corner, out of sight. I wait for Gerard to vanish upstairs before slipping out of my hiding spot and darting along the hallway, taking refuge behind one of the ming vases positioned closest to the sitting room.

"And not exactly living up to the title of maternal goddess," comes King's voice.

"Killed by a curse? Killed by a curse!" shouts the parrot.

"She won't get the chance to live up to it at all with an override chip."

There's a distinct silence inside Devonshire, a stillness, too. Then King says in a scorching tone: "Save the judgment. Old friend."

More silence and my ears twist, desperate to hear every

last detail of this very important conversation. And then..."I heard a rumor you're, ahem, arming your insurance policy."

King hesitates. "They don't provide very much coverage otherwise," he says a heartbeat later.

"An alarming development, I'd say," pushes Lebwitski, and my brow furrows. Here I was, fearing the man in white above all else, when really, it should be King who causes the most trepidation.

"An alarming development? Pray tell, how so?"

"Isn't the notion of robotized killing machines plainly alarming?"

"What did I tell you about passing judgment against your King, hmm? It's not a good look. Don't forget, dear friend, that you *are* replaceable."

"Am I? Because if you lock me up, you won't have anyone to perform these operations."

"Alas, alas, there are other doctors around."

"Yet the more people you tell, the greater the risk that your secret will spread, that all those people down there will call foul, as some of them are already doing."

"Is that a threat, Monsieur Lebwitski?" King asks in a sugary tone. "Because dare not forget that I wouldn't simply lock you up, oh no. Why, your wife and children would be lonely on their own, hmm?"

Even out in the hall, the silence emanating from Devonshire Commons is heavy and uncomfortable.

"Well, then. Since we've cleared up that nasty business," continues King, clapping his hands together, "let's get down to the juicy bits and pieces. Tell me, old friend, how precisely you came to know about my plan to arm the Mavericks?"

"Apparently, you blathered to the whole palace about it. Didn't take long for word to spread outside these fine walls." His voice sounds different, ever so slightly strained. Like a man in a bind.

"I didn't have a choice," King snaps. "Someone already knew and was trying to persuade the House of Weaponry girl to red card the whole damn thing."

"Sounds as though between that and the recent protests, discontent is spreading. It might be wise to lay low, perhaps postpone implementing any more final solutions until—"

"I didn't ask you here for advice on how to rule my kingdom," King growls, causing the doctor to swallow his words.

As for me, I can hardly believe my ears. Doctor Lebwitski, it seems, is no longer content to blindly do King's bidding. I have little doubt, however, that given the imbalance of power between them, King will secure his every desire, even if Lebwitski disagrees on some moral ground. Perhaps he's disagreed all along, although I don't recall this level of tension between them in their previous exchanges.

"Miss Alex?" croons an old voice from behind me, and I jump. I whirl around to see Gerard standing over me, holding a cigar box. "May I ask what you're doing?"

I wave my hand dismissively, far more accustomed to playing the role than when I first arrived at the palace. "I was on my way to the library when I realized that I had tucked my shoes over here just yesterday. Alas, they've disappeared. Would you kindly know where they are?"

The old man shakes his head, the suspicion evident in his eye. Yet my story is convincing enough, I think, that not even he can accuse me of eavesdropping. At least not openly.

"If you see a pair of heels without their owner, I'll be busy working away in the library," I advise, patting him warmly on the hand before crossing the hallway and disappearing inside.

Once tucked inside and sufficiently confident that I'm alone, I curse.

Lebwitski, whether he disdains the idea or not, is here to place an override chip in Aubrey's brain, and even though

Aubrey's been consistently rude to me since I first arrived at Strath Glen, I can't stand by and let something so horrid happen to her. I need to track her down.

With that thought, I pull the door open a crack and stick my head through. Voices still emanate from Devonshire, and I can spot the shadowy figure of Gerard standing amongst the smoke.

Thankful yet again for my socked feet, I slip outside, then take the stairs two at a time to the second floor. Despite knocking for several minutes on Aubrey's door, however, it doesn't budge. When I press my ear to it, no sounds echo from inside, and I take my search back to the main floor, this time using the servants' stairs to avoid King and his guest.

In and out of every room I go, interrupting Evie's studies at one point and James having toast soldiers in another room while playing the jumble. I smile at the Queen as we pass each other in the hall, and just as I start to panic, I remember the sunroom—the one room I have yet to peruse.

———

THE PIANO SITS EMPTY, the window seats are unoccupied. But I spot movement in the attached greenhouse, and I push forward, around a telescope and through the plastic streamers that keep the moist air locked inside with the plants.

Immediately upon entering, my hair poufs, it coils, and I feel like I'm wearing fogged-up glasses. Aubrey and Butch kiss in the corner, surrounded by several Bird of Paradise plants. I clear my throat, and when that fails to rouse them, I cough loudly.

"You again," pouts Aubrey. "I know you young bucks adore me, but this is starting to smell desperato!"

I turn to Butch. "The doctor that we discussed is here, at Strath Glen," I announce, speaking quickly and lifting my voice over the humming of the fans, "to perform the procedure on Aubrey, whom King calls *out of control.* It's imperative you leave the palace immediately. There are cloaks at the back door—"

"The ditch piggy from Quire simply won't get the hint!" Aubrey interjects, looking somewhere between bored and annoyed. "Go, little bird, go!" and she uses both hands to shoo me away.

"Aubrey—"

"Dear little piggy, I don't know how to make my rejection any more apparent. Now, I have a burning in my loins, I intend to make love to my beloved right here amongst the plants, and I must insist you grab your pitchfork and mosey away."

That's it, then. Failure.

With one last desperate look at Butch, I turn for the exit with a heaviness in my chest.

And then I remember Wolfe.

I need to speak to him. He's the closest thing to an ally I have around here, and someone with far more influence than me. I scratch my head, feeling utterly exhausted even though my day has just begun, and head for the servants' stairs.

twenty-four

. . .

AS SOON AS I step foot in Bishop's Aisle, I spot King and Doctor Lebwitski stepping inside King's office at the end of the corridor, the door sealed promptly behind them. I step quickly toward Wolfe's office, the nerves in my stomach making me nauseated and the floating heads suspended in liquid lining the walls doing nothing to ease the sensation.

The blood red carpet, I notice next, is speckled with dirt, as though it hasn't been cleaned in several days, and the timbers overhead are lost in a maze of cobwebs.

Before I can analyze the bizarre state of disrepair, however, Wolfe's nameplate glints next to me, and I knock as quietly as I can, not wanting to capture the interest of King.

"What is it," comes Wolfe's crisp voice. "Oh, it's you," he adds, gazing down his nose at me, not sounding more or less excited by this revelation. "What is it," he echoes.

"I need to talk to you." I don't wait for an invitation. I slip inside, pushing the door closed behind me. I take a seat across from his, considering both the mighty head of a grizzly mounted on the wall behind his desk and the towering pile of paperwork he has waiting in queue.

Wolfe throws open the window, the whistling wind having the double effect of masking our conversation and rendering his office a mess. To his credit, he disregards the latter, seats himself across from me, and waits patiently for me to begin.

"It's Aubrey."

"What about her?"

"Doctor Lebwitski is at the palace right now to place an override chip in her brain. I overheard him and King discussing it. I tried to warn her and her lover, Butch, but Aubrey is refusing to heed my advice to flee Strath Glen. Butch, I believe, will attempt to protect her, but if the blue-coats are present, he will likely be no match."

Slowly Wolfe steeples his long fingers together, resting his elbows on the desk. He considers me with eyes that are hard, dark, and unfriendly, but I recognize that they don't so much reflect his feelings toward me, but rather the amount of thought churning inside his head.

"Did you take care," he begins quietly, "to mask your conversation with Aubrey and this young man?"

I pull a face as I realize my mistake. "I didn't," I admit. Not in the greenhouse.

He breathes slowly, in and out. "Then Aubrey's fate is already decided."

"Excuse me?"

"I refuse to intervene—clear now?"

"I'm afraid not—"

"To stop Aubrey's fate from befalling her would rouse questions, your knowledge of things you should have no knowledge of will undoubtedly come to light, and the next override chip will have your name on it." His gaze cools with a wordless rebuke.

"But—"

"The matter is settled," he reiterates. "Now, tell me, does

eavesdropping on my uncle yet again seem like a wise endeavor?"

"Well, no, but I stumbled upon—"

"Did anyone spot you?"

"Just Gerard—"

"King's butler caught you spying?" he asks, as his brow draws into a tight, unbending line.

"I told him I was searching for my shoes—"

"Your shoes—"

"As I'm not wearing any," I continue.

Wolfe peers under the desk and, upon spotting my socked feet, closes his eyes as though I really do sap his strength. "Why aren't you wearing shoes?" he asks in a voice void of inflection.

"The only ones that fit were the riding boots your mother had confiscated."

He rubs his temple and jots something down on a lined sheet of paper. "Fine. I'll have them returned to you at once. As for the rest of it, take care not to eavesdrop again. The same goes for placing yourself in the middle of matters that don't concern you and failing to adequately protect yourself in the process."

"A woman's life hangs in the bal—"

"As does yours."

I swallow.

"Have you determined who is behind the White Ribbon Campaign?"

"I haven't," I admit. "Although your mother and sister both believe it's a woman."

His brow arches. "Why, precisely, were you discussing such matters with my mother and my sister?"

I scratch my nose. "I, uh, well, your mother came upon me and Evie discussing a notice pasted to the second-floor window, one about the campaign being considered a terrorist organization. That's all."

"Why were you and Evie discussing it?"

"Well," I begin, and I scratch behind my ear, "it's topical."

"It's topical. And?"

"And...And, as she finds the idea of her own impending Selection to be off-putting and anxiety-producing, she was quite, uh, taken with it."

His nostrils flare as he draws himself out of his seat and to his full towering height.

"I warned her," I say quickly, trying to placate him. "I was subtle, but I reminded her that it's now considered a terrorist organization and that the Mainframe is always—"

"Heavens, me!" shouts a voice from the door, one now swung all the way open. Claudia comes bustling inside in a miniskirt, slamming the window shut. "Whatever has gotten into you," she begins, but her gaze snags on me and she falters. "I see the problem," she says in a bracing voice.

I stand. Not only did I fail to secure help for Aubrey, I've sufficiently angered Wolfe by mentioning his sister's political leanings, and now, *she's* here. Time, I think, to go.

"Sit!" Wolfe barks, pointing to my seat.

I sit down promptly.

"What's she doing here?" Claudia demands.

Wolfe stares at her like he'd forgotten about her presence completely.

"Didn't you see the protest a few days back?" she continues. "Soon the Selection system will be out the window, meaning your sham of a marriage to this Quire yam can be avoided completely."

I stare at the side of her face, unbothered by the insult frankly, but transfixed by the meaning behind her message. The citizens of Airo-Aurora are open to the possibility of a different future. A regime that doesn't involve the Mainframe choosing for us our careers and our spouses. And that means, surely, that change will be easy to come by.

"You'll be wise to note that the group behind the protest is now designated a terrorist entity," Wolfe says blandly, his gaze still on mine. Finally, though, he turns his attention to Claudia. "You're here to discuss the missing cargo. Sit, sit," and he motions to the empty chair next to mine.

Claudia considers it, she considers me. "It's a sensitive matter, Viscount, requiring the utmost discretion."

"I'll go," I offer, thinking of the need to track down Monsieur Timothee and Jill.

"Do I have your word, Alex," Wolfe says, striding around his desk to meet me at the door. "Concerning the first matter we discussed, do I have your word that the matter is settled?"

"Yes," I agree. "The matter is settled. As for our most recent discussions," I continue, speaking cryptically and causing Claudia to stare openly at us, "it's something for us to be mindful of moving forward, but I don't believe the time for panic is upon us."

He nods, understanding that I speak of Evie and her newfound leanings, then steps aside. But he catches my arm before I can go. "Thank you," he says gruffly, avoiding eye contact and turning promptly for his desk.

Claudia, I notice, as I walk out the door, looks affronted. Probably she thought that Wolfe and I had no business with one another whatsoever, and it's hard not to enjoy the wave of satisfaction sitting in my chest.

Then I draw the cardigan tighter around me and sigh. Really, I did all I can to protect Aubrey. Whether or not she and Butch heed my advice is out of my hands, and with that thought firmly in mind, I turn my attention to tracking down Monsieur Sawyer.

On the servants' stairs, however, it's Rebecca that I run into. "There's the secret keeper," she says, poking my side.

"I wish my life was that exciting," I reply in an amiable way.

"What were yeh doin' up in Bishop's Aisle?"

"Speaking with Wolfe, that's all. Claudia has his ear now."

"Oh, aye? And that doesn't make the missus jealous?"

"Why should it? He doesn't seem to be taken with her." I pause and stare at the young girl. "Does he?"

"Don't know, like, but I do know it didn't stop 'em from shagging in the past now, did it?"

"Uh, well, I suppose." I decide to change the subject. "Do you know where Monsieur Sawyer is?"

"Why do yeh want to know?"

"He's taking the viscount and me to Quire Park tomorrow, and I'm supposed to touch base with him on departure time," I lie.

"He's none too happy about all those damn chickens in his ride, aye."

"I wouldn't be, either. So, do you know where I can find him?"

"He's not gone around here. Getting ready to drive King is what I'd guess."

"Oh? Where is King going?"

She lifts an eyebrow. "Awfully nosey, you."

"Just making conversation," I reply breezily.

"Aye. Well, he's got a lunch on with the baron of Seymore, like. I and the others have a wager he comes back this afty toasted."

"I'll eagerly be awaiting Monsieur's return then," I announce, scarcely able to believe my luck. King gone, which makes my day significantly easier, even if I am still worried about Aubrey, Evie, and, to some small and silly extent, Claudia. I shake my head to refocus. This is a stroke of luck, one much-needed. After all, sneaking out to Hallah, where Timothee works as a computer programmer, is against King's rules, and didn't I learn my lesson last time?

But with King away, the risk is far less, and the reward is

too great to ignore. After all, if Neo's right, Timothee and Jill are my allies—a team of resistance fighters, so to speak—and the thought makes goosebumps slip over my skin.

Besides, Neo needs Timothee's computer skills for our national address plan to be a success, and I do want that. Yes, the need to speak to Timothee is urgent.

First, though, I go back to my quarters, waiting with my nose pressed to the window until I see the behemoth depart from Strath Glen, vanishing deep into the city. To make matters even better, Gerard knocks on the door with my riding boots just as I'm preparing to leave.

I thank him, pull them on, and head back to the servants' stairs, keeping my eyes peeled for Lebwitski, who could still very well be on the premises. I watch, too, for Aubrey, but the corridors are quiet, I spot no one. The mystery, for now, suspended.

twenty-five

. . .

TYPICALLY I'D TAKE the front door out and into the city, but right now, I head for the back of the palace. Extreme times call for extreme caution, after all. And yet, how cautious am I really being, waltzing around in the middle of the day, speaking with Timothee and Jill? I think about how careful and meticulous Neo is and pause.

Should King review my footage, he'll see me brazenly breaking the rules, he'll hear me speak of matters I should know nothing about to Butch and Aubrey, but, far worse than that even—he'll see me have suspicious conversations with Timothee and Jill, too.

I can't have that, not with a clean conscious. So, after drawing on a cloak from the back closet, I root around for a hat, finally finding a pageboy cap that I pull down low over my eyes.

There. Not exactly an airtight solution, but if I'm careful, it'll block out their faces from my feed.

And then I'm gone, following the same path I took when I snuck to the stables and back from my aunt's place. Once I'm hidden inside city streets and away from the leering palace, I relax a little, but I continue to keep my gaze rooted to the sidewalk below. I don't want my route to be traceable, after all, and when I finally reach the cube-shaped glass building that houses Hallah, I'm careful not to glance at it or the signage.

Things are more difficult inside, I soon find, once I step into the large room filled with a sea of computers. I can't exactly shout Timothee's name, the Mainframe will record that. I can't look at the workers fanning across the room, either. So, with no other option and feeling foolish, I stare at the floor, then shout over the cacophony of clicking, "A word, please!"

I turn away and wait, trying to ignore the painful kink in my neck from staring continuously at my feet and the blood blush filling my face.

"Did you want a word with me, Alex?" comes Timothee's voice over my shoulder. "Or with everyone? Hey, is everything okay?"

I nod. "Can the two of us go somewhere quiet, please? And dark?" I add, rubbing my neck.

"Dark?"

"A closet would be ideal."

"You want to talk to me...in a closet," he clarifies.

"Please."

"Alright. I mean, yeah...whatever. There's a supply closet down here. Come on."

I follow him down a hallway, my pageboy cap still pulled down low, my gaze still cemented to the ground, even when he trips and stubs his toe. Inside a small room, I spot the bottom of a photocopier in the corner and shelving lined with reams of paper. "Can you switch out the light?" I whisper.

He laughs. "Oh, right. I forgot you wanted somewhere dark. Do you have a migraine or something?" he adds as he reaches over my shoulder and snaps the switch.

I lift my head, never more grateful for the dark as now,

and stretch out my neck. "It's best to whisper," I advise. "Actually, it's imperative I do. And no, I don't have a migraine."

"Whisper? Why?"

"For the same reason we're standing in the dark. So that if my feed is reviewed, there'd be no evidence of me meeting with you, and the authorities would have no way of hearing anything I'm about to tell you."

"Uh, Alex?" he whispers.

"Yeah?"

"This is really weird."

"I promise you, it's about to get much weirder."

"Does it have to do with those scrolls?"

I nod, momentarily forgetting that we stand in the pitch black. "I found the scroll writer."

"Oh?" I can hear the sudden interest in his voice. The fact that we're whispering inside a dark closet goes by the wayside.

"His name is Neo, and he's one of the Mainframe technicians. He placed me at Strath Glen on purpose and he gave me your name and Jill's because we're what he calls "outliers". In other words, people who aren't willing to readily accept the status quo. People who've been through hardship, too."

For a while, he's silent. Then he whispers, "To what end?"

"Ultimately? To overthrow King and the Mainframe system," I reply, my voice so quiet I can barely register it. When he says nothing in reply, I add, "I know it sounds crazy—"

"I'm in."

Now I'm the one taking a moment to digest things. "Are you serious?" I finally ask. "Just like that?"

I see the outline of his head bob through the darkness. "I told you what happened to my brother, right? Something bad happened when the bluecoats took him, there's no way he offed himself. Besides, he should've been matched up with his girlfriend all along. Nobody should be forced to marry someone if they don't want to."

I pull back in surprise, but I'm relieved, too—undeniably so. And I'm beginning to see what Neo meant when he said we were both outliers, unlikely to bow to authority.

I lean closer. "It's even worse than that. Do you know what the bluecoats do to people like your brother? People who are unhappy with their situation? Or who speak out against the system?"

He barely breathes. "What?"

"They have a doctor named Lebwitski insert an override chip into their brain. They become completely controlled by the Mainframe."

"Like a robot?" he asks, sounding skeptical.

"If that helps. And it's not obvious to everyone, at least not right away, because the Mainframe has years of data to work with."

"Jesus, that's some sophisticated artificial intelligence. So, my brother…"

"He must've fought them off, and they ended up killing him. That or he really did kill himself in order to avoid the override chip. Either way, it's incredibly sad, and totally avoidable."

He runs his hands through his hair and whistles. "I can't believe it. I just…can't believe it. How do you know all this?"

"Let me finish," I whisper. "Because it gets even worse."

"Is that even possible?" he asks, making a sound of disbelief.

"Have you ever heard of the Mavericks?"

"Woodspeople?"

"Yes, them. They don't have any chips in their brain— the Mainframe knows nothing about them. But King has been rounding them up and inserting the override chips into them too. Without any data though, they're completely robotized, controlled entirely by the system."

"Why would the King bother with all that? Wouldn't it be easier to throw them in jail?"

"He's building an army with them, I saw them myself about a hundred miles north of here."

"An *army*? For what?"

"My best guess is to use them against disgruntled citizens. I mean, why else would he have them?"

"But he's already controlling us through the Selection process and these override chips you're talking about. Isn't an army a little overkill?"

"Maybe not—not if unrest is spreading faster than Lebwitski can work. Or maybe people are noticing that something's off with their loved ones who have those override chips. Maybe they even suspect what's happening, I don't know."

"How did Neo find out all this in the first place?"

"I assume he stumbled upon it in the course of his job. You can ask him yourself if you'd like. He wants to meet with you, me, and Jill—soon."

"For what?"

"To work on our plan to expose King. He'll need your computer skills," I add pointedly.

"Count me intrigued," he says loudly.

"Don't forget what's on the line," I say, shushing him. "If King finds out we know about all this, we'll be the next ones with override chips in our brains."

"Not me," he whispers. "I'd rather go down like my brother. So, what's this big plan to expose the King?"

"Well, we're thinking that at the next national address—"

"We're going to hack in with our own message!"

"Not quite, but you're right about the hacking part.

Instead of *telling* people what's happening, we're going to *show* them."

"What does that mean?"

"It means the Queen, who's always on camera during these addresses, has an override chip implanted in her brain."

He scoffs. "You're kidding, right? He did that to his own wife?"

"From what I've gleaned, she wasn't exactly deferential."

"So I'm supposed to manipulate her override chip during the address?"

"Exactly. You're going to make it obvious that she's not controlling herself."

"Neo has the channels to let me in?"

"You're going to have to discuss that with him, but I think so."

He nods. "What if we take it further? What if we don't just attack her override chip, but we attack *all* the override chips at the same time?"

"So that every family with a bot suddenly knows it? That's *genius*."

"Right? We could turn the public sentiment against the King practically instantaneously."

For a minute both of us are silent, lost in thought, and I imagine success alongside a new dawn for our beautiful Airo-Aurora.

"Which night works to meet up with Neo? I'll be speaking to him Sunday, I'll tell him then."

"Why not sometime Sunday night, after you talk to him? Sounds like the program I'll need to write will take some time."

"Sunday night it is. It'll have to be late, though," I explain, "since I'll have to sneak out of the palace."

"That's fine with me."

"Plus, the more often we meet in the dark, the safer we'll be."

"Right. Our feed. Does this mean I have to watch everything I say and do from this point forward?"

"Absolutely it does," I whisper.

"Cool. So, where should we meet?"

"There's a park not far from the palace—"

"Battery park?"

"That's the one. Around 11:30?"

"Perfect, see you then. Put your head down," he adds, then he flips on the light and walks out the door.

I follow behind him, my gaze once again fixed to the floor. I continue this way out the building, into the bustling streets, and it's not until I'm close to the palace that I lift my gaze, once again stretching out my neck.

And just as I do this, just as my gaze sweeps the streets, I spot a sight that makes my stomach drop, and the swelling balloon of hope and excitement in my chest pop like a pin's been pushed straight through. The behemoth, its snout arcing toward the palace.

King, returning to Strath Glen.

I break into a sprint, crossing the busy intersection against the light, then cut through the apple orchard that stands at the foot of the palace grounds. The heel of my boot crushes an apple causing its cloying scent to lift into the air. I have to dart left and right to avoid the crisscrossed branches reaching for the sunlight. Anything to avoid winding up in King's crosshairs.

Funny. Not so long ago, I stood in this very orchard, staring up at Strath Glen, having just learned my Selection results, with my insides in knots. Confused about how my future could look so different than the one I had envisioned. Fearful of that palace way up high.

Now I know the truth. That my future wasn't supposed

to be this way. That the fear was well-justified, well-warranted. But maybe...just maybe, it will all be worth it.

I come to an abrupt stop at the edge of the orchard. I remember that shadowy figure way up high staring straight down at me, and a shiver runs along my spine. Then I'm running harder than before, across the road allowance, up the steps two at a time. My muscles scream, my lungs are on fire—

"You okay, princess?" Jill calls as I pull open the palace door. An aria hits my ears like a sharp punch, and I jump back, letting the door swing swiftly shut.

"What's gotten into you?" Jill asks over my shoulder.

"King's home," I say under my breath, so the other greencoat can't hear.

"Ah, and you've been breaking the rules," Jill gathers. She spits over the banister and shrugs. "You're allowed outside, just say you were talking to me the whole time. What he doesn't know can't hurt him. Or you," and she winks.

"I hope you're right. And speaking of talking to you, what time are you done your shift?"

"Dinner hour. Why?"

"Can you meet me around back?" I ask, lowering my voice even more. "In the stables?"

Her brow arches with surprise. "What for?"

"The scrolls."

"You have an update?"

"Lots of updates," I confirm.

"Have you told Timothee yet?"

"I just did."

She taps her finger against her chin. "You bringing dinner?"

I grin. "Strath Glen serves dinner quite late, I'm afraid. But I may be able to sneak out some hor d'oeuvres."

"That should tie me over," she grunts. "And hey, if you see any shrimp around, send them my way."

Before I can respond, there comes a squealing that rings out over the wind. The towering front door swings open, my heart stops—

But it isn't King's wide face that crests through the shadows. It's Wolfe. His cool gaze sweeps over us, his eyes narrow as he considers my windswept hair. "You should know my uncle has returned," he says pointedly.

"I am aware."

"I take it you've been enjoying the fresh air here on Strath Glen's grounds?"

"That's right," I say, even though he and I both know that isn't true. And yet, how does he know that?

"He's gone upstairs now," Wolfe continues. Another hard look, then, wordlessly, he vanishes back inside.

"Pillow talk?" Jill asks.

"Not quite," I say, then I turn to the other guard on duty. "Do you know the viscount?"

The man looks almost startled to be addressed, I suppose he's used to me and Jill speaking quietly to each other. "Aye, that was him just now, wasn't it?"

"Did you notify him that I'd left the palace?"

He glances at Jill, looking mildly confused. "I didn't. Didn't see you go, either, if I'm being honest."

I sigh. How, precisely, was he able to keep such close tabs on me when he's been in a meeting with Claudia?

One thing is clear, and that's that Wolfe doesn't want me coming into King's crosshairs. A strategic move, no doubt, and yet part of me—a small, infinitesimal part—can't help but feel touched.

And then my brain wanders to Neo's recent revelation that Wolfe and I are quite well-matched... Immediately I clear my throat and turn to Jill. "See you tonight?"

"Yeah, princess, see you tonight," she confirms.

I slip inside the palace. The corridors are still, eerily so, and the towering ming vases seem taller than usual. No drilling from overhead, no laughter echoing from the corners of the palace, no operatic singing from above. There's no trace of Wolfe either. He must've returned to his office along Bishop's Aisle. Evie, no doubt, is still taking her studies, and who knows what the rest of the family is up to. What I really want to know, now that I'm back, aside from King's current location, of course, is if Aubrey—

"Doe-eyed doll," James suddenly sings in my ear.

I whirl around, heart hammering. "I—didn't see you there."

He bites into an apple and smacks his lips. "Such an innocent cotton-tail, you. Of course you didn't. Why, I was tiptoeing!"

There's a gleam in his eye that shines brighter than usual. Slowly I inch backward, wishing the palace wasn't dead as a doornail right now.

"Cat got your tongue?" he prods. Apple juice rolls down his chin.

"Of course not." My voice wavers ever so slightly, and then I step around him and head for the stairs.

He grabs my wrist before I can make it a foot. "Tell me it isn't so," he says in a heavy voice, one laced with theater.

"Sorry?"

"Are you scared of your prince? Surely not, after I spared you the whip. Would you really have preferred that barbaric torture device over the gentle caress of a prince's lips?"

"I'd prefer neither, frankly."

"What if I were to oust Papa and take the throne as my own, hmm? Imagine, kissing the most important person in all of Airo-Aurora!"

"I'd still prefer not," I say boldly.

"Too cute! Even your anger is like a spring flower. So

unfortunate, I'd say, that all that is lost on that morose old fiancé of yours."

Something flares inside my stomach as I set my gaze on him. "I can assure you that I'd choose that morose old fiancé of mine head and shoulders over the likes of you any day of the week." I yank my wrist free and turn on my heel, leaving a stunned-looking James behind me. Part of me reels. I don't want an enemy out of the prince, I know that. But part of me also bursts with pride.

My mother, never a wallflower, would've been particularly proud—telling off James was a long time coming. Own your ground, she used to tell me. And for the first time since moving into Strath Glen—maybe the first time ever—I feel like I have.

———

AT SUNDOWN, and before Wolfe's workday is finished with, I head to Carnegie Reserve in search of hor d'oeuvres. Only a small crowd has gathered so far, and I find myself waiting for the kitchen to release the first round of appetizers. As I wait, the women in the crowd, all from a neighboring estate, take turns gazing over their shoulders and under their elaborate updos and fascinators in my direction. I hear the viscount's name muttered, alongside a sharp burst of laughter, but I refuse to move to the shadows, I refuse to lower my chin. And then pigs in a blanket and shrimp skewers waltz by. I grab a napkin and a half dozen of each.

More laughter follows me out of Carnegie, but I'm undeterred, instead heading with intention toward the back cloak closet.

———

JILL MUST ALREADY BE THERE—A light is turned on inside the stables—and when I draw near, I can hear the characteristic sound of spitting that carries through the damp air. When I pull open the door, I cover my eyes and ask her to switch off the light.

A second later, we're thrown into murky near-darkness, and it strikes me that the days are getting longer. Winter's end, indeed.

"Why no light?" Jill begins, then she sniffs the air. "Sausage?"

"And shrimp. Princess," I add as I stumble toward her.

"Very funny," comes her reply, and I can see her outline well enough to pass her the loaded napkins.

"Well?"

"Damn," she says as she chews. "Everything I thought palace food would be, and then some. The ambiance could use some work, though. I mean, a dark stable? Care to explain?"

I shush her. "We need to meet in the darkness, and whisper, to minimize the trouble we could get in should the wrong person review our feed."

"Wrong person? Like who?"

"Like King."

"He's still whipping you I take it?"

"Actually, he's up to a lot more than that."

"Yeah? What's he doing to you now?"

"It's not to me. It's to everyone. All the citizens of Airo-Aurora that dissent or are unhappy. He interferes with them."

"What are you talking about?"

I take a steady breath and dive in, explaining to Jill all about the override chips, the Mavericks, the arms deal, and Neo. "He wants to meet with the three of us Sunday night," I finish, "to work on next steps."

"Next steps for what?"

"Dismantling the system. Exposing King. Overturning the Mainframe," I rhyme off.

She whistles. "That sounds pretty damn intense," she says, but even I can hear the hesitation in her voice.

"We have a plan," I continue, "to expose the Queen and everyone else who has override chips during King's next public address. That means Timothee and Neo will have to find a way to access the chips from inside the Mainframe, and it may be handy to have a greencoat on our side."

"Yeah. Maybe," she agrees, as she wipes her mouth. "Is that why my name is wrapped up in all this? Because of my job?"

"It's because you're what Neo calls an "outlier." Timothee and me, too. He thinks, statistically speaking, we're the least likely members of society to go along with the status quo. In other words, we'd make a good team for the job."

"I get that," she says gruffly. "And normally, I'd be all in —you know how much I like breaking the rules. But things have been going pretty damn good for me lately. Like my job. Plus, the fiancé and I are shopping for our own house, which means I wouldn't have to live with my old man anymore. I just...don't want to risk that."

For a while I'm silent. The last person I thought I'd have to convince is Jill. She's completely fearless—braver than Timothee and me combined. But I know how much is at stake—especially considering her father is an abusive alcoholic and her home-life is far from fun—I know how risky this endeavor truly is. Convincing her to put everything on the line isn't something I'm willing to do. Not if she's unsure about it.

"I get it," I say, finally. "I'd probably feel the same way if I were you," I admit, and it's true. Had I been paired with Patrick and slotted to be a librarian, pilot, or pianist like I desired, how plausible would it be that I'd risk it all on a far-fetched plan to destroy the entire system? Not very likely—outlier or not.

"Yeah," she grumbles. "Still, sorry."

I wave a hand. "Don't be. If you change your mind, we'll be meeting Sunday night at Battery Park around 11:30. Otherwise, I'll see you on the front stoop, like usual."

"Like usual," she agrees, and we step outside together, waving goodbye. I head back to the palace, feeling defeated.

Should I have pushed harder? Neo seems to think it's important to have her working alongside us, and he's probably right. Not only is she a greencoat, but she would've been another ally, as well. I groan. Already I feel like I'm failing, and we haven't even begun.

To make matters worse, tomorrow is Saturday, and it's unlikely Jill is working this weekend. That means I won't have another opportunity to convince her to attend Sunday night's meeting. Maybe Timothee could try to convince her, but that would mean another voyage off palace property to speak to him, and besides, I don't know where he lives to make the request in the first place.

And then I smack my forehead. Tomorrow is Agnes's *wedding*. I'd completely forgotten, and the thought bothers me. Because no matter how much I have on my plate right now, from the danger Aubrey's in, to Evie's newfound rebellious streak, to my upcoming meeting with Neo, this is a big day for my best friend, and I pledge that for the next twenty-four hours, my focus will be firmly on her.

twenty-six

. . .

CARNEGIE HAS FILLED with people in my absence, and my resolve to think only of Agnes is tested immediately. Because nowhere amongst the sea of glittering aristocrats is Aubrey. Maybe she and Butch heeded my advice. Or, maybe, she's recovering from a procedure she didn't consent to...

King, I notice next, is in a stormy mood. Could it have something to do with his daughter? Perhaps she really did escape, and a surge of hopefulness shoots through my chest. Or, perhaps it's because things with Lebwitski have clearly soured, and with that last thought, an idea is born.

If I could track down Doctor Lebwitski, if I could convince him of King's evil and dubious ways, might I be able to convince him to abandon the override chip program? I mean, the man must have a conscience, considering his unimpressed reaction to King arming the Mavericks... Even better, King doesn't have to know that the chips are no longer being implanted. And sure, he might cotton on eventually, but by then, with a helping of luck—a heap of it, frankly—King's throne might very well be reduced to rubble.

The risk, of course, is that I'm underestimating Lebwitski's loyalty to King. That everything I do and say will be relayed to King the second I leave. That I'll be the next target for chip implantation, and I can't have that.

I could send him an anonymous letter, written in the cover of darkness, but that idea hadn't exactly panned out in regard to Morocco and her father...

And then, as I draw my attention back to tomorrow's wedding, I notice another impediment to my pledge to focus only on Agnes. Claudia has arrived for the evening, her dress as skimpy as the ones Morocco typically dons. Several women standing nearby actually elbow each other as they stare at her mostly exposed breasts.

I should go back to my thoughts and scheming, but instead, I watch her. Just as I suspected, her gaze stops swiveling when it lands on Wolfe, and I remember her words in his office: one measly little protest, and she thinks the whole system is about to crumple. She doesn't realize the depths King will go to in order to retain power. She is too distracted thinking that the burden of her betrothed—and, well, of me—will soon vanish. That she will marry Wolfe as she always intended and gain the title of viscountess.

And maybe, just maybe, if Neo, Timothee, and I are successful in executing our plan during the national address, she will be right.

I watch as Claudia makes her way through the crowd toward Wolfe, spritzing her mouth with breath spray as she goes, fluffing her voluminous hair, pulling her shoulders back, and pushing her chest out more and more with every step.

Part of me expects Wolfe to dismiss her completely, but he doesn't. Instead, he turns, his gaze dips down her dress, then fixes ferociously on hers. Whatever he says to her gets a reaction—I can tell by their body language that they're now caught in a heated argument. Evie watches them with wide eyes, then she looks around, perhaps looking for me. But really, what am I to do? What am I to make of it?

While I'm trying to deduce the answers to those questions, Claudia suddenly bursts into tears and runs from the room. Wolfe checks his watch, hesitating for several seconds, then, looking put out, follows her out of Carnegie.

I don't care what their drama is about—I don't think so, anyway. Yet that doesn't stop me from tiptoeing through the crowd and carefully drawing open the door. My ears swivel, listening for the sound of sobbing. That or crisply polished loafers echoing across the well-lacquered floors.

Hearing nothing, I quietly move along the corridors, checking each room, each nook and alley, convincing myself that I act out of simple curiosity and nothing more.

And yet, no one else searches for them. I'm even doubtful that Dear Matthew would bother if it were Aubrey and Butch who disappeared under such intriguing circumstances. So, why do I care so much? Is it possible my feelings for Wolfe go farther than I care to admit?

At that moment, I catch wind of it—voices—and my pace slows. I walk around the imperial staircase, still trying to deduce where, precisely, it came from.

The parlor, the one nestled next to Counterdown, and I place my ear along the heavy wood door only to feel the door give. It's unlatched, and I push it open several inches, until Claudia's voice is crystal clear.

"It's an arrangement that would serve us both well," she is saying, her voice articulate and not at all touched with tears.

"And yet I am betrothed to another. There's no chance of you gaining the title of viscountess," counters Wolfe in an equally articulate voice. "I fail to see how your proposal would serve you in the slightest."

"I refuse to capitulate, Viscount, how's that? I wish to rub it in your uncle's nose that the Mainframe was wrong, that we belong together, and together we'll be—no matter what that ugly building spits out."

Dangerous words, I think to myself—discontent is rampant, and I'm sure Wolfe must be thinking that, too. He makes no mention of it, however. Instead, he says, "I believe my uncle has other things on his mind, and your presence, romantic or otherwise, will have no effect on him whatsoever."

"The nation is changing," Claudia charges. "Father thinks it won't be long before we can choose our own spouses, and that means the title of viscountess will indeed be mine."

"There is no evidence whatsoever that change is coming. I feel this whole conversation is a waste of time."

"How about this, then. I don't like your little fiancée," she says coldly. "I don't like her at all."

"That has no bearing—"

"It should, though. Shouldn't it? Do you not have a shred of loyalty in your bones?"

"As I'm betrothed to her—"

"She's awful."

"Has she done something to offend you?"

"She's marrying you, isn't that reason enough?"

"She'd rather not—"

"Which means, what, Viscount? That you aren't getting any action in the bedroom? Consider that another reason why this arrangement would benefit you."

"What are you doin' snoopin' through the door like that?" comes a voice from behind me. Rebecca, and she shoves the door open. Immediately she goes still.

I do, too. Wolfe sits comfortably in a wing chair, while Claudia occupies the other one with her breasts completely exposed.

His eyes round slightly at seeing us standing there, otherwise, his face is impassive.

Claudia, on the other hand, stands immediately from her chair, straddles Wolfe on his, and begins kissing him.

"I'll be goin'," Rebecca says hurriedly.

Wolfe stands abruptly, as if he barely notices Claudia attached to him in the first place. "I'm glad you're here," he says to me in his usual disinterested voice.

I blink, unable to say a word.

"In a bid to avoid unwanted drama, you should know that Claudia has pitched an idea whereby she and I continue a relationship in secret, something I simply don't have time for." With that, he marches out the parlor door.

My eyes slide to hers, and I feel something stir inside of me. Something similar to anger, yet even more pronounced.

Claudia laughs. "He rejected my proposal because he doesn't have time, did you hear that? *Time* is the issue. It's not because he has any feelings for you. Quire rat," she adds.

"I think he was just being polite," I say, causing her eyes to narrow. "After all, if he had any feelings for you whatsoever, he'd make the time."

She pulls the sleeves of her dress up, covering her breasts, and then she walks right up to me. "Do you realize that he was married before?"

"Of course."

"So, you recognize that he's allowed to remarry if his wife dies? Good. Consider it a warning," and then she's gone, shouting, "Gerard, my coat!" to the shadows.

Several seconds later, I'm surprised to see the old butler appear with her coat folded neatly over his arm.

Yes, there's still much to learn about life at Strath Glen, that's for sure. But I'm starting to learn a few things about myself, too.

———

BACK IN CARNEGIE, most of the attendees have already seated themselves, and the kitchen staff begin to serve dinner. I slide into my seat next to Evie, still mildly shaken from the incident in the parlor, and startle when I see the way Wolfe stares at me.

"Yes?"

He smooths his napkin and leans forward in his chair. "Well, Alex?"

My eyes pinch. Then I lean forward, mimicking him. "Shouldn't I be asking you that?"

"Heavens! Whatever are you two discussing?" Evie shouts. "Did you see Claudia here earlier, sister? Such a revealing dress, my! Was it true you upset her, brother, by telling her how preposterous she looks? What—"

"That will do, Evie."

"But—"

"Claudia proposed that they rekindle their romance," I state in a matter-of-fact tone, "but Wolfe rejected it because he doesn't have the time."

"How scandalous!" gasps Evie.

"That isn't the reason," Wolfe declares in a baritone voice, giving me a thunderous look. He lifts a hand when I start to object. "It was a matter of being civilized and not causing more godforsaken drama than was already—"

"She also exposed herself to Wolfe just now and kissed him on the lips," I interrupt, feeling a rush of satisfaction. Perhaps the whole thing bothered me more than I realized.

"Brother!" Evie shouts, throwing down her napkin. "That is unconscionable and completely indecent!"

Wolfe exhales, looking suddenly flustered. "It should be Claudia you are scolding—"

"Should it?" I query. "Because I didn't hear you protesting her state of undress while the two of you were talking."

"Nothing untoward happened, as you know," he says coolly.

"It seems to me it did," I retort.

He lifts an eyebrow and considers me. Evie, meanwhile, watches both of us in turn, not even glancing at the meal that's placed before her.

Finally, Wolfe clears his throat. "I will admit that the whole thing was in poor taste, and I regret that I gave her my ear in the first place. That being said, as we continue to conduct business together, given her position at her father's company, I felt it best to placate her." He picks up his fork and adds, "I didn't realize it would make you so jealous."

I choke on a piece of lamb. "Jealous?" I finally echo, staring at him incredulously.

"Indeed."

"I wasn't...I'm not..." I turn my attention to my meal, ignoring the way my fingers shake as I cut apart the rest of the meat. Suddenly I lift my head. "I'm indignant. Not jealous," I clarify.

He simply waves his hand, now immersed in the paper. But before I can return to my meal, he folds down the corner and considers me. "Has she left the palace?"

"I believe so."

"Did she have anything to say to you before leaving?"

"As a matter of fact, she did."

Evie shouts, "Oh, sister, you're killing me with suspense!"

I'm about to repeat her parting words, her threat of death, of all things, but talk of that would involve talk of Maria, Wolfe's deceased wife. So, I simply clear my throat. "My apologies for misleading you there. She said nothing of importance." I go back to eating my meal in silence, and eventually, the others do as well.

But I can feel Wolfe's gaze return to me periodically

throughout the rest of the meal. I keep mine fixed to my plate, no longer able to decipher the juggling act of emotions inside my chest.

twenty-seven

. . .

"THANK YOU, EVIE."

"It's not every day I get to play makeover," she gushes. She spins me around, admiring me from all angles. "This dress hangs just perfectly on your little figure."

"Isn't it in bad taste to wear white to a wedding? Wasn't it you who warned me—"

"It's *cream*, sister. *Big* difference. And besides, look at the weather! The first day of spring? This is the dress for the occasion, I'm sure. The seamstress did an absolutely perfect job taking it in, don't you find? Isn't it stunning? Do you love it?"

"I do," I assure her. "I just don't remember it being so snug at the fitting."

"Well, it was rather loose, then. Now it fits like an absolute glove, as it should."

"You don't think it's inappropriate?"

She laughs gaily. "But only a prude would! All your bits are covered, quite unlike Claudia last night, hmm? And it drapes loosely over your midsection. What does it matter that it resembles a slip? Besides, this silk is heavenly, don't you find? Isn't it soft as butter? Besides, you saw the reaction this number received at the fitting; do you remember? It simply wouldn't have been chosen if it wasn't smashing and flawless in every way. That reminds me, I have the fitting already scheduled for your wedding dress. Are you excited, sister?"

My wedding dress. I swallow. But Evie waits for a response, so I nod politely.

Agnes, I remind myself. Today is all about Agnes. Not my upcoming nuptials, not what happened last night with Claudia, not my meeting tomorrow night with Neo and Timothee.

I consider my hair in the floor-to-ceiling mirror that hogs the wall in Evie's quarters. Straightened meticulously by a hairstylist, it now reaches my elbows. "You don't think the makeup is too much?"

"Do relax, sister. Mary-Kathryn is a world-class artist. It's splendid, absolutely."

I really should relax. Besides, why do I care in the first place? If it's for Wolfe, I shouldn't bother. He's never been impressed when I've made an effort to look presentable in the past.

Or is it for Quire?

Patrick?

"Are things okay between the two of you?" Evie suddenly asks.

"Between your brother and me, you mean?" I clarify, caught off-guard by the question.

"Yes, that. Hold still for a touch of lip gloss."

"Things are fine," I assure her, although even I must admit my tone is flat.

"Sister?"

"It's just...I don't know. Truly, I don't. Sometimes I feel like there's so much left unsaid between the two of us, and yet, I don't know what there is *to* say."

"An impossible conundrum, it sounds like, and yet one

born from true feelings."

"You think?"

"I do," she says firmly. Then she raises an eyebrow and says slyly, "You really did seem a tad jealous last night."

I swat her. "Indignant. Not jealous. And really, can you believe Claudia? I don't know what Wolfe saw in her in the first place."

She hides a smile with her hand, but not without me first noticing it. "And prior to last night, how have things been?"

I sigh. "Not at their best. But better, lately. I think."

"I thought as much, about things not being at their best, I mean. He really has been a crank lately. And you, you elusive birdie, you're hardly ever around!"

I say nothing. For the most part, I've hardly been around because I've been sneaking back and forth to the stables and into town. And no matter the need to spread the truth, the last person I'm going to pull into my dangerous web of secrets is Evie.

"Do you not enjoy palace life, sister?" she presses.

"Aside from you, I haven't exactly been welcomed into the family," I explain. "Not that I'm complaining, mind you. I realize the Rocksavage clan wasn't actively seeking out a girl like me. Wolfe either, for that matter."

"Oh, but he cares so deeply about you—he must! That black eye he gave James, for instance, that was the talk of Carnegie for ages!"

"Evie, that was delivered out of duty, nothing more."

"Nonsense, sister. James played such games with his previous wife, and Claudia, for that matter. Oh, sure, not to the same extent that he does with you, but he really loves to get under brother's skin, that's the truth. Anyhoo, it never roused brother in the least. There's something about you, I suppose, that he really cares for."

"Let's agree to disagree, shall we?"

A sharp rap on the door interrupts us. "Monsieur Sawyer

is waiting," Wolfe calls in his leaden voice from the other side.

"One second!" Evie replies lightly. Then she turns to me and draws up my hands in her own. "I heard all about the nasty business in Devonshire leading up to the shiner. Are you upset over that?" she whispers. "I imagine if I was whipped by my fiancé's uncle and kissed by his cousin, I'd be none too happy either. But really, sister, really you must give my brother another chance. I caught him recently in the midst of his work duties staring at his shoes, looking so glum I just wanted to throw my arms around him. He cares for you; I stand behind it."

I'm about to say, *don't*, but Wolfe raps again, impatient as ever.

Evie gives me one last imploring look, then throws open the door. "Brother! Don't you look dashing dressed up in black. Why, between the beautiful spring weather and your outfit, it could be the two of you exchanging vows, don't you agree?"

He mumbles something indecipherable and checks his watch.

"And your darling fiancée?" she implores.

It's only then that he glances past his sister and sees me. He looks startled by my appearance—I see the way surprise clouds his normally astute gaze. For a moment it lingers along my dress, but quick as lightning, his temper ignites. "So, you deigned to dress her up as a harlot?"

I freeze, hovering somewhere between mortified, embarrassed, and put out.

"*Brother.* You know as well as I do that this dress is nothing next to what we see traipsing around here all day and night. You owe sister an apology, a big one."

"And what of the hair? And the makeup?"

"She looks stunning, and I know you think so. You're being rude beyond compare."

"Let's just get this over with," he barks over his shoulder as he turns on his heel. "Monsieur Sawyer awaits in Devonshire."

"I told you so," I mutter to Evie as we head for the door.

She smacks her hands together in an epiphany. "Now *he's* the jealous one, isn't it obvious? He doesn't want you turning heads, not when your own isn't exactly turning for him!"

"I don't want to look like a harlot, Evie!"

"You don't, sister. I promise. He really has been irritable lately, hasn't he? Don't take it seriously. And for the record, I think you'll steal the show today at the park. Do try to enjoy yourself, you deserve a bit of fun."

"Thank you, but—"

"And as for you and my big brother, well...you deserve a proper date! Perhaps you'll find him much less cantankerous outside of palace walls."

I think of our disastrous journey to neighboring Myopia and very much doubt that.

Then Evie is waving goodbye, turning for her parents' quarters at the end of the House of Mirrors, leaving me to walk alone, following in the viscount's footsteps. A strange series of emotions overwhelm me, but the one that's the loudest, that lingers the longest—of all things—is nervousness.

What, though, am I nervous for? And who?

I think next of Aubrey. I still haven't spotted her since our exchange in the greenhouse. Then there's my meeting tomorrow night with Timothee and Neo—a high-risk meeting with even riskier plans to hammer down. Plus, there's the matter of Jill. Neo, for one, won't be happy that she's not in attendance. I have to admit that I'm disappointed, as well.

And then I enter the rotunda, I hear the echo of small thuds, and all thoughts of nerves and meetings fly out the window. An overwhelming sense of fear takes its place, and then an aria erupts into the cool palace air, a gust of wind ruffles my hair, and a moment later, King stands next to me.

He whistles. "A fine representative of the family," he says, tipping his head and surveying me. But there's a gleam in his eye I don't care for. A hardness, perhaps, like he's reminding me of my job to do just that. Or, a far worse possibility, like he suspects something is afoot.

No, I can't go down that road. Because no matter my feelings or my suspicions, if I don't play the game, my time's up.

So I smile widely and drop into a curtsy. "It's my honor."

"And as for your first official outing with my nephew?"

"An exciting day, indeed. And a fitting prelude, I'd say, before our own vows."

"Spring always is a busy time at Strath Glen," he says cryptically. "Pray tell, where is your dashing date?"

I cast my gaze down the stairs and see Wolfe standing there, watching us closely.

"Ah, yes," says King, turning to him. "Not often you take time off work, is it, my boy?"

"Indeed," he replies coolly.

I lift my brow, surprised at the tone Wolfe had used. King, however, seems unbothered. "Ta," he says a second later. "I'm off to the loo."

"Ta, King," I call, noting that Wolfe remains silent. Just as I start down the stairs toward him, he turns on his heel and continues his march toward Devonshire.

He doesn't make it all the way when he's cut off by James, and I pause on the stairs as I watch them, silent.

"Cousin, don't you look dressed up something special," James exclaims. Then something shifts across his face, and he squeals. "It's the date, isn't it!"

Wolfe is silent.

"A word to the wise, dear cousin...the first date typically

ends with a kiss, and I can speak from experience when I say that the little lady has the most pillowy lips I've ever deigned—"

"You, are you coming?" Wolfe barks at me, ignoring James completely.

I continue down the stairs, and I can practically feel James's glee as he notices me.

"Heavens," he exclaims. "You'd give any woman around here a run for her money." He shakes his head as though he really can't believe his eyes, then turns back to Wolfe. "Too bad she can't stand the sight of you, my beloved old cousin. Did you know that she queried Dear Matthew on how he managed to live separate and apart from his wife for so long?"

It catches Wolfe off-guard, that news, and I have the sudden urge to smack James. I realize, too, that even if James does succeed in taking over the throne from his father, Airo-Aurora won't be in better hands. In fact, the whole point of life, as far as James is concerned, is relishing in the misfortune of others. He may not match his father's evilness, but he surpasses him in his pursuit of trivial games of maliciousness.

"Keep your nose out of my affairs," Wolfe warns James in an icy tone, then he carries on toward Devonshire, his pace once again brisk. But he adds over his shoulder before he rounds the corner, "Or that other eye of yours will be blackened next."

James winks at me before locking himself in the parlor. With him gone, however, I hear something upstairs. A commotion. A high-pitched voice. That and shouting.

I almost turn around, worried it might involve Evie, but the shouting, the screaming—it's muffled and distant—it must be taking place on the third floor. And then it, too, is silenced. Way up on high comes the pitter-patter of high-heels, down, down—

Aubrey comes careening down the steps, her eyes wild and frenzied.

Instead of feeling alarmed, however, I let out a long breath. This, after all, is not a woman with a recently implanted override chip in her brain. Certainly I've never seen Queen move so quickly or with so much emotion.

When she reaches the ground floor, she hurls herself into my arms and screams, "THEY'VE DONE SOMETHING TO MY BUTCH!"

"What is going on?" Wolfe demands as he re-emerges from Devonshire.

"Such a racket!" James exclaims as he pulls open the parlor door. "Some of us are trying to get some work done," he adds, holding a box of candy.

"My Butch," Aubrey reiterates, her eyes swimming with tears. "They took him, and now he's back, and he's different! He's so different!" and she collapses onto my shoulder in hysterics.

I glance uneasily at Wolfe and can see that he understands. I wonder, though, why Butch was the target of the override chip instead of her. Perhaps Lebwitski refused to perform the procedure on a pregnant woman. Perhaps Butch volunteered himself in order to protect her.

"Is it dear sister's special time of the month?" James asks.

"Go play cards," Wolfe says dismissively, waving his hand in the direction of the parlor.

James looks indignant, but only for a moment. He retreats into the room, munching on gummies.

I pat Aubrey on the back, trying to console her the best that I can, and eventually, her breathing slows, her tears dry.

Then her head snaps up and her eyes beat into mine. "You knew this would happen, didn't you?"

I sense the way Wolfe's long body stills next to mine. Panic erupts in my belly. "No," I lie. "I didn't."

"Yes, you did. You told us to leave the palace yesterday, don't you remember?"

"Uh, well, I was just making small talk—"

"I thought you were merely fondling over me, like usual, but you really knew this was about to happen—"

"I didn't, Aubrey," I insist, sensing the precarious position I'll be in if she spreads this around. "You're misremembering the entire thing."

"I am?"

I nod.

"But I've barely been drinking since finding out I'm with child. How could I possibly be so forgetful? So wrong?"

"You've got a lot on your mind," I say in a soft voice. "You're growing a baby. Plus, you've been so wrapped up with Dear Matthew's return and things with Butch—"

"Oh, Butch!" and she starts crying all over again.

Wolfe vanishes upstairs and returns a few minutes later, in a stroke of genius, with a confused-looking Evie.

"You haven't left yet, sister? Whatever is wrong with dear cousin?"

"Sorry to bother you—"

"Oh, I'm not bothered in the slightest. Makeup studies are scheduled all day, isn't that boorish and unfair? Apparently, I missed far too much between your dress fitting and our dazzling trip to the farm, my!"

"Er, yes, well, do you mind helping console Aubrey? She believes her lover is unwell."

Evie graciously fills my place, rubbing Aubrey's back and hushing her softly. A minute later, Evie leads her upstairs and toward her quarters, talking of the healing powers of a nap.

Wolfe and I look at each other. "Do you see what a dangerous position you've put yourself in by warning them?" he asks in an undertone.

"I couldn't *not*," I insist. Then I add with a hint of attitude, "It's called having a conscience."

"It's called being reckless and, quite frankly, dense," he fires back. Then he taps his watch impatiently and disappears into Devonshire.

I hang back a moment to collect myself. Even Wolfe's tongue can't distract me from the surge of sadness I feel for Aubrey, and I cling even harder to the vision of a free Airo-Aurora. I lean into the national address plan developed by me, Timothee, and Neo. So much rides on it—and it's so fraught with risk—it has to work.

It must.

But I can't linger on that—not right now. I have a wedding to attend, so I smooth my dress and force myself to set aside the disturbing exchange with Aubrey. I'll worry about that and the long list of problems associated with it when I return to Strath Glen.

twenty-eight

. . .

MONSIEUR SAWYER WHISTLES AS SOON as I enter Devonshire, and, despite the knot inside my chest that still refuses to loosen, I grin. When he whistles a second time, I knock him across the shoulder with familiarity.

"Alas, might that Quire blood of yours be running with a hint of purple?"

I place my hand lightly on his shoulder. "Monsieur, I'm surprised! Surely by now, you realize that you can take the girl out of Quire, but you can't take Quire out of the girl."

"And yet you look every part the princess."

"Unfortunately, the Rocksavage clan wouldn't approve of me wearing menswear to a wedding."

"A crying shame, that. I think I'd pay a pretty penny to see you dressed in the getup that brought you here."

I laugh. "I really must peruse my closet for my uncle's double-breasted number—"

Wolfe clears his throat. "When you two are finished with your horseplay, let's get on with it. I have a pile of work awaiting my return." With that, he strides through the door toward the underground garage, leaving Monsieur to traipse after him shouting apologies, and with me drawing up the rear, wondering how I'm expected to get through an entire afternoon with Wolfe, particularly when he's in such a cantankerous mood.

"Oh, the chickens!" I shout to Monsieur. "We can't forget their wedding gift—"

"I hardly think we can arrive at such an event with a cast of filthy farm animals at our side," Wolfe objects.

"But Evie—"

"Monsieur Sawyer will arrange to have a proper coop delivered to their residence this afternoon, along with the chickens themselves."

Having no reason to object to the plan, I slide into the behemoth and say in a low voice, "Chickens aren't filthy."

Wolfe glances at me out of the corner of his eye.

"Shall I pick up the palace's coop at the same time, sir?" Monsieur asks from the front seat.

"We're getting chickens?" I half-shout.

"That will be fine, Monsieur."

I turn to Wolfe and reiterate, "We're getting chickens?"

He merely turns to the window, but Monsieur grins at me through the rear-view mirror as he starts up the engine. "Will you have time to tend to them between your lengthy shifts in the library?"

"Indeed, I will," I reply, smiling.

Then we're gliding out of the palace, the garage door closing seamlessly behind us, into the elements. Typically, it's wind, rain, or snow that greets us, but today it's a shining sun and a light breeze that does nothing but ruffle the uppermost leaves of the apple grove that separates the grounds of Strath Glen with the Mainframe. Monsieur and I chat amiably about the turn in the weather while Wolfe continues to say nothing, his silence unebbing.

It's hard to tell if he's angry about the revelation from James, the debacle with Aubrey, or if it's his normal surly temperament. Or maybe it's because I'm dressed like a harlot. I turn to my own window.

Finally, though, unable to take the heavy silence any longer, I angle myself toward him. "I'm sorry for what James said," I say quietly.

He glances at me coolly. "It's not exactly news," he mutters. "Quizzing Matthew, however, seems ill-guided."

"It was," I admit. "But it was shortly after the fiasco at the Sky Center, so an understandable misstep, perhaps."

He goes back to staring out the window, and a minute later, I do the same.

"Your beloved district," announces Monsieur, as the behemoth's nose arcs away from Central Boulevard, through a small suburb, and into the outskirts of Quire.

"I imagine the florist is busy with today's event," I remark, my nose pressed to the window as we drive by, and all of a sudden and out of the blue, my heart squeezes with profound sadness. It isn't the kindness of the woman who'd give away bouquets by the bundle rather than see them wilt, the beauty of her arrangements, or even the fact that I no longer reside in this comfortable district I so love. It's the countless times I walked this block with my hand tucked inside my mother's, the bell over the door ringing as we entered the shop, the smell of the flowers as we'd pick out our favorite blooms.

It's the intense longing for my mother's presence by my side, especially at this dire time in my life, navigating marriage and revolution. Chickens and change.

When I finally turn away, when the florist's storefront is finally out of sight, I notice Wolfe watching me out of the corner of his eye. I turn to him, but immediately he goes back to staring out the window, and I'm reminded of the vast gulf of space between us, littered with questions and things unsaid.

We drive past the butcher, next, then the old-fashioned

grocer. The memories keep coming, poignant and heart-wrenching ones, so I'm grateful when Monsieur interrupts my thoughts by asking, "What time shall I be picking the two of you up?"

"I'll call," Wolfe replies evenly.

"I assume there will be a dinner served at this, ahem, wedding?"

I roll my eyes. "Yes, Monsieur. Dinner will be provided, and surely a tasty one at that. The district of Quire knows its way around a plate, I can assure you."

The chauffeur smirks. "And the palace food you're served on the regular isn't up to snuff, is that correct, Miss Alex?"

"On the contrary. And yet the home cooking I've come to associate with—"

"The two of you are giving me a headache," Wolfe snaps, swiping a finger across his mouth. He casts a long look at Monsieur Sawyer.

"My deepest apologies, Viscount, sir," Monsieur replies promptly.

Wolfe really is irritable, even for him, and I'm relieved when we pull up to Quire Park a few minutes later.

"Our destination," announces Monsieur with a flourish. He pulls the door open for us, and a minute later, after a quick goodbye, Wolfe and I stand alone in the sunshine.

What I notice first is how out of place he looks. His impossibly tall, aristocratic frame doesn't fit with the cracked sidewalk, the chain-link fence. Even the small houses that line the street are so wonderfully ordinary, so warm and inviting, that it contradicts everything about him. Then, in the midst of me studying him, he turns to me and exhales. "You are friendlier to the chauffeur than you are to me."

Caught off-guard by the remark, my gaze beats into his. "Why should you care?"

"You are to be my wife," he reminds me.

"He's kind," I explain after a moment's hesitation. "And he didn't push me into the hands of a mad doctor, nor did he abandon me at a bus stop."

"I've explained away my actions regarding the first of your complaints, and I've apologized for the second," he intones. "What more can I do?"

"I don't know," I admit. "But probably calling me a harlot isn't order number one."

He eyes me. "You know what the problem is," he grumbles as we start toward the park's entrance.

For a moment, I'm too distracted by the garlands of white pom-poms I spot through the trees to respond. The same goes for the balloons of the same color clustered around picnic tables and the high-top tents. All of Quire looks to be in attendance, I notice once we round the corner. People, young and old, spread through the park, chatting happily and dancing to the music offered by a small band. Children play ring toss and race one another in sacks, and I feel like I've finally come home.

I turn to Wolfe after a while. "Really, I don't," I say. "I don't know what your problem is or why you'd deign to call me a harlot."

He circles away from the festivities and fixes me with a piercing stare. "Polished and prim, just like the rest of them. Don't let Evie or my mother change you."

For a moment, the festivities over my shoulder fade away, and I focus only on my fiancé. *Don't let Evie or my mother change you.* That's what he had said. *That*, of all things... So what does it imply? That I'm well and good, just the way I am? That his ideal mate *isn't* polished and prim like the rest of the royals and their gang?

I clear my throat. "It was made clear to me that I'm representing the royal family and was expected to—"

"I know all that," he says dismissively, waving his hand.

"But God knows it isn't me you're trying to impress looking like that. Trying to show all the neighborhood boys what they missed out on, are you? They already know, Alexandra, rest assured."

My breath hitches. But, before I can parse out what he meant by that, or if I even heard him correctly, he adds, "I told you about the paperwork waiting for me, didn't I?" Once again, he starts forward toward the party.

I follow after him, my head spinning.

Inside the park, Miller is the first to catch my eye, and he smiles broadly. "Aggy's meeting with the officiant," he explains by way of introduction, gesturing to a pergola woven with a vine of white roses. "Is this here your fiancé?"

After trying unsuccessfully to spot Agnes through the roses, I turn to Miller and nod.

"It's a pleasure, Lord Viscount," Miller says, shaking Wolfe's hand and staring at him as though awe-struck. "Can't say I expected a senior member of the Rocksavage clan to grace my wedding, that's for sure."

Wolfe looks downright uncomfortable with the praise, and I grin. But a sharp shriek emanates from behind me, and when I turn, I spot Aunt Jo in a skirt suit bearing down on me. A second later, she crushes me into an almighty hug.

"You're going to break my neck with a greeting like that," I say as I extricate myself and kiss her cheek.

"Didn't think you'd crush like a petal, did I? What's this you're wearing?" She fingers the satin bow that fastens the fur bolero in place. "A tad fancier than your uncle's stained old overcoat, wouldn't you say?"

"Funny you should mention it, I was discussing that very coat earlier, with the chauffeur. I miss that number."

"The chauffeur? My."

I swat her. "If you must know about my outfit, my soon-to-be sister-in-law readied me, and she's far more fashionable than I am."

"Oh, and you expect me to believe you just blindly go along with things that don't suit you? Is that what you're selling?"

Somewhere overhead, Wolfe stifles a short laugh.

Both of us turn to him, and immediately, he returns to his morose self. He extends a hand. "You must be Alexandra's aunt."

Aunt Jo lifts an eyebrow at me, then returns her attention to the viscount. She bows her head and shakes his hand. "Call me Jo. And what shall I call you? You *are* the fiancé, aren't you?"

"I am, yes." His voice is stiff, even by his standards. I can tell he's even more uncomfortable now than when Miller was fawning over him.

"He's referred to as Viscount, Aunt Jo," I explain.

"Viscount." She whistles. "And tell me, Viscount, why I have yet to receive my invitation?"

He coughs lightly into his fist. "Invitation?"

"Don't tell me I'm being snubbed!"

"I believe my aunt is speaking in reference to the wedding," I explain to Wolfe before turning to her. "And who would walk me down the aisle if not you?"

She draws in a breath and fans herself. "But I'd be honored, Alex. I just assumed your groom's father would do it."

"That man hasn't said a single word to me so long as I've known him, not that I've made much of an effort, either. Anyhow, if it isn't you walking me down the aisle, Aunt, it's no one."

She beams.

"My father's disinterest in life is unparalleled. It would be a waste of your energy to take it personally," Wolfe advises me.

Frankly, I'm surprised he bothered to say anything, and I bow my head.

"And you, Viscount," Aunt Jo says, "I don't know you from a hole in the wall. What is it you even do, way up there in that castle of yours?"

"I tend to Airo-Aurora's economic concerns, particularly on an international scale, madam."

"That sounds awfully important."

He nods, curt as ever.

"You promoted my niece to a pilot, that's one thing I do know."

"And now she's carving out a role for herself as Strath Glen's librarian. Her desire to make herself useful is laudable."

"She has hardworking genes in her blood, my boy."

"So I've noticed. I'm given to understand she resided with you for several years. Is that correct?"

"Ever since her parents were killed in that god-awful crash, may they rest in peace. Thought she'd die of heartbreak, but she's tougher than she looks."

His eyes flash momentarily onto mine. "So I've noticed." Then he draws himself taller, "Is your home within walking distance?"

Aunt Jo and I exchange a curious look. "Just around the corner," she confirms.

"What time is the ceremony?" he asks next, checking his watch. All business, but with an agenda, too.

"In an hour. A feast and dance will follow at sundown," I explain.

"Then we have time for a quick tour." He turns and begins to stride toward the park's exit without waiting for confirmation.

Aunt Jo and I exchange another look, then hurry after him.

"It's no palace," warns Aunt Jo once our mismatched group turns onto the sidewalk.

"Of course it isn't," he says simply, crossing the street where my aunt indicates.

I let a car go past before scrambling after them, trying to decipher why he wants to see her house in the first place. I'm distracted from all that, however, as soon as we turn onto that familiar block. Daffodils now poke their way through the gardens that wrap around the little houses, some with windows thrown open wide to let in the fresh spring air. Just as always, the seasons have changed on a dime.

The familiarity is soothing, there's no doubting that. And yet the memories aren't all fond ones. I remember the sadness, too. The rawness of the grief I felt when this street became my home, and for a second I'm motionless, those old feelings washing over me, and it's all I can do not to throw off my heels and sprint to the Mainframe this very second to spend time with my parents' memories.

I'm quickly preoccupied with something else, though, when I spot a poster plastered to a lamppost. It's the same one plastered about Strath Glen, declaring the White Ribbon Campaign to be a terrorist organization and outlawing all involvement with it. That isn't what captures my attention, though.

It's the red paint splattered across it, along with the word LIES, twice underlined, and I feel my brow lift as I study it. A second later, I smile. Perhaps, then, fear is no longer enough to control the citizens of Airo-Aurora.

"You coming?" Aunt Jo shouts to me from up ahead. Wolfe pauses, too, considering me with that distant yet somehow piercing gaze of his.

I hurry to catch up with them, and as we turn up Aunt Jo's drive, I take a moment to consider the house next door. Mary Beth's house, and I look for signs of her son between the curtains or around the property. Nothing today—probably old Mary Beth's at Quire Park, now that I think about it. And perhaps her son has returned to his wife, the chip implanted in his brain precluding any more friction at home. Yes, that would make sense, and the thought makes me shiver, especially since my relationship with Wolfe is nothing *but* friction.

And yet watching the backside of the towering aristocrat scale Aunt Jo's front steps unexpectedly makes me laugh, and I hurry after them, stumbling over the threshold as Wolfe holds open the door.

"It's the shoes," I explain apologetically. "I'm not used to high heels."

"At least you don't appear so minuscule," he offers as he shuts the door behind me.

The house looks just as I remember it, with my aunt's knitting materials spread across the rocking chair and a blanket left where it was used along the chesterfield. The smell is the most familiar. An intoxicating aroma of thyme and garlic lingers in the air.

"Chicken pie?"

Aunt Jo tips her head.

"Don't you intend to stay for dinner at the wedding? I believe a food truck will be attending for the occasion."

"One can never have too many pies on hand. Besides, here's me always hoping you'll stop in for another visit."

The sentiment touches me deeply. "I'm sorry, Aunt. You know my movements are restricted."

She turns to Wolfe, who takes a sudden interest in a picture of daffodils hanging on the wall. She clears her throat, staring pointedly at him.

He links his long arms behind his back and sighs. "I hold little sway over my uncle, who ordered your niece's movements be restricted in the first place. It is my hope, madam, that things will improve for her in time. I'd ask that you withhold judgment of me and my character until I have time to prove myself as an adequate spouse. Now, show me around your home, please."

My aunt's eyes widen at this soliloquy, and mine do too. Things will improve for me in time? Wolfe wishes to prove himself an adequate spouse? The latter is certainly news to me. Or perhaps my aunt's surprise comes from Wolfe's signature brusqueness, as she quickly proceeds to give him a guided tour of the house, leaving me to follow behind.

"Your clothes still hang in the closet," he observes as we congregate in the guest room.

"I'm not permitted to wear them at the palace," I remind him.

He nods, his expression stern. Then he asks, "Do we have time to walk by your childhood home?"

I freeze at the question. "My parents' house?"

"Yes, that."

"Why do you wish to see it?"

He brushes his sleeve of dust, though none sits there. "You've suffered many barbs since arriving at mine concerning Quire. I'd like to see more of it."

"Then see more of it you shall," booms Aunt Jo, looking pleased.

Once again, I find myself trailing after Wolfe and Aunt Jo, more puzzled by the second. Wolfe just might be the least likable person I've ever met, and yet it has taken him almost no time to ingratiate himself with my aunt. Already he's more popular with her than I am with his parents, and I've been sharing a home with them for months. The thought is admittedly deflating. For if all that is true, who truly is the unlikable one?

"I think I'll wait here," I call to them from the street corner. They both hesitate, but I motion for them to continue their walk, and I take the time to lean on a stop sign and breathe. No, walking along the same sidewalk I walked with my parents isn't something I'm ready to do. Neither is seeing the house full of happy memories up close and personal. Besides, I see it enough when I visit the memory bank, and for a while, I'm lost in thought, surrounded by familiar faces, cozy interiors, and the feeling of contentedness and safety firmly in my heart.

A car blasts its horn, and I come back to reality. Soon. I'll go soon, I promise myself. Go to the memory bank, delve deeper into all those old feelings. It used to be a near-daily ritual, but since moving into Strath Glen several months ago, I've only been once, and I wonder if that's why today's return to Quire is as painful as it is. It must be.

"Please accept my apologies," a voice says into my ear.

I startle, but then I see that it's Wolfe, he and my aunt finished with their walkabout.

"I didn't think the request would be so trying for you," he continues. "That was insensitive."

I do a double take at his politeness, his consideration. Then I stand straighter. "We should hurry. We don't want to miss the ceremony."

He nods, and our perplexing little group retraces its steps back to Quire Park.

twenty-nine

. . .

WE RETURN in the nick of time. Everyone has taken their seats in foldout chairs placed out for the occasion. We take the last of the empty seats in the back row just as the bridal chorus begins, and Aunt Jo squeezes my hand as Agnes draws up behind the crowd with her arm strung through her father's. Her short black curls are teased to perfection, fanning out around her head like a halo, and her cheeks are perfectly rouged. Her purple gown skims the grass poetically.

Even though I'm not usually one to be taken by such things, I find myself blinking back tears as I catch my best friend's eye. Then, with one last smile, she sweeps past, and I notice that Wolfe appears to study me out of the corner of his eye. I smile somewhat shyly, not knowing what on earth Wolfe could be thinking as he contemplates me.

A moment later, Agnes and Miller exchange their vows under the guidance of the officiant, and I'm reminded of my own fast-approaching nuptials with the man seated beside me.

There's something almost tactile between Wolfe and me as we watch the bride and groom slip rings onto each other's fingers and seal it all with a kiss. I wonder if he, too, is picturing us standing where Miller and Agnes stand, before a crowd of people and framed in flowers, declaring ourselves to each other, forever and for always.

It's a lot to digest for two people who can barely stand one another. And then...what of the kiss? My palms turn tacky just thinking about it.

"Aren't weddings romantic?" Aunt Jo thinks to gush at that moment.

Wolfe and I nod in a forced, uneasy way. He swipes a finger across his mouth. I bite my lip.

Then everyone is standing and cheering, and the awkwardness between us is broken by the celebratory atmosphere that engulfs us all. Confetti is thrown in the air, the band begins to play lively music, and as the newlyweds have their picture taken, the rest of us move deeper into the park, mingling under the late afternoon sun. Agnes's family arranges coolers on tables under the high top, surrounding them with tubs of ice and plastic cups. A food truck pulls up.

Old Mary Beth, it turns out, is in attendance, and after we say hello, and as Aunt Jo begins discussing tomato plant pests with her, I tug on Wolfe's sleeve. "Shall we get a drink?"

He nods, but we don't make it two steps before there's a flash of purple and Agnes has me in a hug.

"I've never seen you look so posh!" she shouts.

"Oh, who cares about all that," I insist. "Look at you! A truly breathtaking bride, and staying true to your colors, I see," I add, motioning to her dress.

"Who says traditional is best anyhow, am I right?" she asks as she catches sight of Wolfe. He greets her with a bow of his head, and she reciprocates, then elbows me. "Don't think I'm not having some serious one on one time with you tonight, girl. In the meantime, get a drink in your hand. Him, too," she adds, tilting her head at Wolfe and winking.

"We're on our way," I assure her as Aunt Jo nabs Agnes.

The coolers, I discover, are full of an assortment of canned cocktails, beer, and wine. I turn to Wolfe, then turn away.

"Is there a problem?" he asks.

"No," I admit. "It's just a little different than what you're used to, that's all. You know, without butlers serving the beverages and all."

"I don't think I've ever objected to your Quire roots, have I?"

"No," I say, surprised, and I realize I've never stopped to think about it before now.

"Do you really take me for the rest?" he continues. "Do I require a silver spoon to feed myself?"

"Well, I suppose—"

"Please. Despite what you may think, I am not passing cruel judgment as I move about Quire or this wedding. Sometimes I wonder if it's not you who holds the prejudice." With that, he reaches into the cooler, grabs a can labeled whisky sour, and pulls the tab. I choose a sangria, feeling slightly more at ease than a second ago.

Next, I chat with Agnes's parents and, with no other option, introduce them to Wolfe. Describing him as my fiancé still feels foreign on my tongue, and it's still strange to see him interact with people that aren't aristocracy or the people who rub shoulders with the aristocracy. But...I don't loathe having him by my side.

Somehow, he has become familiar to me, and without the oppressive air instilled by King, without the savage barbs of the Rocksavage clan circling me, things between the two of us feel more relaxed, more comfortable than I would've predicted.

Or, maybe it's the crowd.

Because dressed as I am, with the viscount of Airo-Aurora by my side, the Quire crowd looks at me differently, I'm sure of it. It's the way they give me a wide berth, the way they stare my way yet avoid my gaze, as if they think I carry an air of superiority, that I look down my nose at them, when that couldn't be further from the truth.

It almost makes me feel badly for assuming the same of Wolfe.

"Hi Alex," comes a voice over my shoulder.

I turn to a girl I used to school with. Tawny, her name is, and I say hello.

She swishes her hand, casting aside my greeting. "So, I suppose the rumors are true? You, royalty?"

It's then that I catch the glimpse in her eye, an unfriendly one, and it catches me off-guard. "Y...yes," I stammer. "I mean, once the wedding—"

"You don't seem particularly suited to be royalty, no offense."

"Yes, well—"

She leans toward me. "You gamed the system, didn't you."

"What? No—"

"That's what everyone's been saying. That you used your parents' death to trick the Mainframe into—"

"It's unwise to speak of things you know nothing about," interjects Wolfe coldly.

Tawny gazes at him and—not surprisingly, given the shrewdness of his gaze—falters. A moment later, she rejoins her friends, telling them about what just transpired.

"Are you all right, Alex?" Wolfe asks.

I nod. "It seems that not only does my Quire heritage ostracize me from the aristocracy, but my placement in the aristocracy ostracizes me from Quire." It's a depressing thought, especially what I've been accused of. Gaming the system? Using my parents' *deaths* to do so? It makes me sick just thinking about it, but that's not all. There's anger I feel, too.

"You can't please everyone," advises Wolfe as he watches me. "It's senseless to try, not to mention a waste of your energy. People with exceedingly poor character should simply be avoided."

"Poor character, indeed," I mutter in agreement. "Still, it would be nice to have a community to be part of."

"There are plenty of people within Quire and Strath Glen who think fondly of you. Decent ones, at that."

I think of Evie and Monsieur, Agnes and Aunt Jo, and smile. "Your use of the word 'plenty' may be somewhat misguided. Nonetheless, your point stands. Thank you," I add.

He bows his head and, with dusk setting in, we decide to join the queue for the food truck.

"You're moving laboriously," Wolfe notes as we walk in its direction.

"It's the shoes," I explain, wincing. "I think I've developed at minimum a thousand blisters during our walk-around this afternoon."

Wordlessly he extends his arm, and after the briefest of hesitations, I accept.

"I suppose I should've been more sensitive to that possibility when I asked your aunt for a tour."

"Not at all," I insist, watching him closely from the corner of my eye. "Besides, I think she enjoyed it."

"Your aunt was an excellent tour guide, and it isn't often I get to explore Airo-Aurora's neighborhoods," he explains. "And naturally, I wished to see where you grew up," he adds.

I turn quickly to him. "Why?"

"Because you are to be my wife," he says, as though the point is plainly obvious. "Surely your aunt must have been keen to meet me?"

"Oh, yes. I mean...yes." Then I smile and add, "Of course."

"You sound surprised."

"Sometimes I forget...well, nothing."

"No, tell me."

"Well, sometimes I forget that you're actually human, that's all."

For a minute he's silent, then he turns to me. "I'm curious, in your eyes, what makes me less human than the next person?"

"I suppose there really is no reason for me to say that," I admit. After all, my contention that he is heartless isn't completely accurate. He had shown kindness to my aunt, he had stood up for me with Tawny, and besides, before that dreaded moment when he shoved me into Doctor Lebwitski's arms, hadn't he shown how much heart he truly has? Hadn't that emotion in the helicopter been real, raw, and decidedly human?

He stares sternly down at me, then says in an uncharacteristically soft tone, "I asked you to trust me. Do you remember? I asked that you put all your trust in me."

"I remember." Of course I do. It was right before I was pushed into Doctor Lebwitski's arms. Right before, perhaps, he convinced King of my naiveté and saved my life. I angle my body toward him and stare up into his eyes, wondering—

"What can I do you for?"

I blink, realizing that we now stand at the front of the queue.

I clear my throat, remove my arm from Wolfe's so I can step forward, and order myself a cheeseburger and fries. Wolfe orders the same a moment later, and I bite away a smile.

"What's so funny?" he demands, astute as always.

"Nothing. I mean...oh, fine. I was just wondering when

the last time you had a cheeseburger was. Or the last time you had anything from a chip truck, period."

He presses his lips together and sighs. "There was a time several years ago in neighboring Myopia when I found myself famished. I believe, if memory serves me, I ordered something called a poutine from a street vendor."

The mental image of him ordering a poutine on the side of the street makes me laugh.

"Something amusing?"

"I think I would've paid a lot of money to see that, that's all."

"So, how much will you pay me for tonight's cheese-burger then?"

"I don't think you need the money. How about this... If you eat the whole cheeseburger, I'll...cut up your meals for you," I say, picking something at random. "For a whole week."

He extends his hand, and I shake it. "It's a deal," he confirms.

The corner of his mouth twitches, mine does too, and then we're both busying ourselves, staring around the park and decidedly not at each other.

With darkness setting in, I notice the strands of white lights strung around the perimeter of the park and every which way in between. Patio heaters are stationed throughout the lively crowd, offering much-needed heat with the sun now retired for the day, and the band plays songs I recognize as Agnes's favorites—a perfectly fitting wedding for my friend.

As I stare at familiar faces, however—the butcher, for instance, schoolmates, and families from my aunt's street— I'm not sure it's perfectly fitting for me, not any longer, and once again, I think about community. Because even without me being ostracized for becoming 'royal', there are surprisingly few people I feel close to here, not even my peers that I attended school with.

The realization catches me by surprise. After all, I've been adamant since moving into Strath Glen that Quire is my rightful home. That it's full of my people. And yet how true has this ever really been?

Since moving into the palace, I've befriended Evie, Jill, Timothee, even Monsieur. Now that the other servants are finally speaking to me and the other royals no longer care to constantly mock me, they've all become as much my community as Quire has ever been. And Wolfe, where does he fit in?

I eye him cautiously. He eyes me at the same time, and I take a sudden interest in my shoes. He does the same.

When our food is ready, we take it to a picnic table next to one of the heaters.

Agnes and Miller take seats next to us, holding their own wrappers. Agnes, I see, has already changed out of her wedding dress, now donning a flared pair of pants, a crochet tank top, and a jaunty blazer pulled over that.

"Were you guys behind us in line?" I ask.

"Miller's brother was. He picked up our order," Agnes explains as she unwraps her burger and stares lovingly at it. "Man, am I starving. I've been waiting all day for this moment."

I grin. "I'm glad to see married life hasn't changed you." Next, I chance a look at Wolfe. "How is it?"

"I suggest you get your knife and fork ready," he says in a deadpan voice.

"Is this some kind of inside joke?" Agnes demands as she looks between us.

"Something like that," I admit, laughing. Wolfe's mouth bends with a hint of a smile.

Agnes, meanwhile, grins widely. "Interesting, *very* interesting. So. Speaking of love in the air, do I get an invite to your stately affair?"

"We," Miller reminds her.

"Ah, yes. We're officially a *we*. That will take some time to get used to."

"You have been an *I* for eighteen years," I point out. "And if the stately affair you're talking about is the wedding, is it really necessary to ask?"

"Just checking," she says, "seeing as how there's been no invite in the mail. Leaving it to the last minute, aren't you?"

"That's the pot calling the kettle black."

"True, but...there was some disagreement about the invitations," says Agnes pointedly.

"Ah. Well, Evie's working on it, so expect your invite shortly," I say, then avert my gaze from the table. It really is awkward discussing the wedding with Wolfe nearby, and my stomach lurches as I think about the big day. The fast-approaching big day.

"Hard to follow this kick-ass party, though," Agnes says, winking.

"Without question."

"Who are you inviting?"

"Funny you should ask. I was just thinking that I really don't have many people to invite." Wolfe glances at me. "All of Strath Glen will already be in attendance, and I don't have all that many friends back in Quire. You, of course, and my aunt."

"There are tons of people in Quire you could invite."

"Name one."

Agnes stuffs a few fries in her mouth and chews thoughtfully. "Suzy M."

"We haven't spoken since eighth grade. Besides, I don't think being betrothed to royalty has exactly endeared me to anyone." I push away what's left of my dinner and shrug. "I suppose they say you can never go home again."

"Yeah, that. Or, you know…"

"What?"

"Or Strath Glen has become your home. Like, legit. Did you hear yourself a minute ago?" Then in a high-pitched rendition of my voice, she adds, *"All of Strath Glen will already be in attendance."*

"I didn't say it like *that*," I insist.

"Sure, you did. As though *all* your favorites herald from there. You're already a viscountess, admit it!"

I kick my friend under the table. "It'll always be Alex to you."

"What shall I call him?" and she nods Wolfe's way.

"He comes with a long list of formal titles," I reply as I grab another sangria from the cooler. "Viscount will do, although I've heard him referred to as the great Lord Viscount if you're feeling generous."

"I didn't realize you were so funny," Wolfe says chillingly, but even I can see the humor in his eyes.

Miller points his fork at me across the table. "Will you take his surname?" he asks.

"I didn't realize it was optional," I admit.

"This one thinks it is," and his fork shifts so it points at Agnes.

"Hey, I think it's a stupid rule, just like wearing a white wedding dress," she replies, shifting in her seat and causing her blazer to drape open. I catch sight of something on her shirt, soft and white, but she tugs her blazer closed before I can examine it. She says, "I said no to one, and I'll say no to the other."

Miller shakes his head, annoyed, while Wolfe goes out of his way to make eye contact with me. There's a heaviness there, something he's trying to communicate, and suddenly it strikes me. Agnes isn't simply dissatisfied, she's a dissident. A rebel, or at least that's how the Mainframe will see it. And that white thing on her top? A white ribbon—I'd bet my dress on it. She really is a rebel—a supporter of the White Ribbon Campaign and everything—and as much as I emphasize with her, as much as I share her feelings and her vision of a free Airo-Aurora, the danger she's putting herself in is grave.

She needs to know the risk. She needs to know the truth.

Well, Neo had said to spread it, hadn't he? I lick my teeth, trying frantically to sort through my thoughts—the pros and cons, the competing interests—but considering it's the midst of her wedding and Miller's by her side, I opt to say little. "Uh, don't you think it'd be romantic to take his name?" I try.

She looks at me like I have two heads. "Of course not. It's—"

"It's something we're expected to do," I remind her as pointedly as I can. "Just like undergoing the Selection in the first place."

Agnes rolls her eyes, somewhere between annoyed and glum, and I feel bad for not having her back. If only I could tell her this very instant the danger she's placing herself in.

"Speaking of tradition," Miller continues, oblivious to the weighted glances around him, "When are you guys thinking of having kids?"

I spit out a mouthful of sangria at the question. Agnes looks just as uncomfortable. "That isn't... We haven't—"

"It isn't something we've discussed," Wolfe finishes for me in a formal tone. He tidies up our empty food cartons and drops them in the garbage.

"Agnes would be a great mom, don't you think, Alex?" Miller asks.

"Why do you say that?" Agnes demands.

"Think of all the practice you get at the Quire nursery!"

"Yeah, except I *hate* working there."

"You won't hate it when it's your own kid."

"How do you know?"

Miller rolls his eyes. "I just do. Everyone knows it's different when you have your own—"

"Shall we walk?" I say quickly, standing and motioning to Agnes.

"Excellent idea," she responds. She grabs my arm and pulls me away from the others. "Thanks," she mutters in my ear.

"No problem," I say, even though in truth, interrupting the uncomfortable conversation wasn't completely for her sake—it wasn't even for mine. I think of the nursery frozen in time and know how much Wolfe wouldn't want to discuss it. Maybe he never will.

Then I grab Agnes by the arm and pull her close, making my decision in that very moment. "Hide that ribbon from now on," I say into her ear. She tries to respond, but I shake my head and hold her close. "Tomorrow night, at 11:30, meet me at Battery Park. Don't tell anyone where you're going or what you're doing. Don't look at me or the others that will be there. Keep your head down, and don't raise your voice above a whisper."

She draws back and stares at me, clearly trying to gauge how serious I am. Then she leans toward me. "Does the meeting have anything to do with the White Ribbon Campaign?"

"In a way."

"So why all the secrecy?"

"The Mainframe is always watching," I say patiently.

"True, but it doesn't exactly have any recourse—"

"It does," I correct her, frowning deeply and understanding why people have been wearing the ribbons openly. They don't know of the danger, the consequences. "Trust me, Agnes, you must be discrete."

"It's just a ribbon."

"It's *not* just a ribbon. Didn't you see those posters declaring the Campaign to be a terrorist organization?"

"Total bullshit. It's not going to stop me."

"But—"

"I can't pull the plug on the whole thing...not when so many people are—"

"What are you two girls whispering about?" shouts Miller from behind us.

"Girl stuff," Agnes replies without bothering to turn to him. Then she looks meaningfully at me. "Tomorrow night then."

"Tomorrow night."

For a while, we walk in silence, and I know she's taking a moment to digest everything I said. Hopefully, she takes it to heart, too. Finally, she nudges me playfully, more like her normal self. "Seems like you and the fiancé are enjoying yourselves?"

"We are," I admit. "It really is a great wedding, too bad you're not a professional party planner. You and Evie could start up your own business together."

"I'd sign up for that," she says, grinning. "So, is it weird being back in Quire?"

"Kind of," I admit. "A lot of people have been staring. Hey, speaking of weird, how's that mysterious secret project of yours, anyway?"

"Oh, that? It's going okay. It's been a bit of a roller-coaster, and it's a huge time suck—especially with some, er, recent challenges—but overall people have been really receptive to it."

"Wait, so you've told others about it, but not me?"

She laughs. "It's a long story. I'll fill you in tomorrow night, I promise."

"I look forward to hearing all about it," I say, thinking it'll be a late night for me and Monsieur—if he's even available, I realize. Speaking to him about it is something else for my growing to-do list. Then, checking over my shoulder to make sure Wolfe is occupied, I add, "I thought Patrick and his fiancée would be here."

At that very moment, a hand grips my shoulder, it pulls me into a tight hug. I smell gum and beer.

"Patrick!" I shout, grinning. "I was just talking about you, I assumed you weren't here."

"Annie's in bed with a cold. She's sleeping now, so I thought I'd slip out," he explains. He holds me by the shoulders and takes a step back, whistling. "I've known you for as long as I can remember, Alex, and this is the first time I've ever seen you dolled up, let alone *this*," and he laughs. "It's a good thing, too, or all of Quire would be queuing up."

"I believe I should be the only one concerned on that front," interrupts Wolfe, who, as always, is paying very close attention.

Patrick's arms drop from my shoulders at the sound of the viscount's icy voice, but he doesn't shy away. "Are you, though?" He speaks in his easy, good-natured way, and yet he has the viscount's full attention.

Wolfe bristles at the question, but he doesn't dismiss Patrick, no matter his station. Instead, he runs a hand over his mouth and waits for more.

"It looks as though she hasn't had a square meal in months."

"It isn't my job to force-feed her."

"No, but if she were my fiancée, I'd be making sure she was taking care of herself." He glances at me. "I'd make sure she's happy, too."

"And yet she's not your fiancée," Wolfe points out in a restrained tone.

"That's true," Patrick admits. He turns to me. "Is this gown a gift from him? I'm surprised you're not wearing any jewels, not that they were ever your style. Has he been spoiling you?"

"Why should I gift her with things she hates," Wolfe interrupts, seething.

"Again, if she were my fiancée—"

"Again. She's not."

An uncomfortable silence falls on our group.

"It's getting late," I say, eventually. I eye Wolfe, and a series of emotions and feelings thunder through my chest, none of which I can begin to decipher. "Maybe we should go wait for Monsieur."

He considers me, then nods once. After rushed goodbyes mired by awkwardness, the two of us walk toward the park's exit in silence, then along the sidewalks glowing with light from tidy streetlamps. The little circular houses on the other side of the street, with their orange windows and plumes of smoke coming from the chimneys, make me feel like we're in another world. A world separate and apart from Strath Glen.

After Wolfe phones Monsieur and the music from the park grows dim with distance, we are truly alone. My stomach flips with nerves I don't really understand.

"So," says Wolfe, breaking the silence with a crisp tone. "He's the reason why." He pauses on the sidewalk and stares at me with those disinterested eyes.

"I'm sorry?"

"That boy. Patrick. He's the reason you wish our marriage to remain purely contractual. He's the reason why you suggested I take up things again with Claudia."

"No," I reply, surprised. "And I only suggested that in anger—"

"Is it jewels you wish?"

My surprise grows. "It isn't."

"Do you wish to hear how beautiful you look in that dress?"

"Pardon?"

"The dress. Surely you already know how devastatingly

beautiful you look, but perhaps you'd like me to make a scene about it, as he just did."

This time all I can do by reply is shake my head.

"So what, then? What is it you're looking for? Why *him*?"

"It isn't...I'm afraid I don't understand where you're going with all this, Wolfe."

"You favor him, deny it as you might."

Once again, I shake my head—firmly this time. "He's a reminder of my former life, and because of that, he is special to me. But I don't have feelings for him." I know this now without question.

"Then the problem is simply me, so to speak."

I walk right up to him, still nervous, yes, but suddenly determined to say my piece. I clear my throat and begin. "I've learned something about you, Wolfe, and that's that you don't care about me in the slightest. The real me, that is. Not the mere fact of me being your fiancée. I admit that you do care about that—that you want to keep your wife safe— understandable considering what you've endured. But whether that wife is me or Claudia or Agnes or any other woman makes no difference to you. That is why you acted the way you did in the woods and with James, even all this with King. You do care about the abstract concept of marriage. But you don't care about me."

"Who gave you grounds to lay such claims? Do you have evidence to support them?" Under the glow of the street-lamps, I see that he is mad.

I stare at the patch of black fabric on his jacket that meets my eye line. "Well, no—"

"This argument that you make out is impossible for me to refute. Perhaps, then, it's one you've used to convince yourself of my disinterest—could that be it?"

"Hardly. Why would I do such a thing?"

"Because that way, you don't have to feel guilty about the

fact that you have no feelings for me when any fool can see that I, indeed, have feelings for you."

I draw in a breath and lift my gaze straight up to his. The light shining from above make his cheeks look hollow, animalistic. Yet his eyes shine with vulnerability.

"Forget it," he says quickly. "It's neither here nor—"

Without thinking it through, without any forethought whatsoever, I close the distance between us, my fingers wrap around his lapels, and I draw myself to his lips.

The smell of his aftershave, the softness of his skin, the rigidness of his body.

Something warm and foreign floods my insides.

Then the kiss is over, and he stares sternly down at me. But I'm careful to keep my eyes averted, busying myself with my bolero, shifting my long hair to the side as my heart hammers uncontrollably. Since he continues to stare wordlessly at me, I say quietly into the night, "I'm not sure why I did that. The sangria, I suppose."

He coughs lightly. "Yes, I suppose," he agrees. Then as the behemoth turns the corner, he adds quietly, "We don't have to speak of it again."

I bow my head as he swings open the door for me. And not once during the ride home, or even once we're tucked inside our quarters together, do we dare acknowledge one another at all.

It's only then, late at night, do I recall Agnes's words. *I can't pull the plug on the whole thing.* She can't pull the plug on the whole thing. But...pull the plug on what?

Next, I think of my last visit with her at the Quire nursery, her excitement about something she was working on. I remember her mentioning the challenges the project now faces, too.

A secret project...one exhilarating, yes, yet profoundly difficult...

Finally, as though my brain is moving like molasses, I

consider Evie's and the duchess's recent claims that the White Ribbon Campaign was spearheaded by a woman.

And as the darkened room begins to spin around me, I realize with a profound crush of dread that, finally, I've found the founder.

a look at book three:

Scapegoat of Strath Glen

In this heart-pounding conclusion to the captivating Pretty Little Robots trilogy, where secrets and betrayal intertwine, Alex finally unravels the truth behind her presence at Strath Glen.

As Alex uncovers the despicable secrets of the ruling King, she finds herself entangled in a revolutionary's plot. With the weight of all of Airo-Aurora's destiny on her shoulders, she must decide whether to orchestrate the downfall of the King or succumb to the horrifying consequences of being caught.

Together with her trusted friends, Alex embarks on a daring and perilous plan that could reshape their world forever. The stakes are high, the risks undeniable, but the potential for change is immeasurable.

However, fate takes an unexpected turn as Alex realizes that her fiancé, the viscount, is in grave danger. Despite her conflicting emotions, losing him is not an option. Will she be able to protect him while navigating the treacherous landscape of political intrigue and deception?

"Scapegoat of Strath Glen" is a spellbinding tale of love, sacrifice, and the pursuit of justice. Take the final step into the world of Pretty Little Robots and experience the thrilling conclusion to the trilogy. Don't miss your chance to uncover the secrets, face the consequences, and embrace the call to action.

Author Jerri Chisholm masterfully weaves a web of suspense and emotion, leaving readers on the edge of their seats until the very last page.

AVAILABLE SEPTEMBER 2023

about the author

Jerri Chisholm is a YA author, a distance runner, and a chocolate addict. Her childhood was spent largely in solitude with only her imagination and a pet parrot for company. Following that she completed a master's degree in public policy and then became a lawyer, but ultimately decided to leave the profession to focus exclusively on the more imaginative and avian-friendly pursuit of writing. She lives with her husband and three children, but, alas, no parrot.